Two Thousand Million Man-Power

Two Thousand Million Man-Power

Gertrude Eileen Trevelyan

Introduction by Rachel Hore
Afterword by Brad Bigelow

RECOVERED BOOKS
BOILER HOUSE PRESS

Contents

Thus, whereas in China there was an adult working male population of, say, 100 millions, in the United States there was added to the 25 million working males something like two thousand million man power in machinery. And the result is that whereas in China consumers out-number producers by 4 to 1, in the United States producers outnumber consumers by 20 to 1.

From Ian D. Colvin, "Social Survey of the World To-Day: Lines of Weakness Revealed in Western Civilization by the Shock of War and the Reactions of Democracy to Responsibility". In *Universal History of the World*, Volume Eight, edited by J. A. Hammerton. London: The Educational Book Co, 1927.

Introduction
by Rachel Hore

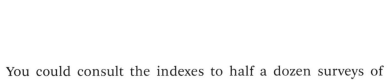

You could consult the indexes to half a dozen surveys of interwar era English literature without finding so much as a mention of Gertrude Trevelyan's name. This neglect is a substantial oversight, for she was a woman whose talent arguably outshone many of the best and brightest writers of the Thirties literary canon. That certain of her novels are returning to print is a cause for celebration: *Two Thousand Million Man-Power* is a jewel amongst them.

Who was Gertrude Eileen Trevelyan? In basic category terms, she was a distinctive experimental English writer who demonstrated an acute sociological and political awareness and was prepared to take imaginative risks with subject and style. She was also prolific and well-regarded in her day: her eight novels were published by prestigious imprints such as Secker and Gollancz and favourably reviewed in places that mattered by critics whose opinions were important. But she died young in 1941 and by the 1950s her work had all but disappeared from public view.

Trevelyan's trail winds back to Edwardian Bath. Born in 1903, she was the only surviving child of Edward Trevelyan, a man styling himself as of 'private means', and his wife Eleanor. She attended Princess Helena College in Ealing, was confirmed at the parish church there, and went up to Lady Margaret Hall, Oxford, in 1923. Later, recalling her undergraduate life, she wrote that she kept 'a position of total obscurity', because she 'did not: play hockey, act, row, take part in debates, political or literary, contribute to the *Isis* or attend cocoa parties, herein failing to conform to the social standards commonly required of women students.' She did, however, shoot to fame by becoming the first woman to win the renowned Newdigate Prize, awarded to a final year undergraduate for a 250-line poem on a set topic. Trevelyan's 'Julia, daughter of Claudius' was subsequently published by Basil Blackwell. She earned a second-class degree.

A context in which to situate Trevelyan and her work can be found in Virginia Woolf's declaration that a woman determined to succeed as a writer requires a room of her own and financial independence. That is exactly what Trevelyan achieved with the help of a small inheritance, living initially in a women's hostel in Bermondsey and later in a series of lodgings in Kensington. In 1932 her first novel was published by Secker. *Appius and Virginia* concerns a scientific experiment devised by English spinster Virginia Hutton, to raise a baby orangutang, which she names Appius, as a human. The narrative is relayed from the points of view of each party, both expressing confusion and failure to understand one another. It was rapturously received, the *Spectator* lauding it as 'a brilliant debut'. The distinguished Compton Mackenzie praised the author's second novel, *Hot-House*, in the *Daily Mail* as 'extremely well done'. It follows the experiences and relationships of Mina Cook, an undergraduate at a fictional college modelled on Lady Margaret Hall. Trevelyan switched subject once more in *As It Was in the Beginning*, a novel that takes place entirely in the head of a woman dying in a care home. This *The Times Literary Supplement* described as 'a book which is almost unreadable in its intensity, but which compels one to go on reading in spite of almost physical discomfort, by the admiration one feels for the author's ingenuity and her uncanny insight into human beings.' Less warm was the reception to *A War Without a Hero*, the last of Trevelyan's novels to be published by Secker, with the *Manchester Guardian* castigating her stylistic tic of presenting unspoken thoughts in 'machine gun sentences generally beginning with the verb'. Happily, her fifth book represented a return to form.

Two Thousand Million Man-Power, issued by Victor Gollancz in their distinctive yellow livery in 1937, is a tour-de-force, the supple prose, fluidity and shrewd insight of a mature writer on display. A masterly piece of social realism that traces the developing relationship of a highbrow but penniless young London couple against an interbellum background of rapid technological, ideological and political change, it also satirizes contemporary bourgeois life and its fashionable belief in endless progress. Robert Thomas and Katherine Bott's story unfolds initially in bedsit land, a country Trevelyan knew well, brilliantly pinpointing her characters' precise position in the social hierarchy. Infiltrated with dark humour, it is no touching love story. Robert is the more likeable of the pair, a research chemist at Cupid Cosmetics who spends lonely evenings trying to concoct a mathematical formula for the nature of time (another interwar obsession).

Katherine, a London County Council school teacher who despises her pupils and holds their attention by fear, is the more ideological, sometimes to comic effect. Her short-lived disdain for the institution of marriage means that for a long time the lovers have to creep about in a ridiculous fashion to avoid Robert's conventional landlady. Later, after they are safely wed and have enjoyed a period of relative affluence, their story turns darker. The novel dramatizes the devastating experience of long-term unemployment with a power that easily matches George Orwell's in *The Road to Wigan Pier*.

Imaginatively, though she may have noticed the technique in John Dos Passos' *USA Trilogy*, Trevelyan weaves into her tale snippets of world news which are taken from real-life headlines, wireless bulletins and newsreels. This conveys the ironic effect that the hapless pair are ultimately unimportant, simply fodder to a vast, pitiless machine that will crush them to oblivion. Sometimes she uses a telescoping technique which offers a wonderful sense of widening out: 'he lit the gas over the uncleared supper table, but put it out again and went to bed. Outside, beyond a blank sheet of brick and a cross-section of beds and wash-stands, the street lamps in Ladbroke Grove were shivering frostily above empty pavements... Up in Oxford Street the last buses were leaving for the suburbs... out in Surrey... down in the farms and manors of the West Country...' All this appealed to the *Spectator* reviewer: 'Miss Trevelyan is an artist... her novels... have always the fascination of a brilliant technique.'

Three more novels followed, the last, *Trance by Appointment*, published by Harrap, but then in October 1940 disaster struck. The flat in Notting Hill where she lived was damaged in the Blitz and she was gravely injured. In February 1941 she died in a care home in Bath. As well as her injuries, her death certificate mentions that she suffered from pulmonary tuberculosis.

Why has Trevelyan not survived when so many of her female contemporaries have returned to the bookshop shelves long years after their death? In large part her personal isolation must be to blame. After her 'position of total obscurity' at university, she hid her gender behind her initials. Her private income was a boon, but also a disadvantage, for although it enabled her to focus on her fiction it meant she did not need to teach, review or otherwise take part in public life. Whether her illness or a natural introversion encouraged this isolation is difficult to tell. She had a small circle of friends, but no cache of letters or diaries survived the bomb. There was no one to keep her flame burning. But now there is. *Two Thousand Million Man-Power* is a twentieth century literary classic and there are more out there waiting to be recovered.

Norwich, 2022

Two Thousand Million Man-Power

by Gertrude Eileen Trevelyan

Chapter I

While at eleven-fifty-five P.M. on December 31st bells throughout London were ringing out, and well-away, the year 1919 and ringing in who knew what, every press in Fleet Street — pounding out New Year Messages by the hundred thousand — was throbbing to one of two burdens: the Bolshevik Peril — "which may yet threaten the very existence of the Western World" — or the imminent ratification of the Peace Treaty, sole ground for self-congratulation in that uneasy age. At that time, on that night, Ireland was in process of being ravaged by Sinn Fein activities, Austria by famine, Russia by civil war, and the United States, Spain and Germany by varying degrees of internal unrest; Bill Jones was sorting mail at the G.P.O., Ted Smith was driving a lorry from Hammersmith to Bristol, Tom Robinson was bringing up the night express from Exeter, Robert Thomas, alone in his room near Ladbroke Grove Underground station, was feeling

a mild but nagging anxiety as to the results of his final examination, six months distant, in the Honours School of Chem-
istry and Mathematics at London University.

The bells stopped; Robert reached for a book and edged
his chair under the gas jet. Along in Fleet Street, soon after,
the throbbing of the presses died down, vans backed, clattering, up side streets, were loaded and driven off, night staffs
came out yawning and lit pipes and dispersed by late buses
or early tubes; throughout the country limbs were stretched
in grey bedrooms and bacon smells began to seep up staircases: England awoke, without undue enthusiasm, to 1920,
the year of peace.

During January of that year the British Press was able
to congratulate itself on the belated report of a Bolshevist
defeat near Pskoff, English governesses escaped from Russia, relief work was pushed forward in Vienna, Jean Dubois
obtained a post as ticket collector with the P.L.M., prepara-
tions were set afoot for the first meeting of the League of
Nations "in order to promote international co-operation and
to achieve international peace and security," Robert Thomas
contracted eye-strain from a too feverish copying of diagrams
from the blackboard, post-offices were raided in Ireland. The
Belgian Minister for the Colonies outlined a project for the
creation of a Congo Cotton Company, a loan of five million
dollars was allotted by the American War Finance Corporation for locomotives for Poland and three million for electrical machinery in France and Belgium, across the Atlantic
four thousand five hundred Radicals were rounded up "from
California to New York" with "a complete gathering in of the
editorial staffs of the communist newspapers throughout
the country," police were shot in Ireland, a "Save-a-Minute"
club was instituted in a large works in the north of England,

factories in Petrograd closed down owing to the dearth of technical experts and raw materials, Ivan Pavlovitch took to raking in Moscow dustbins after dark, an air mail service was inaugurated between Bombay and Karachi, in Central Africa plans were under consideration for the construction of a railway line to join the Congo with the Ituri and Upper Welle, a committee of experts visited Brazil to study an eclipse of the sun with a view to investigating Einstein's Third Critical Test for the Theory of Relativity, the House of the Masses was raided in Detroit and two hundred and eighty Radicals arrested, Robert Thomas packed his notebooks together and went out to lunch at an A.B.C.[1]

Negotiations were now at a deadlock between employers and the N.U.R.[2], Poles and Letts captured Dvinsk from the Soviets, in India the Hunter Commission was sitting on the shootings at Amritsar, Giovanni Rossi, clerk in the municipal offices at Genoa, became worried about his wife, a witchcraft trial was in progress at Bordeaux, the Peace Treaty was ratified in Paris, Robert Thomas walked from Gower Street to Oxford Circus and caught a 15 bus for Ladbroke Grove, farm tractor trials were held at Lincoln, Tom Smith lost his job in a blacking factory at Edmonton, Charlie Jones took to selling papers in Piccadilly, Robert caught a bus for Oxford Circus and walked to Gower Street, Independent Socialists and Communists tried to rush the Reichstag, terrorists were arrested in Madrid, and the first meeting of the executive council of the League of Nations took place in Paris.

In February a record time of rather less than four hours

---

1   Aerated Bread Company café.
2   National Union of Railwaymen, a trade union of railway workers

was set up on the London — Paris air service, German students boycotted Einstein's lectures, food riots broke out in Austria, the Whites abandoned Archangel, the O'Grady British Mission returned to London, Robert Thomas in the lecture hall of University College, listening with strained attention to Eddington's lecture on the Relativity Theory, was filled with a painful ambition to devote the rest of his life to the study of pure mathematics, the Council of the League of Nations resolved that the League should convene an International Conference "to study the financial crisis and look for the means of remedying it and of mitigating the dangerous consequences arising from it."

It is now rumoured that a Bolshevist army will march westward in the spring "to annul the Treaty of Versailles and release the German people from the fetters which are strangling them"; Mr. F. Handley Page prophesies small, privately owned planes within a year or so; Maudie Brown gets a job in a cinema box-office at Barking; Gladys Smith is working for Matric. at Tooting Bec; "the government and the industries of the country are becoming more and more alive to the need of making appointments for chemists more attractive to the best qualified"; Robert Thomas, leaning against a letter-box in Ladbroke Grove, licks the flap of an envelope and posts home to the parsonage in Wales his proposal to spend a year or so on research after taking his degree.

A landlord is shot dead in Galway, Norway and Sweden join the League, Russia makes an agreement with England for resumption of mail service, demobilised men riot in Milan, a Christian Counter-Bolshevist Crusade is launched in London. Round again. Murder of first Republican Lord Mayor of Cork, revolution in Germany, Red advance in the Caucasus, Turkish atrocities in Armenia, daylight murder in Dublin. And round. Machine guns in Charlottenburg, three hundred casualties in Berlin, Poland Russia Armenia Hungary Austria "five million infant victims of disease and starvation," crisis in the Ruhr. Round and round. "Miners' nystagmus is said to cause a loss to the country of at least a million pounds a year"; Rumanian Consolidated Oilfields Ltd. claim a million and a quarter compensation for destruction to oilwells under German invasion; and Robert, jingling two half-crowns in his pocket, a bit nervous, goes to Paddington to meet his father.

"The clergy," asserts the Central Church Fund Appeal, "are suffering greater privations than any other class of the population." "There are people carrying on research work," complains a deputation to the Prime Minister from the British Medical Association and British Science Guild, "who receive less money than unskilled workmen in the service of the Corporation." "Intelligence is in danger," runs the manifesto of *Les Compagnons de l'Intelligence*, "because the middle classes are threatened on the one hand by the power of money, and on the other by the power of numbers." "No, no, my boy," mutters Robert Thomas senior, clambering into a third-class compartment at Paddington with his umbrella knocking behind him on the step. "Things aren't what they were. Learned professions crowded out."

"But," says Robert.

"No, no," he says, "no, my boy," taking off his flat parson's hat and wiping with a very old silk handkerchief around the headband. "No, no, stick to commerce, safety in commerce, fine thing commerce, nothing to be ashamed of."

"But..."

Robert strolls up disconsolately into Praed Street jingling the two half-crowns in his pocket. He wonders whether to go home to his rooms or on to Gower Street for a lecture, remembers he is billed to speak in a college debate at eight o'clock, decides for the lecture and takes a run at a moving bus. On top he cheers up, with the wind lifting his hair: spare time, he thinks, the romance of commerce even; and out at six every day, earlier with luck. He slips in at the back of the crowded lecture room and sits swinging a notebook absently between his knees, with a half grin on his face and the Big Idea hovering, pleasantly vague, at the back of his mind. When the hour is over he crams the unused book into his pocket, gets a snack before the debate, speaks for more than half an hour in support of the League of Nations, catches a bus back to Ladbroke Grove. And in the morning — most mornings — he buys a paper and catches a bus to Gower Street. If the principle of Nationalisation were accepted, the paper assures him, your War Bonds, your War Loan Stock, your War Savings Certificates would be so much waste paper. Ghastly tragedy of Europe's Children, it cries, Save the Children. Necessitous ex-officers: they fought for You. Your gas bill will be more, your electric current bill will be higher, every article of food carried from overseas will rise in price. And are you, it asks him, contributing all you can to the work of the Church to-day? And Armenia: Christianity v. Barbarism, "so long as Barbarism sees us indifferent the peril continues to grow." You will pay more for your clothes — there is no end to the list of commodities the price of which will show an advance. How Will You Help? Honour Your Bond! Nationalisation, the Consumer Pays! Britons! Be Quick! The Turk is Massacring!

Summer: the second reading of the Home Rule Bill is passed by a large majority; relations are discovered between Sinn Fein and Germany; Sweden makes a trade agreement with Russia; the Non-Co-operation Movement begins in India; the League of Nations meets at San Remo; war breaks out in the Ruhr; at the Chemists' Exhibition at Clerkenwell the wonders of modern manicure are on view, and sugar-coated pills of thyroid extract for cretinism, goitre and rejuvenation. "In view of a prejudice lingering in the public mind against the suggestion of simian relationship, this extract is obtained from sheep."

The Surrender to Sinn Fein. Young man's suicide in London taxi-cab: coroner, "It seems to me there are too many pistols about." The War in Ireland.

Ultra-red rays prevent burns from radium, radio telephone stations are opened at Croydon and Lympne for the control of air traffic, Soviet troops muster on the outskirts of Warsaw, Allies and Germans meet at Spa to discuss reparations and armaments, the journey from Paris to London now takes barely two hours, a British trade pact is concluded with the Soviets, Robert Thomas comes down from the university with a half-formulated theory upon, and a glowing determination to examine, the nature of Pure Time, and takes up a post which has been found for him as research chemist to a cosmetics firm with a factory in the neighbourhood of Acton.

Chapter II

Robert pottered about his laboratory, most of the time, with one eye on the clock. He didn't dislike his work but he hardly knew it was there. The laboratory was a converted army hut put down on a piece of meadow-land and along at the side, if he leant from the window, he could see two or three other huts and the one-storied brick main building of Cupid Cosmetics Co. Limited, where they made up great vats of face cream and powder from his formulas and packed them sparingly, with a lot of frilly paper to a box, into shiny cardboard boxes with little flying cupids all over the cover, tied with big, purple bows. A wide shelf ran down one side of the hut; here he had his retorts and burners and mortars, and test-tubes in a rack; he spent his day ranging up and down, with a half whistle, alongside the shelf, analysing samples of powder for the face or teeth or nails, or sticky daubs of cream; in search of recipes for a drier powder or a stickier cream or more economical means of production.

Robert had a boy to run errands and clean the test-tubes and shovel coke into the stove behind the door. The boy was pale and fat, oversized for his age, and breathed loudly. He was called Rodney. Every now and then Rodney would breathe in with a note from the office or a sample for analysis and breathe out again and Robert would get to work with the mortar and retorts, but he had a good deal of time on hand to balance from heel to toe with a half whistle and stare out of the window at the broken-up meadow-land. The grass was long and trampled near the hut; the tarred wall under the window cut down into field and the grass fell back from it in a limp straggling curve like hair from an uncombed parting, leaving a dark line of shiny-smooth unhealthy soil. A good way off, hiding the view, there was a hedge; a board up on the right facing the cinder road said: Freehold Factory Land For Sale. Robert would stare for a time across the field without looking at it; a hand feeling mechanically in his pocket for a pencil and paper. He would lean the paper against the smooth knot in the stained wood wall and jot down a few figures, then go back to the shelf across the hut and begin to potter again. Besides the coke stove with an iron railing round it and a vent-pipe leading to the roof, there was no furniture in the hut except one chair and a small sink and a roller towel hanging on the door. When Robert had finished for the day he washed his hands at the sink and wiped them on the roller towel and pushed them back over his hair and went out, locking the door of the hut. On his way up the cinder road he leaned in at the door of the office and hung the key on a nail in a row of other keys and nodded good night to the clerk. The cinder track led up across the field to a high road, and on a little way, at the bend, he caught a bus for Ealing Broadway. If he were lucky he hadn't long to wait for a train and as he got out at Westbourne Park and walked between high grey houses to his lodgings, his step brisked up. He began to jingle his latchkey against the coins in his pocket. He went up three dusty flights of stairs two steps at a time. His supper was on the table. He ate quickly, with appetite, undiscriminating. Turning his back on the meal he lit the gas over a small table near the window and felt in his pocket for the scrap of paper with the jotted figures. As the gas came up, the roofs outside the window turned dark grey. The drawer of the table stuck, half open. He banged it back and wrenched at it and found a wad of notes and pulled in his chair. The roofs outside turned black against the sky and then the sky blacked out.

The gas sizzled in its wall bracket over Robert's head. Outside, under the dark roofs, sleepers were tossing in frowsy bedrooms; rain dripped from a plane-tree into a puddle of light on the pavement. Along the street and round the corner, in the Underground station, a late train was dropping three passengers on to an empty platform and moving off with a slow scraping groan; horse-vans were crawling up through Hammersmith on their way to Covent Garden, a wet taxi or two rattling in a hurry through the West End where the lights over the theatres were going out; night watchmen were nodding over their pipes; at the side of dark trains, on the long, empty platforms of the railway termini, were knots of activity where sleepy porters were bundling in the night mail; out in the country it was dark and quiet to the west and a red glare hung over the Midlands and North and a clang came up now and then when they stoked the furnaces, and on the North Sea the dark boats rowed quiet beside the nets. Over in Brussels, the representatives of thirty-nine states called to the International Financial Conference slept in hotel bedrooms and their dull boots lay paired on corridor carpets under the turned-down lights. A small Buttons[1] in shirt-sleeves came whistling upstairs and collected the boots and brought them back clean and shiny and purposeful, daylight climbed up over the Channel, fishing boats steered for harbours on the East Coast, milk trains came rattling and smoking up through the suburbs, Robert's arm in a dirty cuff reached and turned out the gas; in the half-light he stood up and turned round and pushed back against the bulging drawer. The drawer jammed and creaked and gave way suddenly; he caught his balance and ran his fingers through his hair and felt his way out of the room and across the dark landing, taking care to shut both doors quietly. His bedroom faced a blank wall, the room was grey near the window; without troubling to light the gas he tugged at his clothes and rolled into bed for a couple of hours.

It was cold in the mornings now. Robert opened the laboratory window to let out the smoke from the coke stove; shivered a bit. Outside, the grass was permanently damp and lying down, it was a broad, dark kind of grass. He put down the window and went across to the bench and began absently to rinse the test-tubes that Rodney had left unwashed. He looked over the day's samples for analysis and set to work on them in a desultory way, whistling quietly to himself, jotting down his findings on a pad splashed yellow with chemical. Presently Rodney came in and stoked the stove so that the smoke came up in gusts. Robert thought of saying something about the test-tubes. He had one in his hand when he

---

1   Hotel bellhop.

turned round. Look here, he meant to say, or How about, but he found he hadn't said it. He was watching Rodney's sulky behind, waiting for it to turn from the stove. He felt shy all at once and it seemed not worthwhile. "Don't forget the door, old man," he said awkwardly, instead. Rodney said nothing and slammed it.

Robert settled back, relieved, at his bench. He wiped the smoke from his spectacles and went on weighing and testing, jotting figures now and then on the curled leaves of the pad. The other part of his brain, the part that was working, put a message through from time to time and he stopped whistling and looked ahead. Sometimes he looked down again after a minute, sometimes he felt through his pockets for a scrap of paper and made a note before he went back to pottering over the retorts. As it grew colder he could feel the steel of his spectacles cutting his ears when he went out of the hot shed. At lunch time he would fill up the hour by stumping up and down the cinder way across the wet field to the road. Now and then he looked in at the doors of the sheds where they made the stuff, but it meant nothing to him. He was glad to get back to his bench, and often he was there before the whistles brought the workpeople crunching and chattering from the main road.

Autumn unfolded over Europe. Fresh rumours of famine came from Russia; D'Annunzio, defeated at Fiume, went into compulsory retirement on Lake Garda; at the Quai d'Orsay they were beating carpets and polishing inkstands for the Reparations Conference in January. Robert, back one night, upstairs three at a time, found a letter with his supper, propped against the butter dish. It wasn't often he had a letter, he looked it up and down with interest. Oh well, only the League secretary, Old Collegiate branch. Wanting subscription. Enclosing fixture card. Robert turned over the card and ran his fingers through his hair and thought vaguely but guiltily that he'd been letting things slide a bit. He stood the card in a prominent position on the mantelpiece and felt better about it. Next day, waiting for Rodney to come back out of a cloud of coke smoke, he wrinkled his nose nervously and responsibly against the bridge of his glasses. "Ever thought much about the League?" Quick and nervous. Rodney picked up the empty coke bucket and went to the door, made a gesture of spitting. "Give me cricket, any day. More of a game, if you ask me."

Better go. One or two men he knew slightly were at the meeting. Afterwards somebody nodded to him across the crowd round the doorway; he nodded back absently and pushed on and out, no time to hang around talking. At the top of a side street he could see the lights of Tottenham Court Road and buses passing, with luck he'd be back and at work by eleven.

He turned away angrily. He'd been staring at a chemist's window, by the bus stop, in Oxford Street: staring, for something to do and without knowing it, at a pyramid of purple Cupid boxes bristling with waxen bows. Filthy muck. He turned away and moved on, disgusted, hitting something with his back, and a woman glared at him. Her face was floury with cheap powder and her lipstick a bad red. Did his turn like that when they put it on? And what did they use the stuff for, anyhow. Women were everywhere, in twos and threes; from the top of the bus he couldn't see their faces, only the hats pulled down like flower-pots rounded at the top and the foreshortened tubs of their bodies. Most of the lighted shops along the route were full of women's clothes. As the streets got darker towards Paddington he began to think about his thesis, but the wind skimming the bus-top made him sleepy; about Westbourne Grove he began to yawn. The gas was out on the stairs; he struck a match on each landing and felt his way by banister up the flights in be-tween. A suggestion of sleep, too strong for him, oozed stealthily from under the shut doors. When he got to the top he lit the gas over the uncleared supper table, but put it out again and went to bed.

Outside, beyond a blank sheet of brick and a cross-section of beds and wash-stands, the street lamps in Ladbroke Grove were shivering frostily above empty pavements, in converging lines dwindling into mist. Up in Oxford Street the last buses were leaving for the suburbs. In streets of crowded tall houses and in wider streets of lower houses and on broad high-roads with houses spaced out by gardens and out in Surrey where new red villas were dropped among the pines, and down in the farms and manors of the West Country, and up through the Midlands and North in sudden huddled stacks and unexpected farmsteads, and in the crofters' cottages and tumbledown castles of the Highlands and in solid Lowland homes and in grey Yorkshire towns and moorland farms and in fishing colonies down the coast, and on the flats of Essex, and in the small new houses beginning to sprout on the extreme northern edge of London, and in the brick and stucco villas, behind tight curtains, and in streets of crowded tall houses, the greater number of the forty-seven million one hundred and thirty-three thousand inhabitants of the British Isles slept or listened to sounds of sleeping. The Reparations Conference had broken down in Paris: Allied proposals; over in Dublin police were potted at from doorways; civil war in Russia was practically over; Poland was making a defensive alliance with Rumania; in London the Reparations Conference was at it again: German counter-proposals. In the early hours of the morning, down off Ladbroke Grove where a coster's barrow here and there was on the move, Robert opened an eye and saw the room was still half dark and shut it again.

Presently he lay on his back and watched the window. Bricks were etched in now, yellow and black, on the wall across the yard; from brightening streaks along their surface he knew it was a fine day. He could hear a van go by and draw up once or twice in the road at the front of the house, and at intervals the higher notes of a street singer and a distant rumble of the Underground over the bridge by the station. The figures of a mathematical equation were lined up on the wall, on the black and yellow bricks. They ranged themselves in order, leisurely, while he watched with lazy interest. With the peculiar clarity of half-sleep he knew at once what it was: the missing part of the formula he had been puzzling out the day before. Queer thing, he thought, the way your mind works during sleep. It was all worked out for him, ready, over on the wall. He thought he would get up in a minute and copy it down. He stared at it, trying to memorise. The top lines were quite clear, as he had seen them on paper only yesterday, but he couldn't be sure of the solution. He sat up sharply to get a better view and found he had been dozing; the noises were louder now in the road and the wall was quite yellow. He wondered whether to get up and work before he was called, but presently he heard the stairs creak and a can put down outside the door. A carpet sweeper squeaked once or twice, perfunctorily, in the sitting-room, and breakfast plates clattered. Out in the road, the plane-trees were coming into bud, and there was a green look about the back gardens edging the line down to Ealing. For a moment he had a ridiculous, elated sense of going into the country as the bus

loped along the main road between half-built plots and factory sites with stretches of misty green hedge left standing
for a hundred yards or more at a time. It was still early summer and he found the laboratory shed full of smoke from the
newly lit stove. He threw up the window to let out the smoke
and noticed that the grass was greener and less lank, sprout-
ing out stiffly from the tarred roots of the sheds. Across on
the work-bench were some tubes and mortars unwashed.
Robert fiddled for a time, sorting them, waiting for Rodney to come in. "See here, my lad," he thought he'd say. But
presently he needed one of the tubes and absent-mindedly
washed it, and by the time Rodney came in it seemed hardly
worthwhile to say anything.

There was a Sold notice on the next plot and during the
summer they began to dig. From his window Robert could
see the men at work on the pegged-out field and dark rec-
tangles of earth lengthening in the high, trodden grass. The
noise of picks and shovels disturbed him at first but he soon
got used to it. Stacks of turf for carting were dumped near his
shed, the bruised grass splayed back at their edge, and broken-down sorrel and ox-eye daisies.

In July he was given a fortnight's holiday. He wrote to his
father that it would cost too much to go home to Wales. He
sat after breakfast at his table by the window and planned
his treatise on Time and looked at the tiles of the house
across the street. When the landlady had finished clearing
the breakfast things behind him he got down on his forearms
and wrote like mad. Sometimes on a hot evening he would
go on top of a bus as far as Marble Arch and hang about with
his hands in his pockets among the crowd on the lit corner
of the park, feeling the air on his head and looking vaguely
at the people. Now and then he would stop to hear part of a

speech on Disarmament or Home Rule, but the constant flux of the crowd prevented attention and if ever there was a point to a speech the wind carried it away. In the dark, up above the moving crowd, the lights would come out one by one in the block of flats on the corner of Oxford Street; a tall smooth-faced block, a challenge, dwarfing the dark, balconied Park Lane houses. He was generally glad to be back in the empty roads of North Kensington. There was little traffic at night, and as the lights went out in the rooms opposite he sat and wrote again under the gas-jet up against the dark window.

By the end of the fortnight he had covered scores of pages with notes; wads fell from the back of the stuck drawer when he had wrenched it straight and rammed it in. He thought that later on, in the winter, he might begin to put them together. He picked up the fallen wads and frowned at them, running his fingers through his hair. It worried him that he could see the thing philosophically — that is he thought he could but he couldn't be sure — but not mathematically. He knew the formula must exist, the precise mathematical formula for the nature of Time. That was what he was out after. He ruffled up the pages of notes and hypotheses with his red, thin fingers; he couldn't say whether this stuff was sound or not, it just came to him. He began to wish he'd taken philosophy at college. But the formula was what he was after. It went by him now and then when he was doing something else, fifty times he'd thought he was on it but it slipped by; when he turned over the wads of figures and signs they didn't mean very much, that he could see. He'd get it some time, he thought, it wouldn't get by him, he'd been on the track of it so often. He wondered whether these theories he'd jotted down were any use, he wished he knew. He thought he'd get hard at it and get the thing co-ordinated in the winter.

Back at the laboratory he found concrete flooring in slabs on the turned field, and walls half-up. From his window he could see a strip of flat dirty grass and at right angles to it the new pink bricks. He felt vaguely annoyed at first at having to lean from the window for a sight of sky and trees at the end of the field, but he soon got used to it, and after a time he didn't trouble to lean. During hot evenings at the end of summer he took to going home all the way by bus and he kept to it as autumn came on: from little strips of public garden spaced beside the high-road, through Shepherd's Bush and Chiswick and Hammersmith, dried leaves were sent whistling along empty stretches of pavement and into the feet of the crowd where the high-road became for a space a local High Street, with shops and station and borough importances and costers' barrows. Not far from Chiswick there was a block of flats, a row of red brick three-storied houses with three brass bells one under another at each door. Modern ideas, reaching right out here. He got off at Hammersmith and took the Underground. As soon as he was back in his rooms and had lit the gas and had supper he got to work.

When it grew colder he had a fire lit. Poppy sellers were prinking up for Armistice Day. Over in Ireland Cosgrave was fighting England for independence and De Valera was fighting England for independence. A bit later, Westminster was passing a treaty making the Irish Free State a self-governing dominion. Over in Ireland De Valera was fighting Cosgrave.

Then early one morning, when Smithfield porters were at work by lamplight unloading beef, and Father Christmases who had to be on the beat in the West End by nine o'clock were yawning in Kentish Town or Peckham, and the fire was out, he thought he'd hit upon his formula at last. He thought he had but he couldn't be sure. The sky was whitish under the blind. He turned down the gas and rolled into bed for a couple of hours' sleep, and when he got up there was barely time for breakfast; he rammed the pages of figures into his pocket to look at later in the day. He glanced at them in the train but couldn't be sure: look it over quietly when he got there. There was a nip in the air when he hurried down the cinder track, he was almost glad to be in the smoky warm shed. He'd just hung his hat on the door and found his overalls and was beginning to see where he was, when Rodney shuffled in with a sample of nail powder for analysis.

He didn't know what it was they were making in the new factory, but by the spring their engines were at work behind the pink bricks. It was some time before he could get used to the monotonous drone and bump, and the vibration was worse than the noise: it seemed as if the bench he worked at had been charged with electricity, full of potential movement. He never could trace that vibration at work on any definite object but it was there all the same, jangling his nerves. Or was it only the noise. Just an impression. He found it difficult now to concentrate while he pottered about the hut, doing jobs which filled a quarter of his time. He took to standing with his hands in his pockets in front of the window and balancing from heel to toe, thinking of nothing in particular, looking at the pink bricks and wondering whether they throbbed or whether he imagined it. The League met at Cannes and the World War Foreign Debt Commission at Washington and the League at Genoa. Robert got used to the machinery after a time but he was more than ever bored with his work in the laboratory. It was seldom now that he got an idea while he was pottering. He pottered and waited for the hooters to go. When they went — three or four nowadays from factories dotted along the road — he was out up the cinder track and on the bus to the station almost before they'd finished. He had given up his leisurely bus ride all the way. He was glad a tube extension was coming down across the fields: from the top of the bus he could see its track cleared through hedges, and hillocks of turf and grit and an uprooted tree or two thrown back on the grass. When the new station was opened near the factory, next year, he would gain quite twenty minutes on the day: his day began when he was back up the steps, past the draggled laburnum tree, up the stairs and through supper and could wrench at the drawer to get it open. Outside, as the laburnum wilted and its leaves were trodden dirty brown on the wet steps, England and France were bickering over an attitude to the Soviets, the German mark in its fall reached nine thousand to the dollar and the Fascisti marched on Rome.

Robert bought a *Morning Post* at Paddington. He seldom read a paper nowadays, but he had an idea the elections would be coming on soon and it might be as well to keep an eye open. Polling To-day, Every Conservative Vote Needed, Premier's Confidence in the Result. Near thing that, he thought, jerked a bit. He took a look through the rest of the paper to see what was going on: German Plea for Moratorium, Egypt's Mischief Makers, Signor Mussolini as Dictator, Pilotless Flight, Melba Sings "Home Sweet Home" at Election Meeting. Robert folded the paper and left it on the seat, with an uneasy feeling that he ought to do a bit more about things. When he got back that night he went straight up Ladbroke Grove from the station to the Council Schools and recorded his vote before he had supper and got settled down to work.

It wasn't long after that that he caught Rodney sneaking a length of copper wire from a drawer in the laboratory.

"What's the big idea," he snapped, sharp quite easily now, what with the noise and one thing and another. The smoke stung his eyes, and when the window was open the thumping of the machines was too loud. "Crystal set, what the deuce is that? Oh, wireless." He handed back the wire, faintly surprised, now he came to think of it, that the youth could take enough interest in anything to work it up in his spare time. "Better cut it then, quick."

He'd noticed there were more of the things about lately. Often now he had to shut the window after supper, against crackling noises and bursts of loud metallic song from across the street. He shut the window and drew the blinds, dirty yellow behind the gas-bracket, and clamped his elbows on the table and his hands over his ears and tried to think. Across the street, in number six, John Jones was struggling to eliminate atmospherics from his reception of London — 369 metres — on his crystal set. An aerial or two appeared daily now in back-yards along behind Paddington. Tenants on a North London Council Estate had been refused permission to install sets on account of the danger of fire. In gardens backing on to the line from Dover to Victoria, aerials were springing up as thick as clothes-props. The B.B.C. was gaining confidence. Jimmy Johns, next door at number three, was tuning in.

Robert jumped up in a rage. He knew there wasn't a chance of their stopping before ten or eleven, and next door, where they had one of the big expensive sets and could even get Paris, later than that. He ran his hands through his hair and stared at himself in the dull square of mirror over the fireplace, because he found himself in front of it, and gave a short, nasty laugh. He felt like that. He picked up the January fixture card of the League of Nations Union, O.C. branch, which had come a few days before and was the only thing on the mantelpiece besides the landlady's ornaments and a pipe he smoked now and then when he thought of it or had that vague, nagging feeling of responsibility. Tucked into the fixture card was a leaflet announcing an open debate on the Ruhr, billed for that evening at the Central Hall, Westminster.

Robert looked at the leaflet. He wondered just what it was, exactly, about the Ruhr. He put the pipe in his mouth and pulled at it and felt through his pockets for some tobacco. A stolid cackle of dance music was coming through the closed window and the higher notes of an operatic soprano thinly pierced the wall to the left. It had been like this for weeks: all the time Mary MacSweeny was hunger-striking in Mountjoy Gaol and Lenin was developing the New Economic Policy and the Italian Fascisti were attacking the Soviet Trade Delegation and Russia was refusing Italian ships entry to Russian ports and the German mark was falling by thousands a week and America was holding protest meetings about Ireland.

There was nothing to smoke in the room, so Robert put the pipe in his pocket and unhooked a muffler from the back of a chair. In due course Mary MacSweeny was released, France and Belgium occupied the Ruhr, the German mark fell to forty-nine thousand to the dollar, and Robert strolled into the Central Hall for a League of Nations debate and met Katherine.

Chapter III

Katherine taught at the L.C.C. Senior Mixed School in Wilberforce Street, S.W. Unscaleable walls of black and yellow brick
shut the school-yard from pavements and tattered shops
and the greater part of the gas-drum at the end of the street.
The yard was paved with cement and gravel worn smooth. In
the ground floor left-hand class-room window there was a
glass jam-jar which had once held flowers, half full of water;
a cord which was used to open and close the upper half of
the window hung in a dismal loop to within a few inches
of the jar. The boys sat on the window side of the room, to
the right of the teacher's desk, and the girls to the left, on
the door side. From the table behind which Katherine was
standing a further line of division, uneven but perceptible,
ran down the room between the two, a ribbon of yellow
ink-stained desk behind desk, to the yellowish-brown wall-
paint: voluntary gesture of sex antagonism on the part of the

eleven-year-olds. From behind the table Katherine could see well over their heads, she talked mostly to the empty desks at the back or the bilious green upper half of the wall.

Katherine believed in progress. She believed in the League of Nations and International Good Will, in Gilbert Murray and Lord Robert Cecil and H. A. L. Fisher, and in the wonders of Science. She liked to think of Geneva as the Temple of Justice: in her mind's eye she saw a large, white building calm and cool beside a lake; of divers on the ocean bed; of great ships, greater and swifter ships, spanning the seas; and airmen alone over deserts; and wireless waves invisibly crisscross in the ether.

Katherine moved across to the blackboard; it stood on an easel on the far side of a blocked-up fireplace. A duster harsh with chalk hung from one of its pegs, she could feel the chalk gritty on her palate as she took up the duster and rubbed, talking over her shoulder at the shuffling class. She hung the duster back, careful not to shake it, and drew quickly, with the chalk breaking in her nails, a rough outline of western Europe. She stood away to the side, facing the class, an arm reached over to point at the chalk lines. As she stepped back her foot struck the fender and made a tinny noise. One of the children sniggered. The fireplace was an old-fashioned one of iron, its high grate half covered by a map of the world: highly coloured, with the British Empire in bright pink and the name of a well-known biscuit firm in large block lettering across the Antarctic. The narrow iron mantelpiece held an open tin of chalks and a pair of black drill shoes with the laces knotted together. On the wall beyond the blackboard was a lithograph of Queen Elizabeth and down at the side, past the door, a chart of historical dates hand-written on sheets of drawing-paper, pinned one below another and added to from time to time by order of Katherine. History was her favourite subject: the upward trend of history. From the vague Beginnings and Dark Ages to Enlightenment, from a dark savage welter of nationalism through its final eruption and collapse in the War to End Wars, to Our Days, to sweetness and light. She would bring it in wherever she could: into geography: Asia, the home of the race; and into botany: as the plant springs from the seed, and at last the flower...; but history itself, preeminently, taught the lesson of a splendid growth, grounded of course on personal sacrifice. She would blink a bit, from the chalk in her eyes, and wonder in a tired, remote way that the children's interest should be so hard to arouse. With extreme conscientiousness she tried to like them. She hated the girls for their giggling and the boys for their sulks and the noise their boots made kicking at the iron supports of the desks. Above all she hated the boys for mimicking the girls' giggles and the girls for looking demure when the boys were rough and noisy. If a boy made rude noises or pulled a girl's hair she sent him to the Head Master, and when a girl looked righteous was suitably sarcastic. As a result both were suspicious and hostile, the girls sly and the boys sulky.

She held their attention by fear: not so much of the sharpness with which she would turn upon them, as of a certain cold fanaticism, an intense intellectual absorption which at times came over her face as she turned from the board and rubbed the fingers of one hand against those of the other to knock away the chalk, and stood with the fingers still together, tips turned a little downwards in a prim gesture she had, while she talked and eyed them coldly. In her face, rather long and regular of feature and scarcely ever ruffled, and the smooth always neat hair drawn from a centre parting there was a coldness which repelled them. Her enthusiasm, cold too, while it compelled their attention was almost frightening. They sniggered. They said Yes Miss, No Miss, the moment she spoke to them, very respectfully, but when her back was turned they mimicked the way she stood and the long hands joined at the tips, slanting downwards.

She could feel the pulse of one hand beating against the pulse of the other. It was late afternoon, her feet were tired in their down-at-heel shoes and the children were restless. It was growing dark on the door side of the room. The lithograph of Queen Elizabeth was black with a grey patch of ruff and the history chart had lost its detail: a light strip with meaningless lines on a darkening, bilious wall. "Shall I put the light on, Miss?"

"No," she said.

A door opened across the hall and feet shuffled impatiently and stopped. In a moment the bell would go and she would line up the children and march them pinching and whispering down the hall between glass cases of barbaric weapons and the eggs of extinct birds. At the door of the cloakroom she would leave them to the mistress on duty, and fetch her books from the staff lockers and put on her hat at the stained square of mirror behind the door.

Already she was in the tram and the High Road shops were sliding by indistinct in the dusk; with a clang they stopped and came up close, Frying To-Night and a hot smell of oil and backs in greasy overcoats, and clanged and slid by: small shops, meanly lit, Boot Repairs and Fish and big, yellow tin mustard placards.

A factory was out, somewhere up a dark turning; from the mouth of the lane the workers trickled and then poured over the wide light road like ink from a bottle. Hooters sounded, on ahead, from factories near the river. Katherine clutched more tightly the pile of exercise-books under her arm and shrank against the dirty glass end of the tram. The street was full now and trade was brisking up: with the dark a single gas-jet in each window shone up yellow and almost gay. In some of the poorer shops lamps winked whitely. The crowd pushed in, hung heavily from the straps. Katherine shrank; through the greasy glass, dodging the driver's back, she watched for the turning where she got off. She thought of workers coming out of factories all over the south and east of London, and on the north, three sides; and of the far west where the belt was closing in. She thought of Robert Thomas and wondered what kind of a place it was that he worked in; and saw her turning, the neat quiet dark side street with empty, decent pavements, and stood up, clutching the exercise-books, and shouldered along the crowd and round the creaking door; got off and clutched the books and thought with envy of Robert and his long quiet working nights.

Robert shot up the wet steps under the branches leafless and anonymous, and up the darkening, cold stairs. The fire was lit in his room; after supper he turned his chair round and smoked a pipe, not so much for enjoyment as to mark a breach with the day. His feet were on the fender and knees out, elbows on knees and one hand cupping the pipe bowl. He was glad of the warm room and the hot food inside him and the work he was going to do in a bit. His mouth parted over teeth gripping the pipe stem and he grinned, abandoned to comfort, at the reddening coals. He thought about the debate last week. He wondered whether he'd turn out again next week. He thought he hadn't too much time to waste. He thought about what-was-her-name, Katherine: taught in a council school somewhere, south of the river.

Didn't look that type quite. He wondered whether there was a debate this week. He looked up for the fixture card but it was out of reach and he settled back to watching the coals.

Presently he went over to the table by the window. One hand cupping the pipe, he dragged with the other at the wedged drawer, rammed it back, bent and pulled, two handed. Outside it was dark, a blade of cold air cut in from under the sash. He dropped the plush curtains to shut out the cold and deaden wireless noises. After thinking for a moment he suddenly picked up a wad of notes and went back to the chair by the fire: moved the pipe further round to the corner of his mouth, balanced a pad on his knee and began to write.

Outside, beyond the curtains, rain was falling in sheets past wavering street lamps; cold February blew across the country. Over in Ireland the Republicans had set with redoubled vigour to the burning of houses, the property of Senators and Members of the Dáil. Through the greater part of Europe governments and peoples were occupied in resisting winter with its threat of disease and famine. Russian Counts were driving taxi-cabs in Paris and Russian Countesses were sweeping floors in French students' hostels. Turkey, in defiance of Allied opinion, was closing the ports of Smyrna and Ismit in the face of the Greek fleet; "incidents" were adding from day to day to tension in the Ruhr. In South London, along a high road where for the most part the blue shop blinds were down and an unveiled window here and there stood cavernous with dark, lurking soap packets and a dull sinister gleam of cocoa tins under a street lamp, and along the wet empty tram lines, and around the corner of a straight dark empty wet respectable side-street walled by straight sheer two-storied poor and tidy red brick houses, and along the dark musty entrance passage of the thirteenth house on the right, and through a door into a gas-lit front parlour, in a straight chair at a centre table covered by a green cloth and with her back to a bamboo stand of ferns, Katherine was reaching for the last of a pile of exercise-books and stretching her back and glancing pessimistically at a popping gas-fire.

With a red pencil she underlined the last sentence of the last essay and slapped-to the book, with a sneer at its shiny stiff slightly curled blue cardboard covers. With a quick, practised jerk of the wrist she flicked the book across the table on to the pile and got up and stared for a minute, because she found herself facing it, at the papery crimped fern on the top shelf of the bamboo stand.

She knew it was time to go up to bed in her back room on the floor above. The people of the house were in bed and she had to be at the school by eight the next morning and the landlady would charge extra for gas. The fire, which worked on a separate penny meter, was out already. There was no means of heating water for a bottle without putting in another penny. She hesitated. Not worthwhile. She carried the exercise-books across and stacked them on the sideboard and came back for her pencil and to put out the light. Her glance fell again on the stiffly goffered polished fern in its red and blue castellated china *jardinière* — so insistently alive and growing, jutting up in fat, bright green spirals with a vigour almost ridiculous in the stuffy cold room — and she wondered how it must feel to be somebody like Robert Thomas, with an interesting job and short hours and time for one's own work, and work to do of vital, absorbing interest.

Katherine, who had never done any, believed passionately in research. She believed, with impartial fervour, in the value of arctic exploration and philological reconstruction and experiments with white mice and the conquest of the air. She believed in Freud and Amundsen and Julian Huxley and that Professor Johann Smithers whose life for forty years had been devoted to the extraction of a hypothetical pre-Indo-Germanic root form of the verb *to be*. Whole-heartedly she admired excavators and commentators and aviators and explorers and biologists and bacteriologists and electrical engineers and the scientific spirit in industry. She believed that at no time in the history of the world had life been so intensely absorbing as in the year 1923. She sighed, prodding the dry mould of a pot-bound fern in the front window of 26 Verbena Road, S.W., that her own part could be no greater in this post-war era of expansion and re-birth: circumstances had forced her to teach, and the London County Council at that time — although she believed that they must shortly do so — did not encourage revolutionary individual experiment in educational method.

Next morning before the children came in, while their yells echoed thinly from the pavements beyond the yard walls, she ran her pencil down the history chart, ticking off items, frowning over recent events and wondering whether anything important had been left out. At intervals a thick line had been drawn across the paper above an important date, and the events so bracketed from line to line given a collective red tide in the margin; in this way the division 1837 Accession of Victoria to 1914 The Great War was seen to be "Industrial Expansion" and the years from 1919 to 1923 "Scientific Discovery" — with the bracket unclosed, dropping away down the page, past unnumbered empty lines. A bell clanged in the roof. A burst of yells and running boots crescendoed across the yard and died down, marshalled unseen into silence. She went back to her desk and found the register. She couldn't remember in exactly what kind of works Robert

Thomas had his appointment: he might not have said. She knew he was an analytical chemist. She was glad she had met him, she wondered whether she would see him again. So few people, comparatively, really cared about things that mattered. It was interesting to have even a nodding acquaintance with somebody who was doing something.

Robert was watching a whitish viscous mixture in a miniature saucepan, waiting for it to cook. He was pottering round the shed, hands in pockets of his white overall. He was back, looking at the pan on the burner, pottering off again, whistling; sharpening a pencil, sorting some files in a drawer. He was stirring the brew, dropping a spoonful into cold water to watch it curdle. He was off again, cursing quietly, wondering whether the stuff would be cooked by lunchtime. He was deciding it was cooked. He was lifting it from the fire and pouring it into an enamel dish and jotting down a note while it cooled. He was trying, at the request of the firm, to produce a shaving cream which would shave without water: three million men, say, in London alone save a minute a day, three million minutes, fifty thousand hours per day saved for Big Business.

Robert was bored. Robert was going out to lunch. He was coming back and pounding powders in a mortar and mixing them to a cream and waiting for them to cook.

He was locking the shed and leaning in around the door of the office to hang the key on its hook, and catching a bus and a tube and tearing upstairs, and eating and working and sleeping and tearing downstairs into a train. He was pottering and travelling and working and travelling and pottering. He was rushing like mad, and waiting interminable hours for a small potful of chemicals to come to the boil. He was eating a poached egg in an A.B.C.

He was mopping up the spilt yoke with yellow spongy toast: yellow shiny yoke slowly congealing, very slowly spreading, with half liquid, rounded celluloid edges. Eggs, untold thousands of eggs, congealing on plates in cheap lunch-rooms all through the city. Eggs broken for minute omelettes in ladies' tea-rooms with marigolds in bowls and blue and orange paint; poached and scrambled in busy food-palaces; oozing over the mashed and sausages at Good Pull-Ups for Car-men. The ubiquitous, the benevolent, the lifegiving egg, the sacrifice, the poured libation: victim torn on arid fields of hunger in afternoon energy to rise again: fertility offered up, red and broken on a plate.

Hens were clucking in dirty farmyards and lanes, a long soft maternal clucking; with a final loud triumphant hoop disclaiming offspring, scuttling splay-legged through the dust. Half-heartedly hens were cackling in hygienic model poultry farms, sixty hens to the pen, in straight tidy small-meshed shining wire cages. Hens betrayed by electric light were getting up at midnight to lay superfluous and debilitating eggs into concealed pails of preservative; hens were in labour in Egypt; the plains of Australia and New Zealand and South Africa cackled to a billion abortive births. Ships heavy with crates staggered across the seven seas, cranes groaned and dockers heaved and swore along the port of London. Farmhouse, new laid, fresh, selected and breakfast: pull-ups and pubs and eating-houses and Corner Houses and tea-rooms and cafés and clubs and restaurants and grill-rooms, and high-capped chefs whipping up the white to meringue in the basements of smart hotels: Katherine, in the staff-room of the L.C.C. Senior Mixed School in Wilberforce Street, S.W., was watching Miss Halliburton boil two eggs for lunch on the small and sulky gas-stove between the door and the staff lockers. The eggs were white, their thick-look-ing shells slightly stained from the nest. They plumped from a grey metal spoon to the bottom of the pan and bubbles came shooting up in spirals through the water and broke on the surface.

Miss Halliburton waited near the stove; her stocky legs in ribbed grey woollen stockings were planted apart in line with its thin rusty shanks on the worn linoleum. Her hand, stuck squarely from the sleeve of her brown machine-knit-ted jumper, grabbed the spoon indignantly above the edge of the pot, ready to pounce. She talked over her shoulder to Miss Vachen and Mrs. Bickerley and Miss Bott who were eating sandwiches from packets at the uncovered table. She was indignant. They were all indignant. They were indignant about a proposal of the London Education Committee to restrict the employment of married women teachers in the service of the Council.

"They daren't do it," Mrs. Bickerley said, flushed and angry. "They can't." She hoped they couldn't.

"Unemployment," Miss Vachen murmured. She was the handwork specialist. Her dress, of some coarse material aggressively handwoven in stripes of green and red, hung loose from her gaunt shoulders, her hair was wound coronet fashion in a greying plait. She had less to lose than any of them. She added, to soothe Mrs. Bickerley, "But it won't pass the Council."

Miss Bott said nothing.

Miss Halliburton looked round suspiciously. Miss Bott was inclined to think herself superior because her father had been a public schoolmaster killed in the war. She was a cut above Miss Vachen, and more than one above pretty snivel-ling little Mrs. Bickerley. She might almost be an intellectual with her straight severe features, but Miss Halliburton was practically certain she had a bourgeois ideology. It was a pity. Miss Halliburton, whose father was a shamefully prosperous butcher in a country town, strove sturdily for the right kind of class consciousness: she would have welcomed a co-worker among the staff. She muttered provocatively, with an eye on Miss Bott, "One of the things they do better in Russia." To give point to her remark she turned the tap of the gas with her left hand so that it went out with a pop, while with the spoon in her right she swooped sternly and efficiently upon the eggs. Miss Bott took no notice.

Miss Bott was Katherine. She got up slowly, folding the paper which had contained her sandwiches, and looked for the waste-paper basket. Miss Halliburton with the boiled eggs rolling on a plate stumped carefully round her and took the chair she had left at the table; noticed, in passing, Miss Bott's tall, good figure and the graceful way she moved in her cheap navy skirt and the thread stockings much darned at the heels. Miss Bott looked for the waste-paper basket and found it on the window-sill, full of dirty pairs of drill shoes. She glanced at it and dropped the neatly folded paper indifferently on top, parting her fingers and letting it fall. "Disdainful, aren't we," Miss Halliburton murmured, partly huffed, partly hoping that Miss Bott would return the chaff. She didn't repeat her remark about Russia. It was hardly safe, you never knew.

Under the window, beyond the yard, some of the children were roller-skating along the farther pavement against a blank wall. Their shouts came up, thin and inarticulate, against the closed window. Katherine went on through the open door, along the passage and down the stairs and across the hall to her class-room. She was glad to get away, the staff-room smelt of lead-pencil and rubber and steaming water and all the chairs were hard. Most of the teachers went home for lunch and in any case there was none of them she cared to talk to. She thought their interests narrow and usually contemptible.

She sat at her table facing the empty rows of desks and ticked over a register, waiting for the children to come in. In a remote way she was sorry for Mrs. Bickerley who would almost certainly lose her job, but the new regulations, if passed, would make the posts of the unmarried more secure. Katherine was a feminist, if she had been born ten years sooner she would have been a suffragette. But she had had to work for her living too unexpectedly, and too urgently, not to value economic security. She had, besides, a vague contempt for married women — content with homes and babies and indifferent to the things that mattered: happy, she thought with a slight sneer, in an emotional and humiliating bondage — which made her, illogically, despise even their efforts to escape. She hoped the regulation would be adopted, and forgot about it.

The table was wide, dirty brown and ink-stained, Katherine sat with elbows fastidiously at her sides, checking over the ruled oasis of register. Ranged on the open groove, up against the beading, were two caked ink-wells, black and red, and an open toffee tin of chalks and a Bible with chalk-smeared shiny cover. At her feet to the left, kicked back against the fender, lay a holed tray half full of empty ink-wells, ink crusted on their mottled china edge. The blackboard stood, smeared blank, on its easel with grey cloth dangling, and the door was half open. In front of her the empty desks stretched back yellow and slanting at different heights, a bumpy waste, to the green and yellow-brown walls. In the high, uncurtained windows ventilator cords dangled against the yellow brick wall and cement floor of the play-ground; the empty jam-jar had been pushed to the end of a sill. The children were outside, unseen; their shouts echoed along the empty wall.

They were marched in, slouching sullenly in line; they clattered and squeaked and flumped between the desks, kicked at the iron supports. Their heads were blobs of uneven height and nondescript colour, tousled or frizzed or oiled, bobbing up and down on the sickly-painted walls. On the blackboard, over the smears, Katherine had written the dates of the Saxon kings: there was a blot, a white round blob with little flecks of white splayed around, where she had brought down the chalk sharply on the board in nervous impatience to emphasise a point. Beyond the glass-panelled door and the dangling chart the hall stretched emptily between its cases of weapons and dried grasses; behind doors on its other sides Miss Halliburton sturdily and Mrs. Bickerley with anxious sniffs were taking classes and Miss Vachen was entangled in a maze of raffia and basket-cane; on the floor above, other teachers were taking other classes and Mr. Blatherston the Head Master lurked in his narrow office at cluttered desk. Under the office were the empty cloak-rooms with limp and silent coats hung on pegs. Outside, the yard was grey and cold and quite empty, the colour of the sky, with the blank yellow brick wall running around behind an empty jam-pot in the window. The children were shuffling up and kicking and slouching out in line, one reaching back to tweak another. Katherine's slim feet in worn black stockings stepped up precisely past the blackboard and the line moved on and out across the hall and broke with a yell in the cold air of the yard. They slouched out and trooped in and on the board the figures of an arithmetic problem were laid precise and clear over the smeared-out dates of kings.

Tension was rising in the staff-room; a weak and yellow sun struggled now over the yard where the children played without their coats, and a handful of depressed catkins drooped from the jar against the window cord. Katherine was concerned about the Ruhr: two French officers wounded at Gelsenkirchen and a German policeman killed and the town fined a hundred million marks; an embargo instituted against the exportation of Ruhr metal products; Belgian occupation of Wesel and Emmerich on the Rhine. Hatred was running high in Germany and indignation in France and nervousness at Westminster. Outside the County Hall several hundred women teachers were assembled to hear the decision of the L.C.C. Mrs. Bickerley, at the staff table, was saying, "They can't do it," and Miss Vachen, "I never thought they'd do it," and Miss Halliburton was hinting darkly about where they did things better. Katherine, behind the fern, under the gas in the front room at 26 Verbena Road, was thinking that if the Bickerley went she'd move up one in seniority on the staff; and Robert, turning over a *Morning Post* in the Underground on his way to the factory, noted that, in view of the grave tension of public opinion in France and Germany, a mass meeting arranged for the following Thursday on the League of Nations and the Ruhr would not take place.

He left the train at its new station in the fields and walked the hundred yards or so to the factory turning. The window of the laboratory was open and he leant out: the sky at the end of the buildings was pale blue, and a damp, growing smell from the retreating grass pierced the throb of machinery.

He came in and found his overalls and instructions for the day and remembered, rinsing a tube, about the postponed meeting. He had thought he ought to go, and forgotten about it; but the news that it was put off, that he could no longer go if he wanted to, made him angry. He decided that he quite definitely had meant to go, that only these mass meetings were worth attending in any case, that it was a matter of international importance and that to cancel it was not only absurd but preposterous, that it was a sheer waste of time to hang around at his branch meetings, that so far as he knew there was no other open meeting for weeks, that it was ridiculous to put it off at the last minute because many people might not see.... That in fact she probably wouldn't see the notice but would roll up to the Central Hall at eight-thirty on Thursday, expecting to find Robert Cecil holding forth on the jolly old Ruhr.

He stopped stirring the brew he was cooking and grinned at it and stirred again. As soon as it was lunch time he went out and lit a pipe and wondered what to do. He felt school-boyish and responsible both at once in a pleasurable mixture, stamping up and down the cinder path with the lit pipe clenched between his teeth in the middle of a grin. He wondered whether Katherine Bott's address would be in the telephone directory; he thought not. He thought she must have told him where she worked, but if so he'd forgotten it. He thought she hadn't. He thought if he went across the river and asked at the first council school he struck it might be the right one, but that didn't seem likely. He thought, with inspiration and a grip at the pipe, that he might stroll down to Westminster on Thursday evening and see whether she turned up. He thought it wouldn't be such a bad idea. He thought he'd go along just on the chance. He went.

They were strolling along the Embankment and talking about Progress.

"Now why?" he said, pulling at his pipe. "Just why," he

said to tease her, "should things get better and better? They can just as easily get worse and worse."

Her face was pink with the wind blowing up from the North Sea. "But think," she said, "but just look at..." — aerial concert over Croydon, sixty-eight aircraft carrying a hundred and twenty-nine passengers operate between London and continent in one week, caterpillar-wheeled cars cross Sahara, Paris night flight.

They turned back and the wind pushed them, propelling towards Westminster. He took his pipe from his mouth and grinned and stuck it back. "Oh yes," he said — fatal R.A.F. crash at Grantham, twenty-nine victims of explosion in British Columbia, hundred and twenty-two miners entombed five thousand feet from entrance in Denver, New Mexico — "quite so, but what about..."

They both laughed and he put her on a bus at the top of Victoria Street. He stood on the corner for a moment writing down the address she had given him, and walked on, grinning, and took a fifty-two.

He stoked up the embers in the grate and wondered whether to work. The wirelesses were hard at it, across the road and next door, and a new one, or a gramophone, on the other side. With a truant, holiday feeling he thought he'd leave it for that night: reached down the fixture card from behind the clock and sat with the card in his hand and feet on the fender until the fire died down again.

"And how about noise?" he said. "How about that?"

"You can't help that," she said, "it's the price of progress."

"Where to," he said, over his pipe.

"Don't be silly," she said.

All the same he was glad they were doing a spot of progressing out at the trading estate that summer. He was glad, as autumn came on, of the good tarred road they laid down over the fields where the cinder track had been, and the new little lock-up shops in a row by the new station, with a café where he could get lunch without going back into town. He was glad of the quick frequent trains which gave him a longer evening, and when there was a meeting on he had time to eat before the show.

Mrs. Bickerley had gone from the staff-room. In the presence of ambassadors and foreign representatives the First International Air Congress — French tackle problem of all-metal plane, Portuguese plan flight round world (Crete — Aleppo — Delhi — Calcutta — Rangoon — Bangkok — Shanghai — Yokohama — Petropavlovsk — Dutch Harbour — Vancouver — Winnipeg — Quebec — Azores), helicopter hovers over fixed point for nine minutes, Amundsen plans flight across the North Pole — is opened in London by the Prince of Wales. Rebellion breaks out in Bavaria, led by a builder's labourer, Adolf Hitler; Lenin dies, Great Britain recognises the U.S.S.R.; Buenos Aires receives an experimental transmission by Beam wireless from Poldhu, Wembley stages a scenic display of London destroyed by hostile aircraft, Robert and Katherine meet in Bloomsbury for a lecture on the Dawes Plan.

"Tell me more about your work," she says as they come out. "Your own work, I mean."

"Oh, that," he says, reddening, pulling at his pipe.

The audience has trickled away down side-streets and they are alone in the empty, artificial stillness of Bedford Square, with a hot August wind blowing through the leaves and the noise of traffic threatening for a distance. "Oh well," he says, modest, reddening. — The Fascist National Council is inaugurated at Rome and twenty-five thousand

Communists are demonstrating in the forest of Garches, ten miles from Paris. — "Oh," he says, "that?"

He has never told anybody about it before, and as he outlines his theory he finds it isn't so complete as he thought, but he slurs over the gaps as they are slurred over in his mind. "Something like this," he says, pointing with the pipe-stem impatiently at nothing. "You see what I mean."

She barely follows in outline what he is telling her, her mind is so busy shying from detail, thinking: This is something Real, this is something Great, this is something new and splendid unfolding in front of me: for this once, for the very first time, most likely for the only time, I am privileged to watch actually in motion, in this quite ordinary-looking boy — for he isn't much more, what would he be, about twenty-two — one of the brave and original minds of science Working Something Out.

"I think it's splendid," she said when they got to the bus. She didn't know what else to say, for anything else seemed inadequate. She repeated, "I think it's splendid."

For, above all, Katherine believed in the boundless capacity and influence of the human mind. She believed in H. G. Wells and Sir Oliver Lodge (earth preparing all these millions of years for a human race, human race crown and flower of all that preparation) and in the dignity of labour; she believed that history is the sum of exceptional personalities. Over the heads of a shuffling, uneasy class, hypnotised by her own words, hands joined wrist and tip and the tips vibrating one against another, she lectured on the significance of Columbus to the green and yellow paint and thought of Robert Thomas and his assault upon the ultimate nature of Time.

She thought what extraordinary luck she had had to make this intellectual contact.

The history chart lengthened on the wall: a fresh sheet of paper and a new row of bright brass drawing-pins; in the jar on the window-sill were three top-heavy crinkled dahlias. Robert, with the heavy curtains drawn behind the gas-jet, was racking his brains to fill the gaps in his thesis.

There were Michaelmas daisies in the jar instead of dahlias, and a leaf left floating on the water half-way up the jar, and nothing. The radiators smelt of paint. Winter came on, busy with hope. A Dawes loan of forty million put Germany back on the gold standard, France and Belgium left the Ruhr, a draft treaty was in preparation: Protocol for the Pacific Settlement of International Disputes. The world, it seemed to Katherine, was turning to peace, the way was open for discovery and advancement; a new and splendid Era — it seemed too good to be true — was in reach around the corner of the year. Invited by Miss Halliburton, she attended a lecture on the Russian Experiment and found it dull. She mentioned it to Robert. Russia, they agreed, would need educating to take a place among the nations of the future; and dismissed it.

The year turned. Katherine, buying stockings in the January sales, thought she might as well get flesh-colour: everybody seemed to wear them now, and really you might as well. Communists and Socialists fought a pitched battle in the streets of Berlin; British Security police discovered a bomb store in Cologne; a five-seater car with twenty-four hundredweight load had conquered the Australian desert. A lecturer at the Royal Society of Arts, on recent exploration into the nature of the atom, asked where radiological research might not lead: it might raise the issue, said he — said Katherine and doubtfully agreed Robert, pulling red-faced at his pipe — as to whether there was any borderline between the man of science and the metaphysician. "You see," she said. "And to think you were bothered about where you were drifting!"

She went to school now with a secret, excited feeling that whatever was going to happen was coming nearer. Sunshine was streaking the floor and making the children fidget, and a handful of limp catkins drooped again from the jar. Aviation for the general public, production of cheap, low-powered planes, was prophesied for the next year or two. The Protocol was marching on.

The Protocol is coming. France rejects the notion that there is no such thing as a German air-force: air-ports springing up: Dutch, Danish, Italian and Russian establishments produce aeroplanes for the Reich. Powder and munition factories in Russia work full time under German engineers: ten thousand aeroplane programme. In Rome a great demonstration celebrates the sixth anniversary of the birth of Fascismo. Naval manoeuvres off Magdalena Bay — "greatest con-centration of naval power ever assembled in the Pacific" — show America powerless to protect the Pacific coast against an attack of enemy air-force. The Government of Great Britain is unable to accept the Protocol. Katherine, with her paper spread out on the stuffy green cloth of the parlour table behind the ferns of 26 Verbena Road, feels terribly flat and weary, and all at once she knows that the one thing in the world she wants is to tell Robert Thomas all about it.

Robert, his window open to the fresh evening, is tidying up a few jobs to the tune of the wireless or gramophone next door. He hums in time as he works, tugging notes from the back of the table drawer:

> *No day's complete dear,*
> *Until we meet dear,*

he hums, and tugs, and stops to grin.

> *And at that meeting*
> *My-y heart stops beating...*

He hums and grins and tugs and stops. For all at once, with a whoop, he knows he is in love with Katherine.

Chapter IV

"Why bother about that," he said. "Never mind the Protocol."
But he saw she did.

The wind was blowing up fresh, April-damp, past Blackfriars and the Tower and over the dark, wide estuary spreading unseen into dark, flat country, from the dark sea.

"The world's all right," he said. "How about letting the jolly
old world get on by itself for a bit?" But he knew she wouldn't.

The wind was blowing up from the dark, distant sea,
fresh and damp, in a wide sweep over Essex and narrowing to
London's docks and up between dark banks of warehouses
and past Somerset House and the high cliffs of the Cecil. It
flicked the opening leaves of the plane-trees into restless patterns against the lamps, and trams lolloped by with a cheerful clang and rattle. "The world's all right," he said, "what's
wrong with it?" and she laughed.

They turned and the wind caught them and blew them

back, walking light on wind, laughing together, blown westward with the small new bursting leaves and the ripple of
the tide.

The wind blew up damp with April; it blew past the
high backs of the Strand, where Mr. Arthur Ponsonby, M.P.,
addressing a Peace Conference in the Essex Hall, was asking
for the enrolment of a vast army of conscientious objectors
in readiness for the next war; past Blackfriars where Mr. Tom
Mann, urging united action in wage demands, was looking
forward to "one of the biggest and finest fights of the workers ever put up in this country"; across from Brussels where
news was coming in of the successful arrival of an aeroplane,
after six weeks' flight, at Leopoldville, Belgian Congo; and
up over Geneva where the newly formed Union of European
Broadcasting was meeting at the League Secretariat; and in
a broad, sweeping rush from east and south, where Communists fought police among the mines of Czechoslovakia
and Mussolini had assumed the portfolio of War Minister
at Rome: over the night plains of Europe where Germany
was converting coal into oil and Industry was becoming Scientific, over the North Sea and over the flats of Essex where
steel and cement houses were going up by the dozen (twen-
ty-one thousand seven hundred and fifty-eight cheap houses
built in England and Wales in first three months of 1925),
and narrowing with a swift piston-push past the City where
sterling was on the rise in view of a possible return to the
gold standard: it came sweeping up behind them and just
before Westminster Bridge they turned together to meet it
and laughed in the face of the wind, waiting to cross, holding
hands and running in front of a tram.

"I'll see you to your place," he said when they got to the bus.

"No, don't bother, you mightn't be able to get back.

Besides I can't ask you in, the people in the house go to bed at ten. It's rather cramping."

"Why should you be stuck in a hole like that," he said, angry for her.

She laughed.

She found the river again, higher up, where it was dark and quiet and the warehouses were low on the far side. Once across, the bus took a turn; she left it and waited for a tram. The tram slid with her along the High Road between the shops where little lights were twinkling among the gay, secret packets of groceries. Summer's coming, she thought. Summer's coming and it's going to be fun. The little lights were twinkling and it was all warm and happy and distantly, comingly, exciting. She didn't know exactly how; but there were going to be a lot of things to go to and it was going to be fun and it was coming.

Robert was coming home from the laboratory. He came out of the Underground humming a tune he had heard from next door. There was a wireless shop across the road and he halted by it, thinking it wouldn't be such a bad idea to get one of the things himself, but all the sets were much too expensive. He turned the corner into the road where he lived and strolled on past the house to the end and round the corner where the barrows of a street market edged the pavement. It was too fine an evening to go in at once, and he had a vague idea of picking up a gramophone cheap. It was a fine evening and this street was full and noisy and his own road seemed quiet when he turned back into it. The privet in the square of front garden was turning light green and the laburnum was breaking scrubbily into bud when Robert came up the steps with his second-hand gramophone in one hand and two or three new records in the other. He put the gramophone on the top step and the records under his left arm and grinned to himself while he felt for the key.

Katherine was prodding the root of the fern in the parlour window: it was putting up tight, brown curly fronds. One of the taller fronds had thrown off its flimsy brown-papery wrapping and was standing upright with a new bright green head ready to uncurl. A pile of exercise-books was waiting on the table behind Katherine and in a minute it would be time to light the gas. She was thinking that knowing somebody who was doing research and making exciting discoveries was the next best thing to doing it oneself. It was almost better, it was more exciting in a way.

Robert played the gramophone to himself for several evenings and got bored with it. He switched it off and tried to work, but as the weather grew warmer more windows were opened in the street and there was too much noise. He hung about from one week to another, waiting for the next time he could meet Katherine. When he came back he felt full of belief in himself and full of work. The wireless fiends were quiet now; he opened the window to the warm night and dropped, elbows first, on to his notes. After half an hour he jumped up and lit a pipe and decided he was stale and might as well ease off through the summer. He wound the gramophone and set it going, up against the open window; wondered fleetingly whether it would carry across the street and hoped it would. One morning the landlady complained, and after that he took to walking home from meetings: getting back tired out and rolling into bed.

Katherine went from desk to blackboard in a mist of enthusiasms pleasantly vague. The windows were open on to the dusty playground and when she dabbed the board with the duster a mist of chalk came out; stray particles hovered for some time after in a shaft of sunlight. In the lunch-hour, with door open for coolness upon the dusty hall, she would go down among empty desks and stand, pencil poised, in front of the history chart, absently checking up dates like items on an account and waiting for afternoon school to begin. In the staff-room Miss Halliburton would be holding forth, stocky and indignant. Katherine smiled and wished she could show Miss Halliburton to Robert.

He was hanging around in the laboratory, waiting for something to cook. It was hot and the next-door machinery was noisy and there were more factories now, on the farther plots, adding to a general purr and vibration: soap and jam and furniture polish and wireless sets. He wished he were back in his room, with the air coming over the roofs and the gramophone on. He wished he could ask Katherine to his place. He wished he were going to see her before next week. There was no reason that he could see why he shouldn't ask her. He wished he'd thought of it before.

She was giving an arithmetic lesson, totting up figures on the dusty board. The children were fidgety with heat and the coming holidays: while she wrote she could hear them behind her, shuffling and tweaking and sitting down clumsily when she moved: restless but not yet out of hand. She ignored them, knowing that if serious noise broke out she could deal with it; that in any case Mr. Blatherston was not likely to say anything in the last week of term. She went on totting up two and two, and thinking of the amazing steps progress was taking in this wonderful summer: experiments with ultra-violet rays in London hospitals; Beam Wireless station at Skegness, at Dorchester, Bridgwater, Bodmin; Swedish dancer flies from Paris to dance at London matinee, to dance at Brussels at five, in Paris at ten; new air line opened,

Berlin — Amsterdam — London; tenders invited for high-power wireless station at Angora, Turks deserting the fez; airship masts erected in Egypt and Karachi for trial flights of R.36 and R.33; world's first air yacht built at Long Island; lecturer to British Science Guild calls for more publicity for science, explanations for man-in-the-street.

"You see," she said. "What people want is a scientist who can write. Not many people can do both, like you."

"No," he said. "Quite. But that's a bit different. That isn't quite what I meant," he said, "popular science."

"That's only a name," she said. "Why be hypnotised by a name."

"Well, yes," he said, "there's something in that. But never mind that," he said. "Why don't we go along to my place, it's only ten."

"Nearer eleven."

They were strolling back along the Strand and a 15 bus drew up ahead of them. He stopped. "I've got a gramophone," he said. "Do you dance?"

She smiled. "It's too late."

"Then come to tea on Sunday."

"I've got to go home," she said, depressed. "Up north. Summer holidays and so on."

He felt for his pipe and stuck it empty in his mouth, perturbed, so that she laughed at him. "Oh, bad luck. Mine's in Wales. But afterwards," he said anxiously. "When you get back."

She nodded. "I'd love to."

He kicked the edge of the pavement, petulant, like a little boy. "You don't mean that."

"Yes, I do," she said, serious all at once, looking away.

They were silent for a moment; jerked back to say goodbye, just friends, cheerful.

"I'll see you in September then?"

"Something like that."

She got on her bus.

Looking back, she saw him standing on the edge of the pavement, hands in pockets and stooping a bit; standing still, irresolute, with the late crowd hurrying behind him.

He watched her bus until it was lost in the jam by Charing Cross, then he started to walk home and walked until he was tired.

He took his fortnight during August and spent it in his room off Ladbroke Grove, determined to get something done. All day by the open window and behind hot curtains in the evening, after business hours when the wirelesses came on, he slogged at his notes, sorting them into files and trying to get them into some kind of order under the main headings of his thesis. When it grew late and the noise had stopped he was glad to throw up the window and smoke a pipe by the empty grate before going to bed. Now and then he'd look at the armchair with its embroidered sleeves and antimacassar and wonder how she'd look sitting there. But it seemed impossible that she ever would.

"I never thought you would," he said.

"Why not?"

"Couldn't say. Just one of those things that seem more unlikely than others."

He was handing out the cakes and buttered buns provided by the landlady for a lady-to-tea. He couldn't have said whether she looked as he'd expected her to up against the antimacassar. She seemed tanned a bit from her holiday, but he was too much embarrassed to take in details. Although they had met so often in other places there was a sudden awkwardness between them at being here: she nibbling a bun in the ridiculous armchair and he hovering unnecessarily over the table. The thought that he had been a fool to ask her trembled gloomily on the edge of his mind, but he toppled it off.

"I like this place of yours," she said. "You've got it all to yourself up here." She thought he had a funny lost look among the much-too-large furniture perched up among the chimney pots. She wondered why she had come.

"Yes," he said, brightening. "Isn't it. Rather jolly I mean. Nobody bothers. Short of playing the gramophone at one in the morning I mean to say."

"Oh yes," she said, "the gramophone."

He straddled a chair and tugged the machine nearer: wound it laboriously and spent unnecessary time over choosing a record. She noticed the table under the open window and wondered if that was where he worked. Now he had got her here it seemed as if he didn't want to talk about himself, or perhaps he was too shy. She thought it had been rather silly to come. When she was away she felt very, very proud of knowing Robert, and she wondered why, now she was with him, they should both feel awkward. The second-hand gramophone jerked and started, with a loud, whirring accompaniment: "Tea for two And two for tea…"

"Dance?" he said.

He pushed the table back against the door, throwing over a cup, and they began to jerk giddily up and down in the small space between the furniture, laughing when the bumps came. Robert was a clumsy dancer — he had spent most of the time at college dances standing out near the door — but he managed to take most of the bumps and that did as well. The record came to an end and the needle scraped loudly. They stopped and Robert reached it off.

Katherine leant against the table by the window and tucked her hair under her cloche hat. "I haven't danced for about five years."

"College dances? Same here. Where were you, by the way?"

"Oh, nowhere. That is, a training college at home. When we had a dance the authorities used to collect a bunch of partners from the men's college next door and hand them round impartially. Unless you had a brother or something to bring, of course. For some reason they always had sweaty hands."

They laughed.

"Other side?" he said, turning the record.

She nodded. "Let's sit it out though."

He looked up anxiously. "Furniture's a bit hard I'm afraid, and I'm not too good at avoiding."

"No, you did it rather well."

The gramophone groaned and whirred. Robert came over and sat on the table and she swung up beside him.

> I want — to be — happy,
> I want — to be — happy...

He watched her sitting there swinging her feet, leaning back on her hands towards the open window. He wished he could see her face better, but her hat came down rather like a flowerpot and hid most of it. He thought she looked pretty much of a kid really, and she'd had a pretty rotten time.

> And I want you — to be hap-py too.

They sat listening to the record until it came to an end; then he jumped down and put it on again, because silence was embarrassing. "I've often wondered what you'd look like in here," he said with a rush, coming back.

"What a funny idea!" she cried. She wished she knew the kind of answer one ought to make to that kind of remark. Awkwardness, which had lifted with the dance, was closing down again. Robert, met outside and walking home from meetings, had been a Person, of similar interests, with whom one discussed politics and work; but shut in here with the conventionally unconventional gramophone and dance, he had somehow became a Man, with whom conversation must be made. Bright conversation. And how did one do that? Neither college dances nor Wilberforce Street school nor League of Nations lectures had taught her how. And it would be terrible to be skittish. She thought Robert seemed at a loss too. Soon she said she must go, and he got up too quickly and walked with her to the tube. But as the train was coming in he gave his old grin and gripped her hand and hoped she'd come again as if he meant it.

The train pulled out with a rattle and shake, plunging past drab house-backs before it plunged into the dark. She was glad she'd been, she was glad she'd seen Robert's place, she thought he'd been awfully sweet the way he'd shown it to her, she thought of all the things she'd wanted to say but not thought of, and said them through the smeared window to the streaky dark tunnel. Robert went down the steps from the station into Ladbroke Grove, jingling the keys in his pockets, and strolled home, grinning faintly at the pavement. He told it he was glad it had come, he'd always wanted to see it there, he'd always wanted to know how it would look; I say, he was saying but without words, this is just about right isn't it. And a lot more. And she was answering... They'd never been so close together, and they'd never been quite so glad to be together: and he was letting himself in at the hall door under the scrubby brown laburnum and she was getting out of the train at Baker Street, wondering abstractedly why she'd come that way and which was the best way now to get home.

Night came on and shook them apart. Dusk came rattling up against the bus windows and the dark, shuttered High Road slid by past the long panels of the tram. Katherine got down at Verbena Road and let herself in and found Sunday supper — brawn and beetroot — on the front room table and the gas turned low. Back down the long High Road and across the river, and across Chelsea and Knightsbridge and on the far side of Kensington, Robert was munching a bun left over from tea and pushing the furniture into place before the landlady could come up and object. Presently she brought up his supper on a tray and he went to bed in the little room looking on to a blank wall, and in the morning the tube carried him rapidly out and away into the newly built country; and behind him, back up the long suburban line and across Kensington and Chelsea and over the river and along the High Road, Katherine was hurrying downstairs from the back bedroom and along Verbena Road, clutching a bunch of exercise-books, and catching a tram for Wilberforce Street, farther out still.

The week went round — school and tram and corrections and tram and school, work and tube and laboratory and tube and work — and swung them together for half an hour in a cold wind, and she hoped he was warm enough, why did he never wear an overcoat, and the clock went round, nearer eleven than ten, and swung them apart.

Westminster Coroner expresses an opinion, in view of frequent suicides, that neurasthenics ought not to go on tube station platforms; French air aces plan nonstop flight to India; cause of disaster to U.S. airship *Shenandoah* is said to be removal of eight of the eighteen safety valves: victims "gave their lives to save the precious helium"; in Hammersmith workmen with brush and whitewash are painting novel traffic control signs on roads: STOP; Robert is stamping up and down the laboratory, waiting for a mixture to cook, swinging his arms and shouting for Rodney, lazy oaf, to light the stove.

The R.33 is launched at Pulham; Cobham leaves Croydon for eight-thousand-mile flight to the Cape; from Genoa Casagrande sets out west in a 500 h.p. hydroplane, Casablanca — Palmas — Cape Verde — Santiago — North Brazil — Argentina. Eastward: vast electric power system installed in Greece; world record for gliding broken in Crimea; Japanese airmen pass on transcontinental flight to Paris and London; New South Wales racing car doing seventy per hour bounds into crowd; Tokyo authorities are troubled by the increasing number of dance halls and cinematograph films; telegraph cables at cost of over two million are laid on the floor of the Pacific; American luxury trains run from coast to coast equipped with barber shops, radio and hot baths; a mouse weighing less than a quarter of an ounce, electrocuted on the plate of a condenser, causes a breakdown for twelve minutes of the transmitting apparatus of the high-power station at Daventry. Katherine, lecturing over the heads of a class and dreaming of progress and Robert, is called back by a small, persistent, hissing noise: one of the boys swishing with his pencil at the dead, dry chrysanthemums in the dirty jar on the sill. "Take that disgusting thing out and empty it," she says irritably to the girl nearest the door, and all the boys snigger.

Robert locks the laboratory and hangs up the key and hurries off home: he feels he'll be able to write a chapter over Christmas, with luck, if he can get ahead with sorting his notes. He wishes he could get a chapter written — get one done he'd go ahead then — because every time he sees Katherine, and that's about once a week, she asks how he's getting on. He goes home and has supper and lights a pipe while he waits for the wireless stations to close down at ten. He sits and smokes, feet on fender, and waits for the noise to stop. Twenty thousand new houses erected in one year, two hundred and seven persons killed in London streets in three months, wireless station, one of the world's greatest, completed at Rugby, motor firm turns out forty-eight thousand seven hundred and twelve cars in 1925 against three hundred and thirty-seven in 1919, it is found necessary to install soundproof floors in a mammoth block of flats in Park Lane, the B.B.C. institutes a transmission of dance music until midnight — "dance music the backbone of British broadcasting" — every day with the exception of Sundays. Robert clenches his teeth and tries to concentrate: he thinks if he had Katherine there to keep him to it he might be able to get more done.

Katherine is correcting exercises under a sizzling gasglobe and thinking about Robert and Science. Science, discovery. From the earth itself: new element discovered at Prague; upwards through man: death of third X-ray martyr of London hospital...

(but Congress of Bloemfontein, Orange Free State, condemns teaching of evolution in schools: "this monkey business" ... "though he did not quite know what evolution meant" ... "the thing an absolute scandal and should be stopped.")

...to the stars. Millikan, from Pike's Peak in California, traces source of radiation in the atmosphere, short-wave rays from outer space; relativity theory shows matter of star, companion to Sirius, to be compressed to density of a ton to the cubic inch; radiation discovered by Millikan, says Jeans, may be derived not only from outside the earth's atmosphere but from outside the galaxy: from the spiral nebulae, most distant objects known in space. Katherine wonders how Robert manages in cold weather, hopes his landlady lights a fire for him before he comes in. She thinks he looks rather tired lately and needs looking after. The room is suddenly quiet. The gas in the grate has stopped sizzling, begun to fail; flame palely dwindling down the sticks of brownish fuel. She reaches for the worn handbag she takes to school and feels at the bottom for some coppers to put in the meter.

There are three pennies in the bag. She forces them into the rusty slot and the fire leaps up, yellow and spluttering. Prime Minister says every economy will be made, however unpopular; dockyard axe scheme will save one million a year; expense an obstacle to speeding up of railways; cotton trade losses reach a million a week, two hundred thousand operatives affected; popular dance tune can earn up to a pound a minute when broadcast. Strikes, doles, subsidies, call for a New Spirit in Industry: for the first time it strikes Robert, drawing his weekly pay envelope at Cupid Cosmetics Ltd. on the New Epoch Trading Estate West, signing for the envelope and slipping it into his pocket in his usual careless way, that if he wanted to marry he couldn't afford to.

"Who looks after you?" She was leaning with her back to the table, craning round at the drab, ordinary houses across the street, thinking that was what he looked at when he worked. She straightened up and started round the room, restlessly, uneasily, noticing little things: the pipe and fixture card behind the stiff vases on the mantelpiece and the rug worn in a solitary patch, where his feet came, in front of the chair. The other chair, a carpet-covered half-easy, was pushed far back into a corner as if nobody ever sat in it. He hadn't pulled it out for her but given her his, perched himself on edges anywhere, wandering from one to another and coming to temporary rests, leaning back on his wrists, feet crossed, feeling for stance. She went across to the bookcase and ran a finger along the bindings: his college textbooks and a few works of reference he had saved up to buy. "Do you mind my poking round and looking at things?"

"No," he said. "I like you to."

She felt there was something aching about the room, something lonely and lost. It made her feel he came in with wet feet and didn't change his shoes, and that when he was too tired to work at night there was nobody to talk to him for half an hour and give him a hot drink so that he could go on again. She fingered the torn binding of a dictionary, with a wild, disproportionate longing to heal. They stood quite still for some time while he watched her fingers soothe the frayed cloth. She knew, achingly, that they were both terribly poor and there was nothing to be done.

She had no shyness with him anymore, she thought there was nothing she couldn't have said. She felt very much larger than he, and protective, and horribly afraid for him that he would say the things he didn't want to and the shyness would come down on them again. She could see him, down below, battling between the things he wanted to say and the not wanting to say them.

She said, sliding the dictionary into place, "How about Thursday week, Euston Road? You'll be there, won't you? Lorimer's sound, as a rule."

He swallowed, and she saw that the things had gone. "What is it? Locarno again?" He banged his fist sulkily, pettishly almost, against the spine of a book and drove the book back against the wall.

"Yes," she said. "But Lorimer's fairly sound."

They went to a lecture on the Spirit of Locarno and another on the Lesson of Geneva. They went to lectures on Disarmament and the New Turkey and poison gas and the Meaning of Fascism — May 1926: undergraduates man railways, M.P.s collect tickets, Katherine walks to school and Robert gets a lift as far as Ealing from a Woman Volunteer, trade declines forty-eight million pounds in the month — and they went to a lecture on What the Strike has Taught Us.

They went to lectures in Euston Road, and Farringdon Road and Red Lion Square and the Strand and Westminster and Hampstead. "No," she said, "I can't come to your place, really, there isn't time. And I always have things to correct on Sundays." Because the room was so lonely and lost that, in a vague way, she was afraid of it.

He would wait for her at the door of the lecture hall and sit by her and walk back with her to get her bus. She was bright and summery in Red Lion Square and shivered a bit in the Strand, and at Hampstead, on a wet winter evening, she wore those high Russian boots that came right up to her short skirt. He would watch her bus rock into the distance and then saunter off, a bit dispirited, to get his own. If it happened to be one of the new ones with tops he would scramble down again and glare at the conductor and wait for the next. He would sit huddled over his evening paper on the unlit bus top, with the wind lifting his hair, and do a crossword puzzle in what light there was because he didn't want to think, because he wouldn't be seeing her for the best part of another week.

Miss Halliburton said, "I do think you ought to come. I do think you haven't given us a fair trial." *Red Flag* at civil service camp; Premier declares war on Communism; Socialist gains in local elections; Communist trial, *Red Flag* at Bow Street.

"It's just people like you," she said, "who ought to take an interest."

Red Spies for British Mining Areas; Zinovieff Wins; Moscow Gold for Miners; Miss Halliburton, trotting earnestly on short legs, walking off Katherine to a lecture on Culture in the Soviets. "It's all lies," she said, turning up her earnest, porky face as she trotted. "Misrepresentation. It's wicked, the misrepresentation. You wouldn't believe."

Katherine agreed politely, she didn't mind very much. She was wondering whether Robert would be at Germany and the League on Friday: it was a point of honour with them, a rule in the game, not to remind one another, it made it more exciting. He always came, but she always wondered whether he would.

The room rented by Miss Halliburton's club was stuffy and they sang a dismal song, rather like a hymn, although Katherine had gathered that religion was abolished in Russia. She wondered what Robert was doing and whether he really worked at his thesis on the evenings she didn't see him and whether it would really matter if she went there again one Sunday. They were out again on the pavement and Miss Halliburton was sniffing from the raw cold. With bright earnestness, between sniffs, she was expounding the position of women under Communism: "You ought to have heard last week's."

"Don't you go thinking We want to get you," she said, "it makes no difference to Us. It's for your own good I'm telling you. It's just educated women like us who've got the most to learn from Russia."

"Oh yes," Katherine said politely. "Yes. Very interesting."

Russian scientist's blood tests, Chinese University founded in Moscow, tractor works at Leningrad, hydro-electric station opened in Erivan — "And Progress, look at Science, nothing to compare, look where you like..."

"Yes," Katherine said vaguely. "Thank you very much. I enjoyed it so much. I mean, it was very interesting."

Miss Halliburton glowed. "There, I thought you would. That's what I say. I do look forward to my Thursday evenings."

"Mind you come again," she called, in a glow, from the platform of the tram. "Only got to say the word. Any time."

She nodded and disappeared inside the tram and it carried her away. Katherine walked on along the empty road, thinking she really might go just once, she hadn't been for so long. Not this Sunday, but Sunday week perhaps. If he asked her on Friday.

She knew it was a mistake as soon as she got there, though she didn't know why, but he seemed so shy and dull. He was fiddling with the gramophone, putting needles in and taking them out again without winding the machine. She had felt glad at coming, but now she felt dull and miserable.

"Haven't you got any new records?"

"One," he said, brightening, and put it on.

> *I am just a lit-tle boy,*
> *Who's looking for a lit-tle girl...*

As soon as it had started he kicked himself. He was furiously depressed at seeing her there in the carpet chair by the fender, knowing she would go again. Under the noise of the gramophone there was a horrible silence in the room. They sat miserably unconcerned, tapping time, helpless under the blare of the unembarrassed machine.

> *Who's looking for a little boy-oy...*

Robert lifted the needle clumsily and the tune ended in a screech and the whirring of the turn-table. "Rotten thing wants oiling," he muttered miserably.

The sudden stoppage of noise left them formal and without conversation. She was annoyed with him both for putting the record on and for taking it off again, and he was furious with her because he had.

"Why don't you have some more tea? That's cold."

"No thanks, it's quite nice."

She cried a bit, angrily, in the tube going home; and in the parlour, under the gas, she set to work on a pile of corrections with tremendous, angry energy.

Along the dark High Road and across the river and the dark, empty park, and down the dark empty cold streets and upstairs, he was kicking defiantly at the fender and saying he didn't care.

She thought he'd been rather sweet really, she thought he was stupid, she thought, with a savage stab at the blackboard, that she wouldn't go there again however much he asked her, she thought he was really rather sweet. She thought, when darkness outside the back window of Verbena Road had blotted out pretences, that whatever happened she must never come in the way of his work and she'd better not go there again however much she wanted to. He thought he'd been a fool, he thought he didn't care, he thought he'd go to Verbena Road, he thought he'd wait until she said something, he thought it would be the best thing for her if she never saw him again, he wondered whether she'd gone away for Christmas, and when he remembered her holidays were going by he thought he was a fool.

High-powered planes released from airship in flight; B.B.C. talks to Australia; aerial torpedo boat for Japan; telegrams by Beam system travel six thousand miles in two minutes; motorist at Brooklands captures three world records in seven hours; photographs transmitted by radio between New York and London: progress drove on and left them behind, small and miserable and reactionary, thinking, What have I got to offer her? I should only be a drag on him.

On the last evening of her holidays they met outside the Essex Hall.

"Come back afterwards?"

"Too late."

"Then come now, instead of going in."

When he had said it they both looked surprised.

"I don't know," she said. They turned back along the Strand.

The bus was cold and stuffy and too full for them to talk. She wondered why she had come and whether it would be the same as last time.

She saw that he had expected her; the fire was banked up against the back of the grate and the supper had been cleared away: a tray of tea-things was waiting for them and he had opened the gramophone on the table under the window where he worked.

She threw off her gloves and hat and sat down gladly by the red fire.

He balanced a kettle on the edge of the coals and wound the gramophone and made tea, with tea from a red canister on the mantelpiece, and she laughed at the efficient way he did it.

He laughed and fixed a needle in the gramophone and put on Tea for Two and they laughed and toasted crumpets, knocking their heads together over the fire. The room was warm and companionable with the curtains drawn. He jumped up and down, toasting and buttering the crumpets and winding the gramophone, and she leant back, half drowsy from the warmth, and watched him and felt she had come home.

He played the records more than once, all but one. Each time he picked it up and put it down and played another, and came back to it and turned it and played the other side; turned it and stared at the label, fascinated, and put it down and took up another. He knew that sooner or later he would have to put it on.

He knew he wouldn't be able to resist putting it on: because he felt like teasing her a bit and because she oughtn't to mind, and because she knew well enough, and because it was a jolly tune anyway, and because he felt like that: the peace of the room, was as tantalising as a sleeping cat. All at once, in a sudden, smashing defiance, he put on the record.

"Don't," she said, breathing sharply, "Besides, it's so vulgar."

He laughed. He told himself that it was a harsh, cynical laugh.

> *I am just a lit-tle boy*
> *Who's looking for a lit-tle girl...*

"What's wrong with vulgarity," he said lightly, defying himself.

Her face was turned away from him, she was looking at the fire. The gramophone ground on, with an intolerable, aching, vulgar nostalgia,

> *Who's looking for a little boy-oy*
> *To-oo love.*

Presently he put it off and she reached for her hat.

"Don't go," he said, not looking at her.

"I must, it's late."

"Don't go," he said, and came across the room behind her.

"Yes," she said tonelessly, "I must," but she sat on.

Chapter V

"What's to be done," they said, walking the Embankment in a biting wind. ("No, I'm not coming to your place again, not so soon, someone's sure to notice.") "Nothing to be done."

He said, "I don't care, I'll chuck that job and get something else, we'll manage somehow, I'm not going to have you..."

"Don't be silly," she said, "as if that mattered, and you know they won't keep on married teachers, and if you chucked your job you mightn't get another, and it isn't that I should mind being poor but I won't be a drag on you like that."

"Come back to my place," he said, "we can't talk here."

They climbed the stairs together, guiltily, an ear on the basement, though they had run up them noisily a dozen times before. "But it's so soon," she whispered, "after last time." They stood still and listened between shut doors on the first landing, but it seemed that everybody was out or asleep.

He poked up the fire. "It's all very well, plenty of people marry on less than I make."

"Yes, but that's different, there's your work. I'm not going to be a drag."

"You wouldn't," he said.

Presently she said, in sudden panic: "But are you sure it's safe? Won't somebody come?"

"Nobody'd come up here. Safe as houses."

"No," she said, "don't come back with me. I'd rather you didn't. Really." She was glad to be alone in the tube, it made things less strange, it made things more as-usual. Everything was happening so very strangely and not at all as she had meant. She wondered what she had meant, but there seemed to be no answer: the tram went lolloping up the empty High Road, and the line of shops with a few late gas-jets alight between black, irregular gaps bounded by in a grin.

She could see in the fanlight over the door that the gas was turned low. She was glad to let herself into the stuffy passage and creep upstairs, she longed for the safety of her cold, empty bedroom. The top stair creaked. One of them, Mr. or Mrs., in the front room, turned and muttered.

"I mustn't be so late again," she said. "Besides, it won't do. Besides, we've got to think this out!"

"I've done my thinking," he said. He put his pipe in his mouth and pulled at it angrily and they sauntered on past Charing Cross, past the corner where she should have waited for her bus, and out into Trafalgar Square.

"Yes," she said, "but that's no good, I won't have it."

"Then what's there to argue about?"

"I know," she said. "That's just it."

They zigzagged recklessly through honking traffic and reached the square under the column, empty now except for the stone lions and the down-and-outs in uneasy sleep on benches. The lighted roadway, a ribbon of noise and movement, seemed to have drawn back, a long way off, and above it the buildings stood up black and sudden, like rocks at sea. "I know," she said in a small voice. "There's nothing to argue about. There's nothing to do but what we're doing."

"Or nothing," he said nastily.

"Yes, I know."

"What do you mean by that," he said, standing still. His nerves were on edge and his teeth ached from clutching the empty pipe. "You mean you'd rather have it nothing?"

"You know I don't mean that. Let's not quarrel about it," she said, small and tired, "it won't make things any better."

"What I can't see," he said, planted stubborn under the toe of a sleeping lion, "is why as things are you can't marry me and take a chance on what I can make."

"You know it isn't that," she said irritably, and stopped because she saw he was misunderstanding on purpose: hurt and angry, and nobody to be angry with. "I won't have you made into a wage-slave, feeling I'm dependent on you."

He drove up his fist against the lion's foot. "Things are improving all the time now. That argument won't hold."

Beyond the dark, empty square and the down-and-outs the roadway was a light, moving fresco along the black walls of the Gallery. The theatres were coming out around St. Martin's Lane and Leicester Square and the West End was light and full of people; suburban roads were empty and discreetly lit and the country slept darkly with flares to the north. Up in Birmingham night-watchmen were putting out red lamps around the excavated site for the new Super Power Station, and with daylight Malcolm Campbell in "Blue Bird" would be doing a hundred and thirty-three miles an hour on Pendine Sands. A bus had crashed into a railway bridge at Glasgow injuring thirteen people, an Anglo-German telephone service was newly opened to the public: the systems were linking up across Europe, on through Austria to the Black Sea. Taxi-drivers were on strike in Cairo, air-mail planes of the Egypt — Iraq service were pushing on to a new terminus at Basra, the arrival of the Air Minister at Karachi had completed the opening of a Cairo to India air service, a raid of two houses in Calcutta revealed thirteen bombs with a store of revolvers and cartridges. Beam communication between England and Australia was ready for an official test, the railroad was pushing on through the jungles and swamps of the Belgian Congo, up in St. Louis, U.S.A., a new electric street-lighting system was in use, put into operation by the broadcast voice of the Mayor; New York business magnates by the hundred were speaking to London on the new transatlantic wireless service, seventy-eight children were burnt to death in a cinema in Montreal, a bus ran into the ditch at East Grinstead, and back across the half-dark night City, in the empty light of Trafalgar Square, surrounded by emptiness and down-and-outs, Robert was rubbing his fist that had banged the black, hard lion.

"Mussolini," said Katherine, moving on, "believes that everybody alive to-day is destined to live through a period of history clouded by tragedy and war."

"So we have," he said, "but the war's over."

"He thinks there'll be another."

"Not that, the League would prevent it. Where d'you see that?"

"Don't you ever read the papers nowadays?"

"Well," he admitted, "I haven't bothered much lately."

They came up out of the dark Square on to the pavement.

"Besides it's all very well," he argued hotly against the

crowd, "but even if there is to be another war sometime you can't expect people to plan their lives for it."

"No," she called, pushing through, "but it isn't only that, it's your work. I'm not going to get in your way. I'm not going to stand in the way of progress."

"Don't worry," he said. "Progress'll look after itself."

Part of the roadway was up at the bottom of the Haymarket; a few passers-by in evening dress had stopped and were staring with curiosity at the electric drill. The air and the ground and the lookers-on and the men at work quavered and throbbed with it; it held a man and shook him like a rat. Robert jerked his head. "That's progress," he said, moving on. "And you needn't think you'll stop it."

At Piccadilly he put her in a bus and caught his own. The electric drill was turning small wheels in his head, a thousand revolutions to the minute. He rammed with his heel at the hollow coals in the grate until a column of smoke came up, thick and blue-grey. He knew she wouldn't marry him and he knew he couldn't ask her again and he knew he would and he knew it couldn't go on, it wasn't fair to her, and he knew it must, and he knew he couldn't let her come there again and when she did he was glad, and he knew she'd go on coming and he knew she must but all the same he said she mustn't.

"That's nonsense," she said, "that's an old-fashioned idea. Besides, fairness just doesn't come into it."

He felt it did and he wished it didn't; he felt it didn't: it didn't.

"And we aren't really doing any harm to society," she said anxiously.

He laughed. "We don't owe society much."

"I suppose," she said, looking at the fire, "we're being terribly modern really." Mayfair full of Bright Young People and night-clubs and drink and dope and pyjama parties in flats and divans in dark corners and broken glass and ash on the carpet and how sordid and horrible it must be in the morning, and huge lit dancehalls in cheap streets, and cheap dance frocks and common scent and showers of cheap common powder and paper festoons and cuddling in the bus and smothered giggles — "But we *aren't* though, are we?" — and Robert's untidy boots nuzzling at the fender and his hands in his pockets and his grin, reassuring: "Not that. We think far too much about it."

"Now if we were Communists," she said, "it wouldn't matter," and they both laughed. She said, "I wish you could see our Miss Halliburton..."

Miss Halliburton's head was jogging along, on a level with Katherine's shoulder, on the ill-lit pavement from the school gate to the turn into the High Road. A pile of mottled exercise-books was tucked snuggly into the bend of her frieze-covered arm, and her flat fat features jogged under her pince-nez. "War did you say? Mussolini? It's as plain as the nose on your face. Capitalist system," she said, "war, it's the same thing. You might as well say one for the other. Don't talk to me about Mussolini," she said. "Banning women teachers from the higher schools. That will show you. You won't get peace or equality either without the revolution," she said, "though you needn't say I said so."

"But do you really think...?" Katherine said.

"Think?" she said. "I don't think, I know. Anyone with half an ounce of sense," she said, "could see that Russia to-day is the biggest power for peace there's ever been in the history of the world."

"You needn't go saying I said so," she said, with a backward jerk at the iron gates. "But it's as plain as the nose on your face."

They slowed up at the corner, by the bus stop.

"Why don't you come along to-morrow evening? Not at the club, I'll give you the address. We've got a fine speaker. Pleased to see you any time. Well, bye-bye," she said, "got to meet my friend." She nodded confidentially and was off at a trot, rolling on her short legs, up the far end of the High Road where the shops grew smaller and faded out and the street lamps dropped away to pin points in the fog and dusk. A lighted tram came crashing down past her and reached Katherine and scraped to a stand-still a little way along the road.

Katherine found the meeting in a room tucked away in a side-street near the river. The room was small and cold. Most of the people there were under thirty and they were all untidily dressed but not poor, the men with red ties or no ties at all, and they all seemed to know one another. Katherine sat on a hard chair with an empty chair on either side and pushed her hands up her sleeves to keep them warm. Presently Miss Halliburton bustled over and perched on one of the empty chairs. "So glad you came, you'll love it, we all do. That's my friend," she whispered with a jerk of the head at a man talking in a group near the platform. His back was towards them, but he looked older than the average. Katherine was a bit surprised to find that Halliburton's friend was a man. She wondered whether they could be engaged, or even... but it didn't seem likely. She blushed, thinking that a few weeks ago she wouldn't even have thought of that. Presently the lecturer climbed on to the platform and Miss Halliburton nodded and hurried back to sit with her friend in the front row.

They sang *The Red Flag*, unaccompanied but with tremendous, straggling gusto: cultured college tenors starting up from an indeterminate undergrowth of drone, and a girl's high voice shooting now and then from somewhere near the door. Then raise the SCAR-let standard high...

The lecturer spoke on the splendid work done by the comrades in China: Chinese coolies becoming class-conscious; and they asked questions and looked pleased and proud and very full of comradeship, and the chairman thanked the lecturer and they all clapped the chairman, and lecturer and chairman and all gave a cheer for the Chinese comrades; and they all looked so happy and proud and pleased with themselves that Katherine felt very cold and out-of-it and more uncertain and muddled than ever; and then the meeting broke up and the door was opened, letting in more cold, and they all lowered their voices as they passed through the doorway and dispersed casually along the dark, suspicious working-street.

"If only we were in Russia, now," she said, and Robert laughed at her, "everything would be so simple."

She sat in the antimacassared chair at the end of the iron fender and darned his socks and felt that it made things better. Somehow. She drove the heavy needle in and out, clumsy and unpractised, and thought about his genius. She thought about how she was darning socks to help his genius, and about how things-were-as-they-were to leave his genius free, and somehow it made things better. He had drawn out the second chair, the carpet half-easy, from the dusty corner by the book-case; looking up between socks she saw him sitting there, smoking, and watching her, opposite across the hearthrug, and thought it was almost as if they were properly married.

She thought it wasn't quite, and thought it was because she was doing it for his genius that things-were-as-they-were; and she felt a glow of sacrifice — she told herself it was that, and she told herself fiercely it wasn't sacrifice working for him, she wanted to do it — and she wished and felt and was sure and was dead certain that everything was all right and things were better-as-they-were, and picked out a new piece of wool from the bundle she had bought for him at Woolworth's and drove it with fierce resolution at the needle so that it missed and shot out past the eye.

He pulled at his pipe and watched her and grinned, and thought if she liked it that way she might be right; and presently they tiptoed out and past the bedroom door that was guiltily shut again, though nobody ever came up until the next morning, and down the stairs and out, quiet on the paved slippery steps and laughing round the corner to the tube.

When he got back he pushed the carpet chair into its corner, straight against the wall, and the socks into a sideboard drawer, on top of the knives, and rumpled up his hair and thought the place looked straight and forgot her unwashed teacup with his own on the table and turned out the light, and in the next room he rolled into bed without troubling to straighten the sheets.

He got up in a hurry and read the paper in the tube and sloped along the fine macadamised road, just in time, and rubbed his hands together in the cold laboratory, because it was spring and Rodney was letting down the fire, and found his overalls and a note from the chief and heated up a burner and put a mixture on to cook. He hung about and went out to lunch and hung about and took the tube home, and that night or the next or the one after he went out when he had had his supper, while the woman was clearing away — "You going for a stroll, Mr. Thomas?"

"Nice night," he'd say, a bit sheepish, "pity to stay in" — and lingered by the gate, lighting his pipe, until he heard a clatter come up from the basement windows, and then moved off quickly to meet her at the tube station.

Sometimes they went for a walk; but more often they came back at once, his key quiet in the lock, and climbed the stairs, and talked or played the gramophone; but they never played it after ten o'clock, she was too much afraid of somebody's coming up. When they came out of the bedroom they were very careful to shut the door quietly, edging around, sliding it to, although he slammed it loudly half a dozen times in a night when he was alone. And on most evenings, before or after but generally after, she would dig the bundle of socks out from behind the knives where Mrs. Blim had pushed them, and feel over the heap for the needle and say "Oh" when it pricked her, and prod at its eye with an end of wool and feel that it wasn't really so dreadful, what they were doing.

Now the World Economic Conference meets at Geneva, the Soviets take part by invitation, the Conference fails; the French Minister of the Interior speaks on the Communist Menace, Soviet headquarters are raided at Peking, British Government breaks off trade relations with Russia; ten Socialist M.P.s entertain members of the Russian Trade Delegation to luncheon at the House. "It's all very well," Robert says. "You can't get away from it, they're the enemies of law and order."

"I don't see that," she said, "really. I don't think they mean it like that, they only want to help people. They're trying to make something so new in a way that people can't understand it. I don't understand it myself, I wish I did."

"Well," he said, "you may be right, I don't know. It doesn't make much difference to us."

"No," she said, "I don't suppose it does."

They said good-bye on the empty platform, and the tube took her to the bus and the bus to the tram and the tram up the empty, lit High Road. The lights were small and dwindling ahead: as the tram came up with them two by two they grew large and blurred through the steamy glass and dwindled again, a lengthening pathway of small, dusty stars, back and back, from her to Robert. She let herself in and turned up the gas and put a few pennies in the meter for the fire and started conscientiously on a pile of corrections. The gas-fire sizzled half-heartedly and she was cold and yawning, and half-way down the pile the red pencil started to run, skating along the lines, with a cross or a tick at random here and there. She slapped over the last book and yawned and stacked them back, and yawned as she bent to pop out the fire. The stairs were steep and short — much shorter than Robert's, only one flight — and smelly; she dragged up them from foot to foot and listened and slid-to her door with the catch held back and slowly released the catch. Although it was May the china jug struck cold when she poured water from it stealthily into the basin.

She got to school early and went over the corrections again and prepared a lesson conscientiously but without interest. The children came in and shuffled and whispered and settled down, and she taught them scripture and then history and then arithmetic and then grammar, and their voices piped up, orderly, one at a time, in answer, with a thick undertone of shuffle and kick and thin, stifled giggle. Katherine walked down to the far corner and back and the shuffling stopped and after a minute or two began again. There were bluebells in the jam-jar on the window-sill and a shaft of sunlight cut across the taller flowers and painted a strip of wall behind them bright yellow-green. The rest of the green paint looked black by contrast. Katherine wondered whether to-morrow ... better make it the day after. But even that was rather soon.

She had lunch in the staff sitting-room and it smelt more than usual of chalk and dirty gym-shoes. As she sauntered

out past the stove, Miss Halliburton nodded conspiratorially
— "See you later on?" — and her little eye seemed to wink.
By the time the children came in for afternoon school the
sunlight had gone from the window-sill, it was lying idle and
meaningless across the yard outside. Before the afternoon
was half-way through it had gone, over the wall.

Miss Halliburton was waiting at the corner of the road.
"You coming to-morrow night?"

"No," she said without thinking. "I'm going out." But I
can't she thought, not so soon.

"What a shame. We're having ever such a good speaker."

"Well, I don't know. I may be able to, I'll see."

"That's right, you come. You'll be sorry if you don't."

Miss Halliburton trotted off, up the High Road, and a
tram came along past her and caught up Katherine and carried her back, down the road to the turn.

She sat in the cold front room with the fire unfit because it
was nearly June and ran over some exercises. She thought she
might go to-morrow night — tram and bus and lights coming
out along the river and tube grinding, dark, and on the steps
with the street at the bottom... "Yes, I knew you would be,
that's why..." — and her thought came back, snap, like a ball
on an elastic: red ink, Fair, and mottled outside of the book,
and the next. No, I can't, she thought between two crosses in
the margin, it's too soon. Better go to Halliburton's show.

The club-room was smaller than she had thought. It was
stuffy and indignant and they took a collection for the comrades in China. Persecution. Katherine thought they were
right to be indignant but she didn't much care, she wondered whether it would be all right to go next day or not.

Next day in the lunch-hour Miss Halliburton brought her
boiled eggs and sat next Katherine at the uncovered table

and talked over the scripture papers for the end of term exam. At the end of afternoon school she was waiting at the corner. "Ever so glad you came," she said quickly with a nod, and was off up the road, a pile of books jogging at her hip.

The tram ploughed along through daylight and the tube was dark; Katherine came out of the tube and found Robert on the steps in the light evening. They went along the street and up the stairs and the door opened and shut; after a minute it opened and shut again, quietly; and a minute later, it seemed, they were very quietly downstairs and out on the steps and it was dark night.

Robert waited until the train was out of sight. He stuck his hands in his pockets and ran down the steps into the street and stood looking around. He bought an evening paper and thrust it, folded to a baton, under his arm and forgot it and walked up and down the street and finally went in. He lit the gas, but the bedroom looked lonely. He put out the gas and went to bed in the dark.

In the morning he woke late and it was neither lonely nor a room but a passage to the day's work: a corridor he sprinted along, flinging off the clothes, slinging in the water can with a splash, spots on the floor, soap ears, tie in a string. It was a street, with a bit of breakfast forgotten in a tooth, tongue digging like mad, fast as feet, out with it and swallow on the steps and in through the closing tube door with an upward gush of bad coffee, swallow in a jolt on to the seat and blow: his ears are hot, he sticks out his feet in front and lights a cigarette; the train rocks him gently from side to side.

He stepped out smartly on the smooth, empty road: the hooters had gone half an hour ago and the jostling crowd of workpeople; now machines were pulsing in the low red factory buildings and the smooth road throbbed. He reached the laboratory on time and threw the window open to the hot, pulsing air; leaned out for a moment and saw between lines of dirtying brick a distant tree-top above a broken line of roofs. He turned back and got to work, weighing and pottering. The shed grew hotter at mid-day and cool towards evening. His time was up before the machine-workers'; he caught a tube with the black-coated crowd from the factories spreading down on either side of the road out into the country; as the train came in sight around a bend they heard the rising groan of syrens and a first, distant rush of feet.

Out and down the steps — he knew she couldn't be there yet — and upstairs and at table, pushing in food, and downstairs and along the street and round the corner and on the steps, to time: but he knew she wouldn't come, not to-night. He went down the steps slowly and bought an evening paper and put it under his arm and walked up the pavement a little way and back, and looked up the steps, and down the pavement in the other direction and quick-turn and back, watching for her and knowing that she wouldn't come. When it was too late he went for a walk, along Ladbroke Grove and up the hill and round the church at the top: he came back in a hurry, sweating with fear that she'd come meanwhile, and hung about by the steps with the sweat on him turning chill, and finally turned home tired and slow, dragging his feet, and into bed,

"But aren't you working now?" she said. "I wish you would. It bothers me that you don't."

She came away dejected, watched the rushing grey-streaked sides of the tube tunnel as they went past towards him. Because if he isn't, she thought, it's no good. What am I doing there, what is it all for. If his genius is going to waste, and through me: and all I wanted was to help him, she thought with tears blurring the sudden station lights. I only wanted to make things easier for him, and why don't we marry then, if it comes to that.

Perhaps I go too often, she thought. I shan't go anymore. Not for a week at least. She drove a bar of red pencil through a wrong word and tried to rub it out, and tears came into her eyes again while she fumbled over the pile of books under the hot, sizzling gas-jet.

Miss Halliburton was alone in the staff cloakroom, between rows of hung, dismal coats. "Yes," Katherine said firmly, "I shall be coming on Thursday." But I can't, she cried out to herself, it will make it so long.

But never mind that. She jammed her hat hard on the iron peg so that the crown was dented. "Yes, Thursday," she said, and the bell went. She stalked away to the class-room, firm and sorrowful. She went from scripture to history and from history to arithmetic and from arithmetic to geography. The class was restless with thundery heat. The windows were open, letting in dust from the playground, and in the jar on the sill there were two wizened roses, dark red: stunted buds. I don't know, she thought. And she went from geography to English.

In the afternoon she called over the register and marched the children down to drill and came back and sat at her desk and wondered: I don't know, perhaps I don't see him often enough, it might be better to go oftener. After a quarter of an hour it was time to fetch the children from drill and march them back for handwork.

She went home and prepared English for the next day and thought of him waiting on the steps, and prepared the geography for Thursday. After geography on Thursday it was lunch-time: "See you to-night then," Miss Halliburton called from the stove.

Katherine came back a step from the passage, to the open staff-room door. "Well, I'm not sure," she said quickly. "I may go out to-night, I may have to."

"Coo," Miss Halliburton remarked, looking up suspiciously from a pan of cocoa. "Busy, aren't you?"

"Never mind," she nodded, fat good humour triumphant over pique. "Come another time."

He was on the steps, they were on the stairs, she was in the carpet chair, darning his socks, and the window was open to the warm night. "Are you working?" she said. "Are you going on with it? I do wish you would."

"Yes," he said. He thought he would, some time soon.

When she had gone he walked up and down the road and thought he'd get to work to-morrow. To-morrow he got up and caught the tube and swung into the factory a minute before time and hung about and worked at high pressure for an hour and hung about and caught the tube back. After supper he threw the window wide open and curtains back and tugged at the jammed drawer of the table. He got out a bundle of notes and unrolled them: each page as it left the rubber band sprang back into shape, a separate cylinder, and rolled irritatingly in the breeze from the window. There was a steady trickle of wireless noises from the street, he had hardly noticed them lately, since he stopped working. He collected the curled pages and tried to press them flat. He held them down with a hand top and bottom and frowned at the rows of figures. He shut down the window to keep out the noise, and opened it to let in air. He gave it up, pushed the notes back into the drawer and went out.

"It isn't much good," he said, "I seem to have lost the hang of it. Get going on it next winter."

"I never did do much at it at this time of year," he said defensively.

"Sure? Are you sure it isn't my fault?"

"Sure," he said.

She wasn't sure, but there was nothing to be done: she thought things must come right presently. She went back to her lodgings and set examination papers and to school and talked them over with the other teachers, and wrote them out and copied them on the duplicating jelly on the staff-room table. She thought he oughtn't to be letting everything go like that because of her, and next time they met she made him go to a lecture on the Washington Conference.

In the lunch-hour he went to the chief's office to see about his holiday, to make it fit in with hers. "I can't say as yet, Mr. Thomas," said the chief. "We will certainly file your request."

"If I can pull that off," he said, "we'll go somewhere, shall we?"

"Yes," she said, and then, "I don't know," and then, "Yes," again.

She sat at her desk next day invigilating for the examination and thought about where they would go.

"Somewhere where nobody knows us. Where we shouldn't have to go on pretending."

"That'd be fine," he said.

"I'm sorry, Mr. Thomas," said the chief. "I'm afraid the best we can do for you is the second half of September."

"So you see," he said.

She said, "Don't let's worry about it, I won't go away, then. We'll have a holiday here, it'll be every bit as good."

She sat at the table under the gas-jet and corrected examination papers; the fern on the bamboo stand was heavy with dark summer fronds. Not to-day, she thought, not for a few days: it'll be the holidays soon.

She stood in a row with the other teachers in the school hall while the Head Master read out the marks: teachers in a sagging, self-conscious row against the varnished wood. The children stood opposite by forms, row behind row, quiet under the master's eye. Only a few days now, she thought, only a day or two.

They were decorating the form-room for prize-giving: the chalks were pushed away in their dusty box on the mantel-piece, back against the wall; a tight bunch of flowers stood up in the window and the walls were hung with sketches from the drawing class and bright coloured raffia handwork baskets. She thought, to-morrow!

Now it's holidays, they said. He wound the gramophone and they danced and stopped for breath and stood, holding hands, looking down on the wet street through the Sunday afternoon rain. "What a shame you have to work to-morrow," she said.

He wound the gramophone and they danced. "But you'll come every day?" One of his hands let her go and gave the table a shove, back against the wall. She swung in his arm and her hands went up to the hair coiled on her ears. She nodded, a hair-pin in her mouth, and pushed the pin into place and his arm came back and swung her round. Presently Mrs. Blim came up with the tea.

"How about her, though?"

"She's all right," he said.

He went to the laboratory and came back and knew he would find her there, by the steps. When it was fine they took a bus to the park or the Chelsea Embankment and walked up and down and came back late to his rooms. "How silly," she said, "we're really half-way to my place, only I daren't ask you there" — and when it was wet they went in and danced until supper and made a lot of noise and after supper they were very quiet.

"It's so peaceful up here," she said.

Twelve people are injured in a charabanc smash at Chiswick, eleven in Wales; a motor-coach collides with an electric standard at Wolverhampton; ten miners are entombed near Glasgow; six passengers are killed and fifteen injured in a train crash in Holland; Fascists fire on a French train at Ventimiglia; R.A.F. plane on secret non-stop flight falls into the Danube; rickshaw coolies riot at Hankow and tribesmen attack Hindus on the North-West Frontier; twenty-five persons are killed in a railway crash in Brazil; two hundred miners trapped by an explosion in Kentucky; New York subway stations are bombed by sympathisers with Sacco and Vanzetti.

"The way the world leaves us alone. Almost as if it knew we had a right."

"So we have."

"I know, only..."

Cars replace horse vehicles in the Vatican; factories are springing up throughout Brazil; eighteen-foot whale is impaled on the bows of a transatlantic liner; a fox is chased through the streets and shot in a back-yard at Muswell Hill;

— "But I'm afraid," she said. "I'm coming too often. Are you sure it's safe?"

"Safe as houses." ——

seven-story building crashes in the City.

Mrs. Blim stood with an uneasy grip on the door handle, her eyes shifted from Mr. Thomas to his breakfast and back again and round to the rumpled cushions in the armchair. "Not these goings-on, I can't have. A lady to tea once a month say, reasonable, and I'd be the last to complain. But not these goings-on, day after day."

"And if you did move," Katherine said, "what's the use. It would be the same anywhere else."

They walked slowly up Ladbroke Grove from the station and up the hill and round the church at the top, round and round.

"If you moved," she said, "it would be the same in a week or two. You can't move every week."

"Or if I moved," she said, "I'd thought of that. Into a flat or something. But the school would be sure to find out."

"Marry me, then."

"No," she said, "you know I won't, it can't be done."

"Then I'll move."

"No," she said, "it's no use."

They walked round and round the church, in the sunset, and the sun went down.

"We'll think of something," he said. "There must be some way."

He rolled into bed in the dark, empty room, and tumbled out into daylight: down and along and round the corner and up the steps, and out on to the wide, light road to the factory. In the laboratory he didn't miss her because she had never been there. But the armchair stood empty — up the road into the tube and jolt and out and down the steps, no good waiting to-night, and up the stairs — tidy, with the cushion slapped flat, straight to the side of the fender. The room was clean and swept, with all the homeliness swept out, and the carpet chair pushed flat against the wall. He bolted his supper and ran down again in case she came after all, and she came, and they went up the street and turned off into a side-road and walked up and down, miserably, and she said he wasn't to worry, there must be some way.

Every twenty yards or so, where a tree overhung the

pavement, or at the farthest point between two street lamps, they passed a couple pressed against the wall or pushed into a gateway. Some of the couples were speaking in low voices and some were quite quiet. As she passed them Katherine would draw away from Robert, just a little and without meaning to: just a very slightly wider strip of pavement between them. He came near again, not noticing. "They're like us," he said. "Nowhere to go."

She nodded, but her face denied it, fierce and frightened in the dark: they're not, we're not like them, no we're not. She came out a step, away from the wall, though it meant coming nearer to Robert: away from the inviting, repulsive wall, the dark wall so hospitable and disgusting.

They took buses to the Embankment and to Hyde Park and on Sundays to Kew and Richmond, and everywhere as night came on there were couples, on seats and on the grass by the tow-path and on the Park chairs. "It's the sameness of them all in a way," she said. "I think it's the lack of uniqueness that makes it so horrible. As if we must be like them, just because..." As if we weren't unique. As if there'd ever been anybody quite like us or quite so miserable. Besides, they don't mind, these people, it's all right for them: they can hold hands, they don't mind where they are.

They walked on, arms swinging, and came near the end of the Park, where a larger crowd than usual was moving restlessly around a number of speakers. Robert spotted the mounted police. "Looks like a bother. Better not get too close."

They went back a little way and sat on some chairs and watched the edge of the distant crowd licking at the grass. At intervals, a thick megaphone voice reached back to them, through the hooting of traffic.

"Sacco and Vanzetti!" She sat up suddenly, pink and

excited. "That's it, a demonstration. Communists. There was going to be one. They want them released."

"You wouldn't think there were so many Communists in London."

They went on sitting, saying nothing. The crowd was flattening out lengthways, straggling into a rough kind of marching order. Indecipherable banners rose and dipped above the thick column. "They're going to the American Embassy," she said. "I remember now."

"Never get there. Police stop 'em."

"Oh, most likely."

After a time the procession gave a jolt and started.

"They're like us," she said. "Persecuted. And why? It's all so senseless."

He got up. "Sure to be a row. Better get away before it starts."

They walked slowly back towards Kensington Gardens.

"Persecuted," she said, and felt better about it.

"After all, what harm do we do anybody. It's so senseless," she cried, righteous and almost happy. "That horrible old woman. It's all so *wrong*. Now in Russia that kind of thing simply couldn't happen."

"No?" he said. "I suppose not. But unfortunately we don't live there."

"But don't you *see*? Communism isn't a thing that belongs to one particular country. It just happened to start in Russia. If you *believe* in freedom, it doesn't matter where you live."

"No, but believing in it won't make you free."

"But you've got to believe," she said.

They sat on a bench at the end of the Serpentine where the water-tanks lay dried up between the stone walks, dirty brown tumps of weed on their muddy bottoms.

"All the same," he said, "that doesn't help much."

He sat there staring at people going by and wondered what to do. He knew what people did do but he didn't like to suggest it. They both sat there a long time without saying anything.

"I suppose," he said, "the obvious thing to most people would be an hotel." He laughed nervously. "But that hardly seems to meet the case."

"Hardly," she agreed, as if it were obvious.

Presently they had supper at an A.B.C. and walked across the Park and he saw her into a bus.

At Victoria she got off the bus. She wanted to go to Grosvenor Gardens, to the American Embassy. Without knowing why, and with a sick daring, she wanted to know what had happened, she wanted to see for herself. She stopped at the turn, not daring to go farther. Except for a couple of mounted police on guard outside the Embassy the road was quite empty, but the pavement, the smooth, unimpressionable pavement, had a trampled, sinister look, it bore for her the invisible print of ten thousand harried feet. She stood for a moment staring in horror at the empty road. She turned and walked away quickly. And if I were a good Communist, she said, smiling to herself, I shouldn't feel there was anything degrading in the hotel idea.

But then it wouldn't be necessary, she argued.

Though in this country it would.

Besides, she said in the tram, it's only an idea. There's no difference really between one place and another. It's only the kind of people who go there.

But it wouldn't mean we were like those people, she told the green plush table.

She stared into the dark mirror tipped over the dark back garden, and her eyes stared hotly back. Besides, it isn't fair on him. It isn't. We can't go on like this.

Next day she went back, she took a tram and a bus and a tube: it's for him, it isn't fair, and we shouldn't be like them, and what does it matter where. And if we were in Russia we shouldn't need to, but I'm a good Communist, she smiled, and after all why not.

"Look here," she said and took his arm, "why don't we go to an hotel or somewhere."

They were strolling towards the corner where the buses ran round. "You wouldn't like that," he said.

"Yes," she said, "I should, I should really, really I should.

"I'm a good Communist," she cried, with a high laugh. "No, don't laugh," she said, "I believe I really am."

The hotel was near Paddington. Katherine waited in the narrow hall. It was not very different from the hall of Robert's house, and the treads of the stair-carpet were not much more worn, and the damp smell of cabbage was only a little damper, but it mattered a good deal more. IT mattered. Robert was inside the small dingy office, paying. She wanted to run away but was afraid to. Nonsense, she thought, it doesn't make any difference, of course not, how can it. Of course it doesn't, it's nonsense, it doesn't matter at all.

"Sorry," he whispered. "Couldn't manage anything better."

"Do you mind?" he said as the door shut.

"No, of course not," she said, "of course I don't," and for a minute or two she didn't.

The sheets smelt of dust and a broken spring jingled angrily. "We must be good Communists, all right," he said, and laughed close into her hair.

"They're wonderful people," she said, and they both laughed, because they were determined they'd be happy and it shouldn't matter.

Through a chink between the dusty curtains, grey daylight

cut across the iron bars and rusty brass knobs. A bus passed outside and its passing vibrated in the rattling spring. Over in Hyde Park thousands mass for march on the American Embassy to demand a reprieve for Sacco and Vanzetti; Paris Communists call for a twenty-four-hour strike, demonstrations proposed throughout the world; bomb explodes in Basle and two in Buenos Aires, dynamite explosion in Missouri, pitched battle in Chicago, machine-guns mounted on the wall of the Charleston State Prison, a hundred thousand dollars-worth of insurance against explosion, strike, riot and civil commotion taken out by citizens of Boston. Sacco and Vanzetti granted leave to appeal.

Down Grosvenor Road banners bob over heads of marchers. *L'Humanité* claims victory for international proletariat: American capitalism forced to yield. Demands amnesty and release of martyrs. London Trades Council bans Communists from executive. Bombs explode in Buenos Aires, in church at Cleveland, Ohio, machineguns and searchlights sweep Boston streets, Sacco and Vanzetti executed. Procession charged by mounted police, thirty pushed through open gateway fall into area. Katherine sits up and pulls on her shoes, the broken spring groans under her, the sheets smell of dust.

"Better get out as soon as you're ready." Robert stared down at the grey dirty street and cursed himself for bringing her there. "Not too good," he said without looking round.

"Not really," she said in a dull, flat voice. She rubbed her hands together to wipe off the feel of the sheets.

They slunk downstairs without looking at one another, on tiptoe, although nobody cared, and along the narrow dirty hall and past the office and out, defeated.

She washed hard in the white china bowl over the back garden: she thought nothing could wash off the feel of that hotel. She thought it was silly to feel like that, what did it matter so long as they were together, but she knew it did matter and she knew he felt it too. They went for walks now in the evenings on wide light roads and avoided the dark, overhung side-streets. Walking on the wide, light pavements she could feel proud, proud of her love. Their love. Not like what People called "love." And why should we cheapen ourselves, she thought fiercely, why shouldn't we keep our ideals. If we haven't got those, what *have* we got.

She took to coming up to town earlier in the day and wandering round the park until Robert was free in the evening. Now and then there would be a little group of people gathered around a Communist speaker, and she loved them because they were defeated, but she never stopped to listen.

"Oh, I grant you," Robert said, "a lot of the feeling against them has been worked up for political reasons. Or trade. That comes to the same thing."

— *Red Peril*: Atrocities in Russia, religious persecutions, reign of Anti-Christ! Menace of Communist Sunday schools, "our innocent children."

No Immediate Danger from Bolshevik Peril: Blockade raised from Russia, America becomes anxious to resume trade relationship if this would not involve active recognition of the Bolsheviks, talk of a delegation to establish commercial relations with Western Europe, Anglo-Russian agreement for resumption of mail service.

Red Régime at Last Gasp, Coming Crash, Doomed Russia: Soviet trade delegation visits England and seeks permanent London offices. British trade pact concluded with Soviets.

Russian timber undersells Canadian: Atrocities in Timber Camps!

New Economic Policy ("coming round to capitalism");

death of Lenin (main danger removed?): Great Britain recognises the U.S.S.R.

Labour disputes, trade losses: Premier declares War on Communism, Communist trial at Bow Street.

General Strike, Moscow Gold for Miners: Communist Menace! British Government breaks off trade relations with Russia.

China; Sacco and Vanzetti (Britain taking no risks): Soviet War on Religion! Blasphemous cartoons!! Children taught to spy on parents!!! Revolting Pictures!!!! Bolshevist Leaders' tyranny over workers!!!!! Labour breaks with Russia.

"Oh, I grant you that," he said. "That crazy rocking. Pushed by cash and funk."

She went to his rooms once before school began. All the doors on to the stairs were shut and the house might have been empty, but it had a faint creaking sound of listening. Katherine went up defiantly, "I don't care," she said, "we have a perfect right." His rooms looked swept and empty as if they had been empty a long time and almost as soon as they were back in the sittingroom it began to get dark. The damp September twilight was hostile and suspicious; she wound up the gramophone to put a wall of noise around them.

"Look out," he said. He was afraid Mrs. Blim would pop out when Katherine went down and be unpleasant.

"I don't care," she said, "we may be persecuted but we're in the right."

She wanted the wall of noise to shut out their thoughts, Mrs. Blim's and the others'. Nobody else knew: but what they'd think if they did. And to shut out that hotel at Paddington. Before she went she scooped out his knotted socks from the back of the drawers, behind the knives, and stuffed them into her handbag.

He laughed at her: "What on earth does that matter?"

"I want to do them," she insisted. "I *want* to." And as she went with him down the dark suspicious stairs with the bag clutched in her hand she suddenly knew that it mattered enormously, though she couldn't think why, unless it was that she had the right.

The children were new, boys and girls, up from the elementary schools. For a week or so they were quiet and awestruck, in awe of the Senior School and in awe of Miss Bott; after that they began to shuffle and snigger. The paint was new and smelly and there was a large new register with the fresh names, and the long white chalks were new: but Katherine was not renewed, she felt tired and bored and as if she couldn't go on with the term when it was barely begun. She took down the history chart from the wall and rolled it and put it away in the table drawer and chose two children, a girl and a boy, to rule out a fresh sheet and start again, with ten-sixty-six at the top and the rest empty to fill as they went.

Miss Halliburton asked her to the club. "I think I'd like to join," she said. It filled one evening a week, and the meetings just now were very lively and angry and full of hope, and she felt these were the only people who were Getting Somewhere. She took Robert to one of the club evenings but she felt awkward about Halliburton's seeing them together. When she could she went out and met him, and on the other nights, after the corrections were done, she sat under the sizzling gas and darned his socks.

She thought about progress and about Robert: about what she and Robert were going to do for progress — what she was going to help Robert to do for progress — and what progress was going to do for them. Things were going faster and faster: bishops were calling for a ten years' holiday for science, scientists were experimenting with synthetic foods, new designs in cars and Paris creations were flashing by radiophotograph across the world ("it is possible, thanks to the radiophotograph, for a new Paris hat or costume to be worn in New York twenty-four hours after it has been designed"), a ten-thousand-pound fleet of British cars was hurtling across the desert the suite and harem of an Arabian king, two and a half million people were huddling to the dogs at the White City track alone ("greyhound racing, one of the greatest counter-irritants to Socialistic revolution we have yet seen"), Robert, alone in his rooms, was tinkering at a crystal set to prevent himself from thinking about Katherine.

Mysterious explosion at naval cordite factory, new German plane a revolution in aircraft, Fascist officers shot at Ravenna, rioting in Nagpur, "India's Joan of Arc" goes to prison, Brooklyn secret bomb factory discovered; at Geneva, at the fourth session of the Preparatory Commission for the Disarmament Conference, Litvinoff is proposing total abolition of armies, navies, and air forces. "There," she cried, "what did I tell you. They're the only people who want peace. Peace and progress. There's no other way to peace."

"Yes," he said, "I believe you're right. You must be right."

They took to going to meetings again, smaller meetings in smaller halls. They took tubes on cold evenings to outlying suburbs and heard intellectuals in red ties lecture to shivering unemployed on dialectical materialism, and a shrill-voiced woman M.P. harangue working-class mothers on divorce reform and free love.

"We *are* Communists," she said, "aren't we?"

His mind shifted uneasily. "Why bother about a category?" He couldn't understand that need in her. "Why want to *be* anything?"

"But we are," she insisted.

"If you like."

She took last year's history chart from the drawer in the class-room and dipped a pen in the red ink and ruled a new line across, horizontally, above the year 1917. Turning the chart sideways she began a new bracket extending up the page from that date, hesitated as to where to close the bracket and ran it off unclosed at the top margin, labelled it Age of Capitalism. From 1917 downwards, with an opening bracket, she called Dawn of Socialism. She blotted the lines and wondered, elbows on the blotting paper, whether to make the division on this year's chart on the wall. Inspector. Probable dismissal. Miss Halliburton's motto — her out-of-school watchword — came back to Katherine: "That won't help the revolution!" With a smile she rolled the chart and slipped it back into the drawer as the children came clattering in from break.

She watched them take their places: the future proletariat. Few were ragged, but the clothes of nearly all were thin and their faces were blotched with cold and they had a general under-nourished look. She was glad that they and their children were going to be well fed and clothed, but she doubted whether even they would gain much from an intervening revolutionary period. She thought the insistence of Miss Halliburton and many of the speakers upon the necessity for a "bloody revolution" was a mistake, and a pity. She said, "Why shouldn't they go on from where we are? Why knock everything down first? Surely that can't help anybody." She thought progress would do everything, in time, if you waited.

The cold, distant light of fanaticism crept into Miss Halliburton's eyes. She shot it suspiciously at Katherine. She said, "That only shows you haven't grasped the ideology…"

Robert said, "What I don't see is why they want a levelling

down. Why not a levelling up?"

Katherine was ready. "Because the proletariat run the country. They're in the majority. If they stopped working, production would stop, there'd be no food, nobody could live. You've got to base everything on them because they're the most important section of the community. You've only got to look at the General Strike."

"Well," he said, "if that means anything it only means they've got the power to hold the country up to ransom. That isn't saying they're justified in doing it. Besides, the General Strike failed."

"Yes," she admitted.

"The fact is," he said, "you'd never get that kind of revolution here. Doesn't suit the English temperament."

"I think you're right," she said, cheered. "I think the revolution will come gradually. Of course, we can't do without it," she said, "there's the whole question of freedom. But I do think it will come peacefully." She hoped it would. She thought the revolution would be a splendid thing, but she did want it to happen without unpleasantness and without too much insistence on the proletariat. She hated this creeping down the stairs, even if it was only once a month, in fear of a prying Mrs. Blim and coarse, sullying remarks. Or even looks. She had a vague, only partly conscious notion that after the revolution all hearts would immediately discern the essential purity of her wanting to sleep with Robert. Her conscious mind might have doubted this assumption, the subconscious kept it safe and warm. When they reached the street they walked openly, feeling brave, because there was no other way to walk, past the basement window; and by the time he had put her in the tube Katherine was boldly defiant. "I shouldn't care if she *did* say anything, we've got a perfect right." As soon as she got in she lit the sitting-room gas and began to darn his socks.

Halliburton took to dropping in in the evenings, to bring a club notice, or on school business, or simply for a chat. At sight of the socks and the dropped, twiggling wool her little eyes hardened and her mouth laughed. "What!" she laughed, her thumb flicking a sock over the plush cloth. "You doing that job? Got a guilt-complex haven't you, that's what wrong with *you*."

"What do you mean?" Katherine hardly knew how to account for the socks. She dug a needle in and out of the cloth and tried to look offended and very stiff. She could feel herself flushing.

"Coo," commented Miss Halliburton good-naturedly. "Touchy, aren't we. No offence meant. Only you wouldn't catch me doing a job like that for *my* friend."

"Oh," Katherine said. She wondered how much was implied, and how much Halliburton knew, and how. So Halliburton's "friend" was that: how surprising. She was very much annoyed, although she knew it was unreasonable. She began to talk coldly about the end-of-term charades.

Presently Miss Halliburton got up to go. She jerked her head cheerily over her shoulder at the handful of socks. "Don't mind me mentioning *that*, do you? Seems silly, doesn't it, being particular over a thing like that. Among friends."

After that Katherine took the socks upstairs and darned them under the hissing shadeless jet in the cold bedroom.

Once a month they met in his rooms and they met, in between, at bus stops and in tube stations and at the doors of small, out-of-the-way political meetings. The months turned slowly, full of things dreadfully important which some-how couldn't matter quite so much as they ought to have mattered: things that they hotly argued about, walking up and down wide, white pavements with a quick jerk away and a raising of the voice at dark close movements in corners.

"Dreadfully important," she said. Cotton operatives' wages cut; Communists declare open war on bourgeois Labour Party; Soviet plan for abolition of armaments; "Communist Trial" appeal dismissed; Optimism at Geneva. "Dreadfully important," she said, with the strained, tense look in her eyes as the month dragged on. She was tense and taut and everything was dreadfully important, and she dragged him off urgently and tensely to Hampstead or Hammersmith or East Ham, to a meeting on free speech or the will-to-peace or Labour's betrayal. And then it was lighter in his room than it had been the month before, a queer, restless urgent light from the drooping sunshine laid along the street outside, and when she went home with the pile of socks, out of a kind of obstinacy and a kind of pride, and sat on her bed and darned them and sent down word to Halliburton that she was out — though Halliburton must know quite well she was in and could even hear her giving the message, but that wouldn't prevent her coming again worse luck — things ceased, just for a day or so, to be quite so desperately important.

Optimism at Geneva, British Army estimates reduced, Italians break world air-speed records. Buds were breaking into green on the laburnum over the steps and the window of his room was up for the gramophone noise to go out and the wireless noise to come in. The crystal set he had begun to make stood in the corner by the pushed-back chair; he would finish it some day.

Four hundred and seventy Chinese drowned in a colliery, one thousand and thirteen Communists arrested in Japan, seven garment workers injured by bomb explosion in

New York, increase in British exports: upward trend of trade, and buds are yellow over the grey steps; mysterious escape of poison gas at Hamburg, anti-Italian riots in Yugoslavia, sixty Italian war-planes leave on a mass manoeuvre flight of two thousand miles, anti-Fascist bomb kills nine and injures forty-one in the Italian consulate at Buenos Aires, the laburnum is out now over the steps, and a stunted lilac sweet and heady, in the back garden at Verbena Road, and Miss Halliburton comes to club meetings in striped washing-silk frocks, sleeveless, with her red arms breaking through: but Katherine never brings Robert to the club, she is afraid of what Halliburton might say about her friend: she rushes him up and down London on hot buses, on the hot, covered buses though he grumbles, because nearly all the open ones are taken off by now and they can't wait, they haven't got time to wait; and on front, inside seats over the hot pulsing engines of buses, and through hot blasts of air down into the tube; and plunges to and fro with a hot, feverish ramrod restlessness between hot halls and the school smelling of hot asphalt.

Robert came back to his room, he was tired, he wanted not to think. He wanted not to think about Katherine, he wanted to think about Time and his thesis, but he couldn't do that because he wanted to think about Katherine. He had read about a new test — the final test — of Einstein's theory being carried out in California and this had reminded him of what he had been going to do. He was still going to do it. He was going to do it when the weather got cooler and when it was quieter and when Kath stopped running about and when they were able to see one another without running half around London and when she changed her mind and married him. With trade improving he thought he might take a chance and try for a better job. He wanted not to think. He threw up the window, he was used to the wireless noises by now and thought they wouldn't upset him. He dragged the drawer open and threw out some notes and turned them over, but whether it was the noise or the heat or Kath or what, they didn't make much sense. He took a pen and dug it at a pad and sat looking stolidly at the jottings he had made two or three years before. By the time the room got cooler he found that it was midnight and he had been thinking along quite different lines: vaguely and stupidly speculating about the origins of the universe and what was the good of it all. And he and Kath. What was the good. He rolled up the notes quickly and thought he'd do more another day now he'd had a look at them and went to bed.

Meanwhile robots speed up work in city offices: machine opens thirty thousand letters an hour, writes, adds, subtracts, addresses, stamps seven thousand envelopes per hour and signs one hundred and fifty cheques a minute. London passenger traffic increases by one hundred and ten million in one year, over three thousand million passengers in twelve months, average four hundred and eighty-three journeys per annum per head of population. London's public increases by five hundred thousand in five years. In a room in the Strand joint meetings are held by wireless with sister society sitting in New York. Round the world in a minute. From a tower in the Indian jungle visitors watch specially preserved tigers kill tethered buffalo under powerful electric lights. Back in Cambridge Voronoff lectures on monkey-gland grafts for rejuvenation. Mechanically propelled vehicles on the roads of England increase by a hundred and fifty thousand in one year, "baby" cars are rushed on to the market. Television is here! Deaths from heart disease have increased by four hundred per cent says doctor, night-clubs, cocktails, ciga-rettes, rush of modern life, emotion increases intra-vascu-lar strain. Miss Halliburton eating lunch thinks how white and nervy Bott's been looking lately, she wonders how things are, with her and her friend, she thinks she'll find out one of these days when she can get her to herself.

Secret stores of arms were discovered in Hanover and Hamburg, six men were killed during German minelaying practice in the Baltic, Leningrad staged a trial gas-attack "to discover how best to repulse British air-raids," Katherine and Robert stood about in the rain on a Sunday afternoon at the edge of an anti-Fascist demonstration in Trafalgar Square.

"I saw you yesterday," Miss Halliburton simpered. "You and your friend. You didn't see me, did you?"

"No," said Katherine. She moved to the pavement edge and peered for the tram. There was one in the distance, sway-ing leisurely and stopping. "Oh, in Trafalgar Square. Splen-did, wasn't it."

"I hadn't seen your friend for a long time.

"No?" The tram was coming nearer. She stepped out into the road and hailed it unnecessarily. "So sorry, I really must run." The tram drew up with deliberate intention. She went to meet it and got on before it had fully stopped. It waited for a long time before it went on, she could see Hallibur-ton looking annoyed on the pavement, wondering whether to come across. Finally the tram clanged and Halliburton turned away in a huff, up the road.

Robert had to take his holiday early, while the exams were on. The staff-room table was littered with paper and copying jelly and wads of long new jelly-copied question papers, and Robert was lounging by himself in the Park and through the West End, wondering whether he'd run down to Wales for a week-end to see his father, but it cost too much, and staring into windows in Tottenham Court Road at the new "modern" furniture, and even the not-so-modern furniture, on the new, attractive hire purchase system.

"Look here," he said, "I'm going to ask for a rise. Things are looking up all round. And it doesn't cost much to furnish, the way you can do it now."

"No, no," she said, "you mustn't risk it. They wouldn't give it to you. There's still so much unemployment everywhere."

"But what's the harm if they refuse?"

"No, no," she said, "you mustn't do that, you mustn't risk being refused. Besides, it's no good," she said, "all the arguments still hold. And it's all very well to talk about hire purchase but how are we to pay the instalments. Even if you did get a rise. If I gave up my job and we both had to live on yours. No, you can't," she said, "it's the same thing, I won't have you tied up Besides, we're both good Communists aren't we? We're not going to knuckle under to a lot of bourgeois ideals."

She felt bright and tense and capable, with a sense of holding something taut in equilibrium. The staff-room table was stacked with written answer-books tied with red tape. She collected her piles and took them home and corrected them until she was tired enough to sleep, and went to school to invigilate and to a staff meeting to make plans for prize-giving, and met Robert and took him out to Lewisham to a discussion on Maxton and Cook's break-away from Labour. "It's all very well," she said, as if it were the most important thing in the world, as if it mattered to her half so much as Robert, "but are they going to fight for affiliation? Are they going to identify themselves quite openly with the party? If not they're no use to us," she said.

She went away for a week, with a sense of holding on to

strings. "I must," she said, "I haven't been home for so long."
She went north with the strings tautening behind her, Robert and all the things that were happening that they ought to be watching together: the signing of the Peace Pact (world's biggest Zeppelin built in Germany, "robot" target ship for gunnery practice at Wilhelmshaven; Russia's air progress, six factories for military machines; thirty-one dead in Italian submarine, four killed in French bombing plane, R.A.F. "air-war" over London) and the World Peace Conference at Prague.

She stayed north for a week and Robert went from his rooms to the factory and back six times. He was in no hurry to get there and no hurry to get home. He dawdled after hours, putting things away. Rodney had gone and he had a new boy, fresh from school. The boy was slow and anxious; he had out-of-work parents to keep, on his first job. If Katherine had been waiting Robert would have sprinted off at five-thirty sharp and left the kid to find his way about, but as it was he hung around to show him where to put things and how they went. On Sunday he got out his notes and sat over them for a long time, dreaming vaguely about the source of world energy and whether it were inexhaustible: electricity used up and the world slowing down, dropping back into a torpid ice-age, life frozen out, a dead mass, like the moon. He yawned and jumped up and ate his supper hungrily and lit a pipe and grinned, remembering Kath was coming back to-morrow.

There was a new term, there were new children. They sat up straight and quiet, cowed, but after a few days they began to shuffle and giggle. One of them brought three drooping dahlias for the jam-jar in the window. Katherine took down last year's history chart and set them to drawing up another. She rolled the old chart and put it away in a drawer. 1928, the Five-Year Plan. How she wished she dared put that on the chart, but she knew it wouldn't do. She and Halliburton talked it over instead one evening when Halliburton dropped in: some day that'll be the only date that matters, they said. That and 1917. Halliburton dropped in less often now, or else Katherine was out when she came. She was generally out. Once a month she went over to Ladbroke Grove, and two or three evenings a week she and Robert went to meetings: to protest meetings in sympathy with the French comrades (nineteen workmen killed by collapse of building in course of construction at Vincennes) and to lectures on the Five-Year Plan. "Isn't it dreadful," she said, "they tried to build without an architect, just for economy. That's the capitalist system."

"Well," he said, "you can't tell, the contractor himself may have been hard up. It's the same everywhere." Four injured in collapse of five-story house in Finland, thirty killed at Prague constructing building of inferior concrete, four killed and unknown number buried by collapse of brewery in Malta, three injured in fall of three-story building at Belfort. "All over the place. It's not so much the system. It's the modern spirit: hurry and big buildings, cheap and showy, and everybody half broke."

"I suppose it's one side of progress," she said. She still believed in progress, she couldn't help it. When she remembered, she knew that there was no real progress outside Russia; but all this modern striving was feeling towards it, all the same, she said.

"Like the talkies," she said. She had never cared much for the cinema, they could only afford cheap seats: thick, whispering darkness and holding hands. But they went now, once or twice, because the talkies were coming in and this was something new and significant. And they went to see the Graf Zeppelin in a field near London: the snub-snouted monster nosing over a hedge.

She got back very late nowadays and let herself in quietly and lit the gas and sat up alone, correcting, until her back ached and she was too tired for sleep. Once or twice she caught herself being nervy with the children, and when she taught with hands joined, tip to tip, the fingers of one tapped irritably against the other.

Over twenty-three million a year received for car licences, two hundred and fifty-three thousand visit the motor show at Olympia, three hundred and nine London traffic deaths in summer quarter, increased efficiency of tube trains increases noise, engineers baffled: woman doctor calls for more sleep "quiet, sound and undisturbed"; coroner comments on motiveless suicides: "mystery of their minds," "depression," "extraordinary cases," "had the world before him." (Rejuvenation successes, missionaries supply Voronoff with monkeys, vistas of life opened up.) "Strange to think how lightly youths nowadays regard their lives," says the coroner, "how quickly they seem to develop a sort of *tedium vitae*."

"Queer thing," said Robert. "As if the balance of population had to be kept somehow. Same thing with civilisation." Television and wireless for Enthronement Day in Japan: films of ancient ceremonies rushed by plane; Rhodesia's progress: natives use cars, cease to kill twins, buy savings certificates; bishop blesses new submarine for Chile; North Wales miners veto pit-head baths, Bradford woman sets fire to Birth Control caravan, atavistic child in North London prowls around cot "like an animal" and gnaws through clothing.

"The fact is," he said, "we've got so far we shall have to go back presently. The turn of the wheel. We keep getting warnings all the time." Man and wife electrocuted by wire-less aerial entangled in high-power transmission line; passenger blown out of plane, five fatal railway accidents in a month, gas explosions in West End, hippopotamus charges train on Natal North Coast Railway.

"And it wasn't even killed," she said, laughing.

"No, but we're doing our best." Oil pollution destroys sea birds, Exmoor ponies threatened with extinction, cow electrocuted on live rail.

"But you can't help that kind of thing," she said impatiently. "It's a necessary part of progress: only the reverse side. Besides," she remembered, "you can't even talk about progress here. People here are going in all directions, they don't know where they're going. Look at Russia. You've got to look there to find progressive purpose."

"Russia?" he said. "They're going the same way. Look at them." Moscow's first underground railway to cost two million; Soviet signs contract with America for two-million-worth of electrical apparatus; Soviet naphtha syndicate secures French market; Soviet new power schemes; Five-Year Plan includes manufacture of tractors, aeroplanes, turbines, synthetic rubber, and artificial fibre; Conservative M.P. would like to see resumption of economic relations, calls for a "gesture" from Russia...

"Shows how they're working round to capitalism."

...Moscow and Leningrad Soviets allow Christmas trees, "reprisals being incompatible with freedom in religious views."

"See?"

"That doesn't mean anything," she said, "except that they're open-minded. Besides," she said, "whatever they do is different. Industrialism there means something different. It's all in the ideology," she said, her eyes burning with vague fervour. "Facts don't mean anything. It's the ideology you have to look at."

"All right," he said. They were in his room, it was Boxing Day, he didn't bother, he hoped they'd have better luck this next year: Higher standard of life in Germany, Boom in America. He grinned and pressed down the red coals with the heel of his boot. "All right, have it your own way."

Early in the new year they gave him a laboratory assistant and a rise. The assistant was a very young man named Graham in a very new clean white coat. He had just come down from a new university. He was anxious to please, and shy of rowing the boy. He did most of the cleaning himself, he said the boy was no good. Robert smacked his chest with his arms to keep warm in the cold, smoky hut (they talked about giving him a new laboratory when times got better still) and Graham shovelled coke into the stove. Robert wondered whether he'd ever looked quite so green as Graham. He thought he must have: he'd been twenty-two when he came and now he was thirty. It made him start, to think he'd been nearly nine years in this place: it had been in the country when he came and now the ribbon of factories wound out a long way beyond the Parade where the shops and cinema and tube station were. Even looking deep in away from the road there was hardly a tree in sight, only small new saplings in the gardens of the small houses they'd built on new, unfinished roads for the factory workers. He knew Graham lodged in one of those. Looking at Graham he felt superior and experienced and rather pitying. He asked Graham how he managed to get through the evenings out here.

"Oh," Graham said, and flushed, "I'm trying to work a bit on my own."

Robert began to feel superior and pitying and then he

wasn't quite sure. He gave Graham a quick, suspicious look. "Ah?" he said indifferently. Well, he thought, things are easier now. A damned lot easier. Young blighter may pull it off. — Big drop in unemployment, (Free Trade speaker predicts grave financial crisis), steady rise in coal output, the Road to Prosperity. — Better for all of us, come to that.

He lit his pipe thoughtfully and strolled up to the tube station, leaving Graham to lock up. From the train he watched the almost unbroken line of new factories and house-backs and frosted gardens and thought about his job. He wondered how it was he'd stayed in the same job for more than eight years without noticing it. Things happened from day to day and made a year, and there you were, eight of them. It wasn't a bad job, he thought, he'd been right to stick it, things were looking up now. He'd thought once or twice of chucking it but Kath hadn't wanted him to, afraid he wouldn't get another. Kath was right. Kath ought to marry him now, now things were looking up. It wasn't fair on her, the way they were dragging on. It suited him all right in a way, but this hole-and-corner business got on her nerves though she didn't know it: women were like that. And the teaching was too much for her, the old girl was getting a bit thin and jumpy. Poor old Kath. It wasn't fair on her. And he'd be glad to get out of those digs and into a decent house somewhere, where they could sit and talk like civilised beings instead of trailing half round London to talk in the tube.

He remembered this was an evening he wouldn't see her, she had some teachers' meeting on. He thought he'd go over his notes and see where he stood, it might be time to see. After supper he unwedged the drawer under the window and turned them out; they were pushed in, rammed to the back, in rolls and files and loose, crumpled leaves from notebooks and uneven, roughly folded wads crammed into used envelopes. He unpinned and untied and straightened the rumpled sheets and flattened them under books. Without troubling much about their content he began to sort them into neat piles, classified under headings. When he'd got them sorted, he thought, he'd be able to see where he was going. He worked steadily and mechanically and was surprised to find that it was midnight.

"I'm so glad," she said. She was really glad that he was working steadily again. She thought: I knew he would, when things got more settled and there was less to worry about. "We oughtn't to go out so often in the evenings," she said, "so that you'd have more time."

"Well," he said, without exactly agreeing or disagreeing, "if I can just see where things are going I'll be able to get ahead."

They went out on three nights a week and Katherine took to going to the club again to fill an evening and Halliburton dropped in oftener, as she used to. Halliburton would drop in with a Party pamphlet and a pile of corrections, and when they had talked over the pamphlet she would sit and correct by the sizzling gas-fire that spurted up blue and loud when Katherine chinked in the pennies. As the evenings grew lighter they pulled their chairs to the window, on either side of the bamboo stand with the pushing, sturdy fern, and Halliburton talked about her friend. "Don't talk to me about marriage," she said. "You won't catch me putting my head in *that* trap. The sort of trap marriage is in a bourgeois society.

"Oh well," she said, "when you come to retire, both of you, that's different. No one minds settling down then, do they. When you've both of you got your pension, and neither's going to be a drag on the other, then it's different, if you see what I mean.

"You don't mind me talking like this, do you?" she said.

"It isn't often you can talk to someone that sees eye to eye."

Katherine told Robert: "But don't you see, it isn't *worthwhile*, this bourgeois sort of marriage. The kind we should have to have. With the world as it is marriage is just a trap for both of us. It's just degrading. Anyway now, when we're both young. It isn't worthy of us," she cried.

"Besides, now you're working again you've got to go on and finish your book. I'm not going to get in the way of that."

"Well," he said modestly, "I hadn't thought of it exactly as a book."

"But of course you're going to publish it! If you're not going to give it to the world, to the future," she said indignantly, "why are you writing it at all?"

"Well," he said, "when I began I didn't think of it like that." He fumbled. He wondered how he had thought of it. It had never occurred to him to think how he thought of it. "It just seemed to me there was something in my head I had to put down. And that it might be a bit different from what some other chap would have in his head." His eyes took on a puzzled look; the explanation seemed to him inadequate. "As if it were the individual part of me I had to do something with," he said, and laughed nervously. "The part that was my own, different from the other fellow. A bit absurd, when you come to think of it.

"But I expect you're right about it," he said.

He thought poor old Kath was such an idealist, or else so practical, he didn't exactly know which. But as he got the notes straightened out he had to admit that there seemed plenty of material there to fill a book when he could get down to it and see what he'd been getting at exactly. Now and then he came across a scribbled sheet he couldn't make fit under any heading. He would look at it, puzzled, for a minute, and put it aside with a query mark in the margin. When he had done for the day he pinned these sheets neatly together under the heading Miscellaneous. He thought he'd soon see where they ought to go when he'd picked up the thread of the argument again. Soon get the hang of it.

"It's the future we've got to look at," she said. "We've got to build for the future, and progress."

High speed rail experiment between Cherbourg and Paris: speed reaches ninety-three miles an hour. French Air Minister is present at the inauguration ceremony of a new fleet of luxury air-liners. (New French submarine launched, special arrangements for mine-laying. Dynamite in German town. Mussolini advocates "war-like education"; thirty-five Italian bombing planes make a tour of the Eastern Mediterranean.) The Kalahari Desert is crossed by car. Persia bans the turban. Legal evidence is given by wireless from New Zealand to Philadelphia. New York plans a huge "super-city" with a population of twenty millions. Baldwin's message to the Empire: of the Empire: "We are bound to think of it less as a human achievement than as an instrument of divine providence." "You've got to look forward," she said.

The summer term was hot and dry. Katherine came back fagged from school; she put up the window with its modest lace petticoat and opened to the room a bare, indecent patch of street. Air came in as the evening cooled and the ferns were coated with dust from the pavement underneath. Halliburton dropped in, with the eyes small in her hot, puffy face, and they talked about the Russian films that were trickling past the censor at last, and the Soviet demand for recognition preliminary to the placing of trade orders, and the Moscow Art Theatre, and their doubts about the Labour Government.

Halliburton dropped in, and her eyes were redder than

the heat made them, deep behind her puffy cheeks. She was upset. Katherine knew she was upset but she didn't want to hear about it, she hoped Halliburton would drink her lime-juice and go away and not say anything, so that she wouldn't have to say she was so sorry.

"It's my friend," Miss Halliburton said, and gulped into the lime-juice.

"Oh," said Katherine, "I'm so..."

"No," said Halliburton, "there's nothing wrong with *him*. I wish there was, the dirty tyke."

She swallowed and pulled herself up. "I'm not one to deny anyone their pleasures. I've never asked what he did with his time, have I? I'm not that sort. I don't believe in that possessive outlook in sex, that bourgeois feminine outlook." She fixed Katherine uncomfortably with her little red eyes. "You know as well as I do what I think about *that*. *I'd* never have minded what he did, and he knows it." She drew up her short, puffy person; too indignant for dignity. "But when it comes to betraying the Cause, when it comes to *marrying* her..."

She got up. "Well," she said, "I expect it's silly of me talking like this. Everyone's free to do what they like, aren't they. But to see him let himself down like that, to see him come so *low*... I can tell you," she said, "that's what upsets me more than anything. That he should lose all his loyalty to the Cause like that, when he was always so sound. Letting himself get dragged right down."

She pulled out a greasy puff and stood on tiptoe to see her nose in the mirror of the overmantel. "It just shows, doesn't it. It doesn't do to depend on anyone, even what you'd think are the most enlightened people. It's no good blaming them," she said, and dabbed with increasing heart. "The majority of people just aren't ready, they can't grasp the ideology. They can't see an inch beyond their own noses, and when you think you've dragged them a bit of the way they have to fall back in their own dirt. It's the same with everything, you gain in one place and you lose in another."

Judge goes by plane from Capetown to conduct witch-craft trial in Darkest Africa. Californian desert conquers motor transport: seven die of thirst when car breaks down.

"But we shall win," cried Halliburton, cramming back the puff into her thumbed leather bag. "Civilisation must win in the end, you can't stop it. You can't stop the Revolution!

"Well, so long," she said, "see you to-morrow."

Katherine sat and stared at the flat, close-curtained houses across the street, red-grey in the dusk, and a splash of light along the pavement, under a lamp-post. She felt shaken. She knew in a remote way that it was dreadful for Halliburton: that she must be forty at least, no, forty-five: that she'd meant, and always meant, to marry when she retired and got her pension: that the chances of her finding a new "friend" were not worth reckoning. It was a tragedy really, but she didn't want to think about it. She thought busily and insistently how lucky she was not to be like Halliburton, how lucky she was that Robert would never let her down. She wondered how old Halliburton had been when she first met her friend. As young as she, Katherine, was now, most likely. And had she really waited all those years, fifteen years or more, to be let down at the finish? How dreadful. But how lucky Katherine was.

Oh yes, Katherine was lucky. Katherine was so dreadfully lucky.

This hot, dry weather was so tiring, she said. She could feel herself getting more and more fagged, snappy with the children. She was snappy at staff meetings, over the exams, and before the end of term she was even snappy with Robert.

She was glad at first that he'd fixed his holiday to cover half of hers, the second half of August; but then she didn't know. "Why couldn't you make it the first half," she grumbled. "You know I've got to go home some time."

"I thought you'd rather go home first and get it over."

"You might have asked me."

She knew she didn't care which it was, but she felt angry and nagging and thought it was like him not to ask her, to fix it all on his own, and then she was angry because she knew that wasn't fair.

"Well," he said, "I can change if it you want to. Expect Graham would change."

"I don't know. It doesn't matter."

"Where shall we go, anyway, now we've got the chance?"

"I don't know that I can," she said irritably. "It's too risky staying somewhere like that. You never know who else may be staying anywhere. I can't risk my job just for the sake of a fortnight's holiday."

"What?" he said. He stared at her. "But we've always planned to, only it never fitted in. You never thought before that we couldn't manage it."

"It's all very well," she said, and began to cry angrily. "It's all very well for *you* to talk like that. You don't risk *your* job if somebody sees us." She sat in the carpet-seated chair and turned to the empty fireplace and wouldn't look at him.

"Well, look here," he said, feeling he had a grievance. "I don't see what I've done. I thought you wanted to go home first, but if you want it the other way about I've offered to change. And as for going away I don't see why it's become more difficult now than we've always thought it would be.

"Well, look here," he said angrily, "what *do* you want? I've offered to change..."

She wiped her eyes. "I don't care," she said stonily. "Do just as you like."

She sat staring away from him at the frilly papers in the grate; the hot dusty air from the open window hardly moved around them. The air stood between them, hot and dusty and full of hostility. She thought it was just like him to be like that, and he couldn't imagine what it was all about but he thought it was very thick.

"The fact is," he said, "you don't know what you do want. So you aren't likely to get it."

She got up and powdered her nose, feeling hurt and angry, and went to the door. Hurt and angry, he opened it for her. They went downstairs. "Well," he said on the steps, "what are you doing, then?"

"I've got to go home," she said. He looked at her, hurt and puzzled. She looked at him but didn't see him: she saw a stupid face not caring what happened to her: just like a man, she thought, why must men be so typical. He wondered why she suddenly had to be feminine and unreasonable: feminine in the way they'd always laughed at.

"So you're going for the whole time," he said levelly.

"Quite likely."

"I see."

They said good-bye politely at the tube station.

"When do you go?"

"On Monday, probably."

"So I suppose I shan't see you again."

She knew he wanted to ask her for Sunday but wouldn't because he was hurt and sulky. She wavered. But if he can't ask, I don't see why I should make a move. "I don't suppose so, I shall be packing."

The train was coming in.

"Good-bye," she said and held out her hand. "Write to me, won't you?" She got into the train and it began to move.

Suddenly she was frightened. She sat quite stiff and still in terror with her eyes wide open on to the moving blur of house-backs. The train plunged into the tunnel and the lights came up and the windows were blacked out, the inside of the carriage was snug and self-contained, swinging safely through night. She settled back in her seat and smiled. Poor old Robert, she thought, I'll have to write him a nice letter. And if I got back a week before term we might manage a day or two somewhere.

Robert went back to his rooms and felt sorry for himself and after a day or two he began to feel sorry for Katherine. He thought, poor old Kath, she's nervy with the end of term and the weather and what not. He spent Saturday wondering whether he should try to see her, but decided against it. He thought she'd feel better when she'd been away a bit and he might as well get down to some work. At the end of the first week her letter came and he thought it was just as he'd thought, she was herself again; she'd be back in another fortnight and meanwhile he'd get ahead with the work and have time to see where he stood. He put the letter away with a comfortable feeling of everything being satisfactory and nothing in a hurry.

Now and then in the evening he took a bus up to the West End and strolled about or went into a cinema. It seemed quite strange at first to be going to something by himself, to have a fine evening ahead and nothing to do with it; it even seemed, unaccountably, very slightly exciting. Poor old Kath, he hoped she was having a good holiday, she needed it. He strolled along Oxford Street and stopped outside a dance hall. He thought it was a good long time since he'd danced, and he'd never been much good at it anyhow. He was moving on when he thought it was only ten, too early to go home, and it might be amusing to watch the dancing for a bit, besides he'd heard they had instructresses in these places that you could pay to dance with. Wouldn't do him any harm to rub up his steps. He went in past the commissionaire and the ivy geraniums in tubs and took a ticket at a desk and went down a few steps, wondering what he'd come for, into a large, stuffy room full of jazz, and when it was getting on for eleven o'clock he met Sheila.

Across the river and along darkening tram-lines the gas was fizzing busily at 26 Verbena Road where the landlady's daughter and her young man were using the front parlour, now Miss Bott was gone on holiday. Up the High Road and off to the left, Wilberforce Street Schools were dark and shut up, with moonlight cutting in through the high uncurtained windows across the desks. Farther out still, Halliburton, bereaved but sturdily self-sufficient, was packing for a visit to the too-prosperous butcher, retired, in the West Country. Up in the North, Katherine was looking from a window across her stepfather's handkerchief of garden at a red factory glow in the sky and wondering whether she would write to Robert that she could come back sooner if he liked, or wait until he suggested it. On the northwest of London, in a very new small brick house, so new that the walls of his room showed patches of damp in the blaze of the electric light, Graham was holding his head and trying to concentrate on his work after a hard and conscientious day of carrying on single-handed while Mr. Thomas was away. Inwards, off Ladbroke Grove, Robert's room was empty, with the used supper plates on the table waiting for Mrs. Blim to take them down in the morning when she laid the breakfast, and along

Oxford Street Robert on a plush bench with his shoulders thrust back against a tub of palms and his legs stuck out straight on the slippery floor where the couples slithered out to the whining of the band, was feeling in first one pocket and then another.

"Do you mind if I smoke a pipe?"

Sheila stared at him curiously. "Do what you like," she said, and yawned. "I want a drink."

He put the pipe down on the table and looked round for a waiter. "What shall I order?"

"You can't get a drink here, at this time. Better come round to my club."

"Club?" He wondered what sort of a club — ladies' club, that was — would serve them with drinks this time of night. "Isn't it a bit late?"

"Night-club, you ass." She gathered up her cloak and laughed contemptuously. "You don't suppose I dance *here* as a rule. I came here with someone," she said, taking a perfunctory glance round, "but he seems to have buzzed off. Aren't you coming?"

She had started off across the floor, between the dancers. He seized his pipe and hurried after her and caught her up at the door, and then wondered why he hadn't let her get away in the crowd.

"Not worth a taxi," she said, "it's only round the corner."

It was strange to be walking in the street with a woman in evening dress. The ordinary look of the people on the pavement made him feel he might as well go home: if a 15 bus stopped anywhere near them he'd make an excuse and get on it. But just then they turned a corner and were there.

The night-club was down a great many more steps than the dance hall, it seemed to be in a cellar, and there was some argument before they could get in. Sheila went into a little lighted cubbyhole of an office and spoke to a man who sat there and poked her head out again into the dark passage. "What's your name. I've got to write it down."

"Roberts," he said, with a sudden gush of caution.

She entered it in a book and came out again and led the way to some swing doors. "What comes before Roberts?"

"Tom." He felt such a glow at his own promptness of inspiration that he thought this place was going to be good fun.

The cellar was very small and very full of smoke and the walls were covered by huge, jazzy patterns as if somebody had thrown paint at them. In place of the massive plush settees of the dance hall the furniture was very thin: mere skeletons of tables and chairs. When he examined them more closely they were made of metal tubing. He thought this must be a very expensive place; he was relieved when Sheila ordered whisky instead of champagne.

There seemed to be a lot of new dances he'd never heard of, but so far as he could see it made no difference what the dance was called. People drove ahead, backing their partners up and down the room and avoiding collision by a miracle, or toddled amicably in a corner. He walked Sheila round once, but the floor was much too full for him, he was glad to get back to the table and order her another whisky. Every few seconds she nodded to somebody among the dancers or at the tables, but in a distant way, he thought, as if she wanted to keep them off. It occurred to him that she mightn't be too proud of his looks and the way he was dressed. Most of the people there, but not all, were in evening clothes. She had given him a cool and comprehensive look-over before issuing the invitation, but now she seemed to be taking no more notice of him, she was looking across his shoulder at the seething room. He wondered why she had brought him. Her fingers, curled around the glass, had the nails varnished crimson and her face was perfectly made up. With an expert's eye he judged that it was also an expensive make-up. Grown philosophical with the heat and whisky he reflected that it was a queer thing to know comparatively so little about women and so much about what they put on their faces. He had an uneasy feeling that he'd said nothing for some time. At the end of the whiskies, her fourth and his third, he asked her to dance again.

"No," she said, looking him over calmly. "You don't dance very well, do you?" She got up. "But you can take me home if you like."

The air in the street went to his head, but it seemed that it didn't matter, she lived only just round the corner. Round the corner again. Back round the corner. No, round another corner. Round several corners.

There were very few people in the street now and in any case they didn't worry him. He had a feeling, not unpleasant, that he needn't worry, that she'd tell him what to do next. Around a corner and another and several more she turned a corner and stopped at a door in what seemed to be a street of smart shops. At the head of a staircase she unlocked a door and switched on the light. One of the rooms seemed to be full of white enamel and white sheets like an operating-theatre. "I'm a masseuse," she said and led him into a sitting-room. He had another whisky to clear his head. It wasn't much good, but he didn't worry much, it was a pleasant feeling that he needn't worry and she'd tell him what to do next.

South of the river, a good way out, Miss Halliburton was lugging her suitcase along a side-road to an early tram; Katherine was staring from her bed at the permanently clouded

Lancashire sky between the lace curtains and wondering whether there'd be a letter from Robert; Graham was waking guiltily to the factory syren and dressing with nervous haste for the responsibilities of the day; Mrs. Blim, getting no answer to her knock, was slopping down the shaving-water to cool outside Robert's door and plumping sulkily downstairs again to the basement. Robert was sitting up, was leaping out in horror, was half-way into his clothes in the small, square, modern-furnished, plain carpeted bedroom with the light coming in under the blind, wondering if he could by any miracle get out before this woman, who was called Sheila, woke up. How did he know she was called Sheila? This puzzled him. He sat on a stool in front of the dressing-table to think it out. The stool was made of the same kind of metal tubing as the furniture at the night-club. In the long glass he could see himself on the stool, in his braces, with his hair tousled, but it didn't strike him that it was himself. A movement of the bedclothes behind got him scrambling to his feet. He sat down again. All right so far.

As he put on his tie and stared with distasteful recognition at his horribly drawn and untidy face in the long glass of the very low dressing-table, a new, horrible problem struck him. Ought he, should he, was she... He felt in his pockets, nothing there but some silver. Seven-and-six? Oh well, of course, that was to say, he'd paid for the whiskies the night before. Quite impossible, though, to leave seven-and-six on this expensive dressing-table. Or how about going? Clearing? Hopping it? Behaving, probably, like the worst possible cad. No, he'd have to wait till she woke, nothing else for it. He shivered at the thought of what she might say when she did. But look here, he argued, taking himself firmly in hand, this wasn't any prostitute. No tart this. Certainly not.

Not even one of those glamorous, expensive ones you heard about, that you'd never think. Or she'd never have wasted so much time over him as she had last night, would she Must be one of these modern girls, independent, whims, that sort. And if that was so, well, there couldn't be anything much worse than trotting out this seven-and-six. On the other hand if she were, and he tried to slip it, and she turned nasty... Turn nasty anyhow, when she saw that was all he'd got. He sweated and shivered, fingering the three half-crowns, and measured with his eye the distance past the bed to the door.

Sheila turned and yawned. "What's the time?"

She sat up, wide awake, brisk and competent, and tugged a wrapper from the foot of the bed. "Good lad, I'd never have woken, and I've got a client at ten." She was out, fitting her feet into mules, snapping up the blind. "You'll find the kitchen other side of the sitting-room. Just put on the kettle and I'll be across before you can look round."

He found himself in a minute kitchen, fumbling with the matches; driven out by frying-pans in a bustle; at the table, opposite her, blinking.

"What's up," she said, looking at him for the first time while she buttered her toast. "Got a head?"

"No," he said. "Yes. It doesn't matter."

Her hair was smoothly waved, as unruffled as at the club last night, and her face seemed as perfectly made up. She smiled into her coffee. "You're rather a queer person, aren't you?"

"I don't know," he said. "No. I mean yes."

She ate in a business-like way while he fiddled with some toast and watched her. When she didn't look at him he could think clearly. Get a clue, somehow. "I was wondering," he said suddenly, "what do you believe in? What's your philosophy of life?"

She gave him a long, amused stare and went on with her breakfast. "God," she said, "you aren't only *queer*.

"Well," she said, "you're queer but I like you. So I don't mind telling you if you want to know. Work hard and have as good a time as you can, that's all the philosophy I've any use for."

The door bell rang.

She jumped up and put on a starched white overall which had been waiting on a chair. "Now you'll have to shoot off. That's my client. Don't show up till I've let him in, and then the door's through there." The bell rang again.

"Here, I say," he said, "look here."

She pulled the sitting-room door to behind her.

When he had heard the door of the consulting-room shut, Robert looked out into the hall. He wondered whether to wait or whether he ought to write a note or something.... He turned back into the sitting-room to look for a pen. But there was a suggestion of hostility in that closed door with voices murmuring behind it: shooting him out. His hat was on a rack in the hall, he took it and went downstairs. Out on the pavement, he turned several corners at random and found himself in Bond Street.

On the bus he lit a pipe. It was a hot, dusty morning and the pavements were full of women shopping in thin summer dresses. Now that he was clear of the Mayfair flat he thought how amusing the whole thing had been and he had to laugh at himself, rounding the corner by Paddington.

A jug of cold shaving-water was outside his door. It reminded him unpleasantly that he had not been there since the day before: this had not occurred to him: it put things in a different light. He wondered whether Mrs. Blim had noticed he wasn't there, and what she had thought. In the sitting-room all the furniture looked newly dusted and was pushed impersonally against the walls; his breakfast was on the table, the clean plate waiting between knife and fork and two rashers side by side on the dish in front of it: quite cold and lustreless. All at once he remembered Katherine.

He thought: Good God; Kath. He went out again.

He walked a long way, trying not to think about her. When he couldn't help thinking about her he tried to think he hadn't let her down. He told himself she wouldn't think anything of it. A thing like that. She believed in Russia and free love and not letting yourself get repressions; she was broad-minded, she was *modern*. Was she? Sheila was.

Sheila was five to ten years younger than either of them, she was post-war. She was young and hard and her nails were lacquered crimson and she had a hard, bright assurance which was genuine through and through, not a protective shell for self-mistrust. She did, without thinking, all the things they talked about without doing them. Sheila hadn't a pre-war parsonage upbringing to react against. Sheila wasn't afraid of not being modern; Sheila was not conscious of being modern. Sheila was modern.

Kath talked a lot about being modern, she'd say she didn't mind, but she'd mind like hell. She'd say she didn't mind because she'd be afraid of being narrowminded and old-fashioned: not afraid so much of Robert's thinking her so, but afraid of being it. That was the trouble with a lot of people nowadays: the half-generation between the war and the post-war. They'd been brought up in one world and jerked out into another, and they hadn't lived the war themselves to get there naturally. Packed away at school, getting trained in the old traditions: then finding the war generation had altered it all. Robert knew he was old-fashioned, but he couldn't help it. He couldn't help feeling he'd behaved like a cad. Thirty-five million cars were in use throughout the world, three million cinemas in Britain were in process of installing sound apparatus, in the United States an aeroplane flying at ninety-five miles an hour was dropping seed on a hundred and sixty acres of ground, America was exporting motor-tractors to Europe at the rate of sixty thousand a year, within a fortnight the world's air speed record was to be broken by an average of three hundred and fifty-five miles per hour, and Robert was tramping the dusty August streets telling himself he had acted dishonourably to Katherine in spending the night with Sheila, that he wouldn't see Sheila again (he turned sharply at the end of Bond Street, back towards Marble Arch) and that as soon as Kath was back he'd ask her again if she wouldn't marry him.

He was glad she stayed away until the end of the month, it gave him more time to think; but however much he thought he thought about the same things. He thought he'd tell Kath, and then he thought it might upset her; he played with an idea of going to see Sheila once more, but he had a suspicion she would laugh at him, and, besides, he didn't know her address: he told himself it wouldn't be fair to Katherine. He thought he'd behaved damn badly to Kath and he'd tell her all about it and let her slang him as he deserved. And then he thought it would only upset her and there wasn't much point.

Katherine wondered why Robert didn't write. She had thought he would be sure to write presently and ask her to come back. When he did write she wondered why he didn't ask her. She wasn't going back early unless he asked her to. He said he was glad she would be back soon but he didn't ask her to come sooner. She thought she wouldn't see him until she'd been back at least a week. When she saw him on the platform at Euston she was glad, and then, looking at him, she was suddenly afraid, about nothing, and then glad again. Because it was the last day of the holidays she went back with him to his rooms before going to Verbena Road and he asked her to marry him.

"But why particularly now?" She smiled. He must have missed me a lot. She smiled and talked about the Cause.

"Damn the Cause. As your friend Halliburton would say, 'that won't hurt the Revolution!'"

Halliburton.

Oh yes, Halliburton. But then Halliburton's different. That's quite different.

She knew for the first time how afraid she had been of losing him.

Nonsense, what utter nonsense. Halliburton, nonsense. Halliburton's a fool, she was asking for it. But how lucky I am Robert isn't like that. She told herself he was looking ill and worried, it wasn't fair on him to keep him waiting longer, and she agreed.

They were married on a Saturday at the end of October, without telling anybody about it. The heat of summer had broken at last and rain was falling steadily. They came out of the register office together and alone and stood on the pavement in the rain waiting for a bus, because he felt too bewildered to think of calling a taxi and because it would have seemed to both of them stupid and a little indecent to mark the occasion by behaving in any special way. They stood on the curb as if it were any ordinary afternoon, two people so very ordinary-looking that nobody gave them a glance, with the shut, ordinary door of the register office behind them; and traffic ploughing indifferently past crashed out their bridal peal. Vast railway works improvement scheme.

Sensation flight R.101. Conquest of peace is imminent. Wall Street. Soviet plane completes first flight, Moscow — New York twelve thousand miles. In Italy, successful trial, six thousand horse-power bombing plane. Giant submarine is launched by France. Panic strikes New York stock market. Prosperity; no danger here. Bank rate is down by half per cent. Huge figures in road fund report, increase in driving licences. Gas suicides; air suicide. First. Air crash, train crash, bus crash, planes crash. New race to come through gland control. Progress, prosperity and peace.

Chapter VI

Katherine stayed at the school until the end of term. As autumn wore on, the new long chalks got broken and littered her table with dusty pieces and when she wrote on the board the short chalk ground into her nails. The desks, which had been scrubbed during August, grew smudged and ink-smeared, and the newly moved-up children lost their awe, they shuffled and sniggered. In the jam-jar on the sill the last autumn flowers withered and hung for a time, dead and smelling, and at last were removed. The jar stood half full of yellowing water with a piece of brown leaf stuck on the glass above the water-line, and the playground outside was yellow-grey with fog. At the end of the road, trams clanged and the small shops grew pinched with winter poverty and the gas-fire in Verbena Road sizzled blue and cheerless. But somewhere across the river, on the way to Robert's, there was the flat they were going to take; they looked for it every Saturday afternoon.

It was in Chelsea or Bloomsbury or Hampstead, in one of the new model blocks, painted white and clean, and so full of labour-saving appliances and the rent was so low that there would be plenty of time and money for the things that were worthwhile. They looked for it every Saturday afternoon but they hadn't found it yet: the new blocks were far too expensive and the new small houses were too far out: Katherine said No these houses were suburban and bourgeois, they must live among intelligent people who were interested in the things that mattered. They went over the ground again, looking at "converted" houses where rents were lower: houses whose floors were being turned into flats.

Robert said, laughing at her, "Since we've been so bourgeois as to get married we mustn't be too particular."

But Katherine had thought it out. "You see," she said, "we didn't marry for bourgeois, conventional reasons. *Our* marriage isn't bourgeois. We married because we wanted to, that's quite different, not because we were afraid." Her forehead wrinkled with the effort of remembering: stray sentences of shrill-voiced women speakers in stuffy halls: and the effort of piecing together. "We weren't afraid of public opinion," she said, "the basis of bourgeois marriage. We did what we wanted without interfering with anyone's freedom, and that's the true spirit of Communism. We haven't hurt anyone," she said, "or given up our own freedom, because we haven't gone into this in the bourgeois spirit. And so long as we live in a capitalist society," she said triumphantly, "we have to compromise, we have to do the best we can for ourselves. That's the true spirit of Marxism. People who keep kicking against the system," she said, "like poor old Halliburton, simply don't get anywhere. They simply haven't grasped the ideology."

She still saw poor old Halliburton now and then because she was sorry for her, and because, she thought, it did one good to talk sometimes to people who saw eye to eye with one. And Halliburton, though she was all wrong on the marriage question, poor old thing, was terribly sound on most things.

Now that Katherine had grasped the ideology: now that she had decided that marrying Robert had been the very best thing to do, in fact the one thing she obviously had had to do in order to be a good Communist, she was more than ever enthusiastic about Communism. She and Halliburton were tremendously thrilled at the instalment of a Soviet ambassador — So the government had to give in! — and the report of the British Workers' delegation to Russia; tremendously indignant at the new campaign against Soviet anti-religious policy. "It's just jealousy," Miss Halliburton cried indignantly. — Introduction of five-day week, short hours, high wages, ideal working conditions, huge industrial development. — "They're jealous because Communism has succeeded."

"I can't think why they've started this again," Katherine said. "Just when we'd renewed diplomatic relations."

Robert laughed. "What, religion again? The good old funk-hole? Take a look round and you'll soon spot the bogy."

Third International "seeks by teaching and propaganda to undermine the existing fabric of civilisation." Communist plot discovered in France, powder magazines blown up, bombs in Bordeaux, bombs on the Riviera; bombs in Rumania, four in ten days on track of the Orient Express; Viceroy's train bombed in India; shots at Argentine President; hundred and fourth bomb in a year explodes in Chicago. Riots in Germany, mutiny on the *Emden*, riots in Australia, Samoa, Haiti, Nigeria, All India Congress shouts for revolution.

True purpose of Soviet policy, war against God and

religion! National protest, Call to Churches, appeal for funds. Blasphemous cartoons, atrocities up to date, corruption of school-children, shaking hands with Antichrist, devils in human guise!

Soviet leads in air armaments, fleet of a thousand planes.

Red war on religion, protest meeting at Albert Hall, England's united front, French protest meeting, emotion of huge audience! British protest fund reaches ten thousand!!

"And you'll notice it isn't primarily the Church," he said. "Several bishops refused to sign. It's political and capitalist funk, through and through."

"How bright of you," Katherine admired. "I should never have put it all together like that." She wished Halliburton could hear him, he was so sound. She was even surprised at times at how sound Robert was; much sounder, really, than poor old Halliburton. She felt particularly sorry for poor old Halliburton each time she set out with Robert to look for the flat.

The "converted" flats they saw were neither modern nor labour-saving. They had the stove on the stairs or in the bedroom, or the bath in the kitchen, or no bath or no sink. Their rents were as high as those of the new suburban houses. Katherine said, "If we lived near the factory you wouldn't have so far to go. And there's no need to be suburban and bourgeois because we live in a suburb. Besides, Primrose Green is hardly a suburb. Really."

The new house was square, in a little plot of garden with a very new tree. One corner of the house was cut away to form a covered sun loggia and the kitchen was white-enamelled and full of labour-saving appliances. They began to like it because it was modern; one of a group washed out over the fields by the last wave of progress. They still believed in progress. — Baby born on express, rocket car inventor has nervous breakdown, stockbroker's suicide, young man refuses food: no interest in life. — They thought of the house as an island of advanced thought in Primrose Green; without conscious intention either to rebuff or uplift the inhabitants, they saw it at the same time as a fortress and a jumping-off ground for the things that mattered.

Katherine left the school at Christmas. The classroom was hung with paper festoons for the end-of-term party, there was a bunch of holly on the window-sill and on the board A Merry Christmas was picked out in holly-berries secured by drawing-pins. For a week the children had been noisy and restless and she had left them alone. When they had gone she took a look round the room, but there was nothing to sentimentalise over. She was glad to go. The children were the citizens of the future, but of a too immediate future. They were the wage slaves of three years ahead. They had the slave mentality. The germ of freedom was not in them. The people are not ready, she thought, that will have to come. She left the half-filled history chart on the wall for her successor to finish or discard as she chose. When she had got back to Verbena Road she remembered the charts of past years in the table drawer, with the red ink lines through 1917. The school would be shut by now. She was annoyed for a moment, and then glad. She no longer had anything to fear and she smiled to think of the new teacher hurrying indignantly to the Head Master to clear herself, or, perhaps, with a glow of guilty pleasure disposing quietly of the charts.

Robert was glad they had taken the house. Instead of the long tube journey in the morning he only had to catch a bus. The bus carried him from the half-built roads and avenues of Primrose Green along a strip of lane with high hedges — they'd be green in summer, if they hadn't been cut down by then — to the end of the concrete road which ran down through the Trading Estate. He was even able to get home for lunch. And in the evening, leaving Graham to lock up as a rule, he would sprint for a bus and try to get home before Kath expected him, to give her a surprise. Turning, as his bus rounded the corner into the lane, he could see bowler-hatted men — the men he used to travel with — trudging to the tube. Katherine had made him give up his bowler. He had always hated the thing, but felt he had to wear one to the factory. Katherine said Nonsense, nobody would say anything; and nobody did. He wore a soft hat now and took it off on the bus; and she made him wear a high-necked knitted pullover instead of a waistcoat and tie. She said there was no point in his looking bourgeois when he wasn't.

Katherine had gone without telling Halliburton she was leaving. She didn't want to tell Halliburton. She said it would be tactless to let the old thing know she had got married: Halliburton was all wrong on the marriage question. She thought of her once when she read in the papers reports of the Women Teachers' conference: demands for sex equality and equal pay. They were quite right, she thought, to agitate about it. But Halliburton was all wrong. Teaching narrowed one. She, Katherine, was right to get out. Into a larger world.

The sitting-room — they called it the living-room — was furnished in scrubbed oak, very nearly, with a plain grey carpet and a grey pottery jar on the low window-sill, and no pictures, very modern. Robert thought there ought to be some colour somewhere to liven it up, but Katherine said No, it ought to be like that. Next to the living-room was a small dining-room, just large enough for a refectory table with hand-woven rush mats instead of a cloth, and two chairs. There was a hatch for Katherine to pass dishes through from the kitchen and fetch them on the other side. Robert said he ought to do his share, but at lunch-time he had barely time for the meal, and in the evening they had a snack, hurriedly, or ate out, to have time to go to things. They went to the protest meeting against Russia at the Kingsway Hall: they went to hear the Communist hecklers. Women interrupters were carried out at the back of the hall and Katherine wondered whether Halliburton was among them. Soon after she forgot about Halliburton.

There were about two thousand people at the meeting. "All the same the campaign seems to be fizzling out," she said. "You don't hear so much about it."

"People getting tired of it," he said. "Besides, they think they've found out nothing much is going to happen." — Mr. MacDonald burnt in effigy on anti-Christmas tree. — "Nobody minds that." — Five-Year Plan of economic development shows signs of failure. — "That'll cheer them up."

"How *can* they say that," Katherine cried indignantly. — Five-day week, nine hundred miles of Turkestan — Siberia railway built since 1926, Palace of Proletarian Culture to go up in eighteen months at a cost of five million roubles. — "And to think that the only interest people take is in the wretched monastery they have to blow up to make room for it."

The local newsagent, one of the small new lock-up shops on the new wide white Parade by the tube station, refused an order for the *Daily Worker*. Katherine was proudly indignant. It made her feel pleasantly independent and superior to put the man in his place and reject an alternative paper. One of the things she had gained by marrying Robert. For some time she bought a copy of the *Daily Worker* whenever she went up to town. She always meant to send a subscription direct to the offices of the paper, but whenever she thought of it she was too busy.

The bedroom was very modern too: twin beds, and rush matting instead of carpet, and a tallboy with a mirror on top, much too high to be convenient. Katherine didn't mind, she had no hair to do up now. She had had it bobbed as a gesture of independence on leaving the school. She parted it in the middle and brushed it smooth. She felt superior in not waving it. — Woman worker with bobbed hair dismissed from German factory. "Reactionism again. The Fascist spirit."

The papers were boosting Fascism. Italy, the ancient ally of England; Fascist trade organisation, the worker as partner; famous Italian speed-ways give a lead to world motoring. Fascism meant Italy. The National-Socialist party in Germany was sometimes called Fascist in brackets, and a small notice appeared to the effect that Herr Hitler, its leader, had been awarded damages in a libel action against the *Münchener Telegramm Zeitung*, this paper having alleged that he had deserted the monarchist cause for republicanism.

The successful trials of R.100[1] were completed. A Dutch scientist was working out a scheme for the production of artificial rain. A Beam wireless service was opened between England and Japan. A pilot flew over six thousand miles of African jungle to carry anti-hydrophobia serum to a missionary. Agricultural machines in France were grading and marking eggs at the rate of a hundred and twenty a minute. Escalators were speeding up, the biggest building in the Empire was in course of construction at Olympia, Katherine and Robert were in their white-enamelled kitchen one Sunday afternoon, washing the tea-things in instantaneous hot water and hanging them to dry in an electrically heated rack.

1 A commercial dirigible first flown in December 1929.

"We ought to have a child," Katherine said.

"Too risky at present."

She wiped her hands and went into the living-room and sat on the deep window-sill beside the pottery jar and folded her hands on her knees wrist to wrist and tip to tip. "We could afford it now," she said. "Things are improving everywhere." — Many millions for electricity, new London tube costs seven million, more work in shipyards, recovery in sight; big railway plans, British films optimistic, huge developments coming. — "And the Cosmetics Co. is going ahead."

"We owe a lot," he said. "Instalments on the house and furniture. We ought to get clear.

"And the world isn't safe enough," he said. "The world's getting ready for war. We've no right to push somebody into it."

"The Five Power Conference," she objected. "Naval disarmament."

"Yes I know," he said impatiently, "but you've got to look at the other side." — America's air strength fourteen hundred first-line machines; pacifist pictures banned from French exhibition.

"But isn't it our duty," she said, fingers tapping tip against tip. "The world needs more of the right kind of people. It needs leaven. It's the wrong people who are having families," she said. "You and I: it's our duty to bring into the world somebody else who will think in the right way."

"As for that," he said with a grin, "the kid might turn out a thorough-going Tory."

"Nonsense," she said, quite sharply.

He walked up and down, serious again and stubborn. "I don't consider we're justified. The furniture ought to be cleared off, we ought to be free of debt."

She was annoyed with him, not so much for holding out

as for his pessimism. She had made a rule never to lose her temper with him; in any case it was time to take a tube to the West End — "We really ought to have a car" — for the theatre. The Thomases hardly ever went to the theatre except on Sunday: to productions of banned plays by private societies.

The Thomases were highbrow. When Mrs. Thomas went into the back-yard to hang washing on the line she carefully took no notice of the back-yards to right and left over the low palings. She hurried over her business and hurried in: she had a horrified fear, based on advertisements of various laundering commodities, of neighbourly gossip over the fence, from line to line. Housewifely and bourgeois. She need not have been afraid, nobody spoke to her. The Thomases were known to be highbrow.

They knew the Grahams of course. Graham had married. His wife was a nondescript little woman and was starting a baby. Katherine asked them in for bridge, Robert was glad she got on with Mrs. Graham: Graham was a decent fellow and did more than his share of the routine work which Robert found so tiresome. Katherine felt very superior to little Mrs. Graham: not because Graham was under Robert in the laboratory, but because little Mrs. Graham was such a weak-minded, well-meaning little thing. Katherine had long talks with her about Communism and progress, and Mrs. Graham said admiringly, "Oh, do you think so? I never thought of that."

It was the idea of Mrs. Graham's baby which made Katherine think that Robert might have been right after all. The Grahams had a much smaller house than the Thomases: an older house: an ugly little house on a noisy road, with practically no labour-saving appliances. How absurd, Katherine thought, to start a baby on Graham's small salary. Why, the woman would be nothing but a slave to it and Graham, she wouldn't have a moment to develop herself or keep up. Even Katherine, heaven knew, had no vacuum cleaner yet, and they had no car or phone: so inconvenient.

"You may be right," she said. "It may be wiser to get settled first. And fairer, certainly."

They agreed to wait for two years and at Easter they got a vacuum cleaner and began to pay for it on the instalment system.

"You ought to finish your book," she said, "I'm sure it'll make a lot of money. Everybody's interested in science now, not only specialists. Look at the way they rushed to the Einstein film in New York." — Film lecture on Einstein theory, four thousand five hundred rush hall, police called in to regulate crowd.

He laughed. "You have to be an Einstein for that."

But he got out his notes after a week or so and looked them through. He was under no delusion that his theory would make money. He did not suppose it would ever be published. He wanted to work it out for his own satisfaction. They turned the small second bedroom into a study and he worked there on Saturday afternoons and in the evening when they weren't going out or having the Grahams to bridge. He worked by the window over the newly made garden, and as spring came on the bulbs they had planted began to flower and presently the small new trees were green and pleasant. He got used to the neighbours' loudspeakers and hardly noticed them. Katherine said they ought to have a wireless but he thought they ought to pay for some of the other things first. Some of his early notes puzzled him but he put them aside and began to work out the formula again: the formula for the nature of Time. He thought a bit and looked out of the window and whistled to himself and pottered with his pipe and his notes and was happy. In the evening, as a rule, he went out with Kath. They went to meetings and to private showings of Russian films and private play societies' productions and sometimes to films and plays of the commercial theatre: because Katherine said it gave them something to talk about when the Grahams came.

They thought they really ought to get a car before Robert's holiday, but decided they couldn't afford it yet. They took a train to North Wales to stay with his father. Katherine was enthusiastic about the village. "Such lovely unspoilt country, no pylons or anything."

"Medieval in fact," Robert agreed. He teased her. "How about unspoilt Russia and industrialisation? How about power stations on the steppes?"

"But that's different," she said. "A huge undeveloped, backward country. They had to take it in hand. But here it's different. You need some places unspoilt, to rest in."

R.100 crosses the Atlantic, Amy Johnson returns from Australia, pilot does non-stop flight to Malta and back in twenty-six hours, on a warm, damp August morning milk is being delivered by donkey cart at the vicarage gate, and up the lane water from a mountain stream is falling freely and wastefully over some stones into a deep pond. Progress, and peace. "I shouldn't say anything to the old man about politics and all that," Robert suggested nervously. "Only upset him."

"Of course not," she agreed. "There'd be no point." She thought Robert's father was a sweet old man and the vicarage was sweet, and the village was a sweet place.

When they got back to town they had the telephone installed, it would save Katherine's going out to shop in bad weather. She liked the feeling it gave her of being in touch with things; she liked to feel she could ring up anybody she wanted to, though she seldom did. She was glad to be back. She was glad to be in the Centre of Things. It was a pity they lived so far out. But when she thought about it, and particularly when she took up the phone to ring a Banned Play Society or a West End store, she could feel Things all around her, Getting Done. It was exciting. Tube extensions, and the new B.B.C. building going up, very modern, — "We really must get a wireless," she said, "it's absurd," — and the North Circular Road, and Great New Oxford Street Store, and slum clearance in Chelsea. Communists in eviction scenes: "I can't think why they should object," she said. "How can we get improved conditions until we've pulled down some of those dreadful old cottages. So childish. Going against their own interests."

Robert pulled at his pipe. "Well," he said, "you can't expect them to see it in the abstract, when it's their own homes that are coming down. You can't expect them to take a long view."

"That's just it," she cried irritably. She was getting irritated by the Communists. "The people are so short-sighted. The country simply isn't ready for Communism yet. How can you give people freedom when they don't know how to take it." During that autumn she stopped going to meetings in outlying halls, it was too difficult to get back to Primrose Green at night; if they had had a car it would have been different; besides the country wasn't ready for Communism and it was sheer waste of time trying to give people what they weren't able to appreciate. And Robert had caught a bad cold one night waiting for a late tube connection at Hammersmith. Robert stopped going to meetings too; he had only gone because Kath wanted to.

She was still tremendously thrilled of course by what the Soviets were doing, the "real" Communists: Arctic expeditions, airship cruise. Just as she was thrilled by the Paris — New York flight and the Pacific flyers and Piccard's first attempt to go ten miles up in a balloon. Even though it failed. "But he'll do it another time. Or somebody else will. There's never been such a time," she cried, in an echo of the schoolroom, "since the Elizabethan Age. Never since then have people had this feeling of the world opening out wider all the time. A new world." — New atomic theory. New scheme for universal indexing of knowledge. New anti-aircraft gun. — "A feeling of expansion, you know what I mean. Some new discovery every day."

She was a little depressed by the unemployment figures and the Serious Plight of British Trade.

"That's nothing," Robert assured her. "A stunt against the Labour Government, that's all. I don't say there isn't unemployment, plenty of it, but many concerns are booming. Look at the motor industry." Besides, he could see it at the factory. The cosmetics trade was working full time.

He was glad of the winter. He was glad of the long, dark evenings when Kath didn't want to go out. He got her the wireless set — on instalments: the vacuum cleaner would be paid off in a month or so — and pottered round with his pipe and his notes and strolled in now and then to hear a broadcast and pottered back to his notes and pipe. They still went out once or twice a week to Interesting plays, and the Grahams came in for bridge occasionally, but it would soon be time for Mrs. Graham's baby. Katherine was glad they had agreed to wait.

Robert talked a good deal to Graham at the factory. They had a new brick laboratory now, with radiators and no smoke, and a couple of clean boys under Graham to carry messages and clear things up. Graham was a very decent chap. He told Robert he wished he could afford a more modern house for the wife; as things were it wasn't fair on her. He said what could you do though, he might not get a rise for years. He was trying to finish his own research, to qualify for a better job, but there was never any time. There were a few things he could do to help when he got back from work, such as carrying coals for the next day, and he had to leave home early in the morning.

Robert thought they'd been right to wait. He thought that all the same Kath wouldn't have been in such a hole as Mrs. Graham. He wondered if they need wait so long as two years. He thought he wouldn't have minded carrying coals if it had been necessary, and he knew Graham didn't mind either. Graham was anxious and Robert would be anxious, but he'd be glad too. He thought it wouldn't be fair on Kath though, without more security behind them. He remembered that it was he who had first suggested waiting, and why. He thought after all the world was no more likely to blow up now than at any other time; if one waited one might as well wait for ever. He thought, well he'd keep to the agreement, not mention it again until the two years were up. He wondered what queer sort of barbarous survival it was that made a chap want a kid of his own. Not because, like Kath, he hoped it would be a specially good one: but just wanting it.

In November the inquiry into the R.101 disaster was in progress, French airmen flew from Paris to Calcutta in three and a half days, a motorist summoned for dangerous driving blamed pedestrian: "might have damaged my car"; the number of registered unemployed was over two million; Graham came home with Robert for his evening meal while Mrs. Graham was in hospital having her baby. Graham was worried.

He told them he wondered how to get help in the house for Vi when she came home and had the baby to look after. Katherine said they might get a girl straight from school, a girl ought to be cheap. She thought the girl might also be useless. She offered to look for a girl. Graham was very grateful but he went on being worried. Katherine thought how wise she and had been to wait. She forgot that it was Robert who had suggested it. She thought how true it was that only a woman could see these things clearly: that by the time they decided to have the baby they must be in a position to give it the best possible advantages to make it grow up into the right kind of person.

She began to take an interest in Robert's laboratory work. She tried to think of ideas for him to work up. She said, dusting her nose with powder under the downward tipped mirror of the tallboy, "You invent a lot of stuff to put on the face, but how about something to take it off?"

"Been done already," he objected. "Cleansing creams and lotions, plenty of good makes."

She flicked the puff over her pale, smooth skin. "Yes, but how about something new and instantaneous, for people who make up heavily? Rouge and mascara and lipstick," she said scornfully, turning from the mirror. "Something that would dissolve it all with one dab. Rather like turpentine cleaning up paint."

He laughed. "That doesn't sound very scientific.

"Still," he said, looking out of the window and jingling the keys in his pocket — he was wondering whether he could decently clear off into the next room and do some work or whether Kath would want him to go out with her because it was Saturday — "it might be worth looking into. Might be something in it."

When he was alone, chewing his pipe in the back room and looking from the window over the wintry garden, it struck him there might be money in it. If he worked it up on his own, not as a routine job, he might sell it to Cosmetics Ltd., and get a small royalty on sales. And considering how that kind of stuff sold he might make a decent bit. And all that kind of thing meant a bit more security; being in a better position in a couple of years' time. He began to jot down tentative formulas on the paper in front of him, the paper he used for his own work.

He began to let Graham go early, because Graham was in a hurry to get home, and when the firm's work was done he would stay late and boil up his private mixtures in little pans and watch them curdle. Sometimes he would even go back to the laboratory after supper.

"Besides," Katherine said impatiently, seeing him absent-minded, — No business sense, she thought, — "it surely can't matter so much. Even if it has much the same things in it as all the others you've only got to give it a different name and advertise a lot."

In the New Year, Italy proposed to eliminate women workers from industry and replace them by unemployed men. Fascism. Katherine was indignant. Indignation recalled her momentarily to Russia. "Do you see this," she said, spreading the papers — she read two or three, to keep abreast of things — over the living-room carpet around the low chair and pushing them with her foot. "Another hue-and-cry. Soviet labour conditions."

"What's up then? The dumping scare?"

"It's probably that," she said contemptuously. The electric kettle whistled from the kitchen and she left the papers and went away to make the tea.

— Soviet timber dumping affects America and Germany. Soviet wheat dumping a serious blow to British farmers. Russian timber undersells Canadian. British Government White Paper on Soviet labour conditions. Russian lumber camp horrors, affidavits from counter-revolutionary refugees, brutal methods of production, War on Soviet Slavers! —

"I wonder how long we shall go on getting up moral scares against Russia," he said as Katherine came back with the tray. "I suppose until they cease to be a Menace, or until we need them. And when we've done with them it will be somebody else. Like the German atrocities. Just as God is always on Our Side."

Katherine sat down. "What hypocrites the English are," she said indignantly, turning the wedding ring on her finger. "They always have to find some moral reason to back them up in what they want to do." She got up suddenly and swept all the papers away into the paper rack, because they messed up the carpet: the plain, modern look of the room. "But about the trade depression," she said. "Does it matter? Is it serious?"

"Oh well," he said, "you can't deny there is depression, in certain trades."

"But you're not feeling it at the factory?"

He laughed and lit a pipe. "That's a bit different. We don't depend on the usual trade reactions. We, and I suppose the dress trade and a few more, depend on human nature. So long as women are human," he said and laughed, "and, naturally, so long as we keep an eye on the trend of fashion, we can't get knocked out."

"Suppose natural faces come into fashion," she teased him.

He chuckled. "Take a darned lot more stuff to make 'em look natural, most of them. We'd sell a whole lot more that way."

"Besides," she said, sitting back easily and lighting a cigarette, "I don't think things as a whole look so bad. People in America seem to think there's another boom coming."

"Oh," he said, "things aren't so bad. Might be a lot worse. In my opinion we've turned the corner."

Campbell does two hundred, two-forty, two-forty-five miles per hour! Dutch line demonstrates faster airliners. Air Ministry prepares for attack on world's long-distance non-stop air record. The Pope turns on electric power installation for the Vatican State. Films boost British goods at Buenos Aires. By the end of February Robert has completed his formula for Cupid Complexion Solvent and offered it to his firm.

"You appreciate the position, Mr. Thomas," said the Managing Director. "As things are, we could only offer you a small sum down for your formula. But if you cared to take a rise in salary and give us the right to market your Solvent on those conditions...?"

Robert hesitated. "I was thinking of a small royalty on sales."

"And a small royalty on sales, naturally.

"In fact, if I may point it out, you would gain considerably by this arrangement. An additional pound or so a week so long as you remain with us..." The Directing mouth smiled. "And I hope that may be for many years, would amount to appreciably more than the sum we could offer you at present.

"Let me be frank," said the mouth, curling. "Your services are valuable to us. On the whole we should prefer to have you attached to us in this way. What guarantee have we," bantered the mouth, "that with your sum down, comparatively negligible though this must be, you would not remove to another firm? And we can't afford to lose you, Mr. Thomas. We prefer to offer you a worthy salary, in keeping with your value to us, and ensure your collaboration."

Robert accepted an additional two pounds a week.

"I think you were right," Katherine said. "How much would they have given you, down?"

"He didn't say. Called it small. Not more than a hundred at the most, probably."

"And this way you get that much extra every year! I wonder they did it. Surely it can't pay them."

"Don't know. The stuff itself won't cost them much. They haven't got to install new plant for it."

"But of course, as he said, that makes you stay with them. That's really the best part of it, isn't it, it shows how keen they are to keep you.

"I told you trade was going to boom," she cried.

"Not trade, human nature. Boom in human nature," he said, and grinned.

They got a car at once, on instalments. They drove up to the West End, to theatres; and in the lengthening evenings and at week-ends they drove outwards, in search of unspoilt country. Robert decided to leave the book until the winter: it wasn't fair on Kath to shut himself up with it. While he was out Katherine ordered ready-cooked food by phone from one or other of the big stores, and passed the vacuum cleaner over the carpets and chairs, and when he got back they only had to take the meal out of the refrigerator and the rinsed dishes from the drying rack and eat, and they were ready to start.

Sometimes they took a run around the Park and along the Embankment — "Doesn't it seem years ago?" — and once they crossed the river and drove past Verbena Road and Wilberforce Street. "How *could* I?" And they ran up to Leicester Square to the Epstein exhibition, to see *Genesis*.

"I don't like it," Katherine said. She was puzzled. She

hated it. It said something to her that she didn't want to hear. She knew, at the same time, that it was modern, and art, and anti-bourgeois, and significant. "Though it's technically clever," she said quickly, "and tremendously impressive of course."

"It's barbarous," he said. "Elemental, that's the word. In feeling, I mean."

He stared at it. "Astounding, you know, that it could be produced to-day." It stirred something in him which had nothing to do with Kath or Primrose Green or the car parked outside or Cupid Complexion Solvent: something so obscure and fleeting and uneasy that it was sensed and turned back before recognition. "Undoubtedly a work of genius," he said coldly, dismissing the statue.

"Oh yes," she agreed, "of course."

Now and then at the week-end they took Mrs. Graham and the baby for a run in the car. The baby was thin and cried a lot and Mrs. Graham looked tired. She was quiet and grateful, but gave an impression that she would nag Graham, or cry at him, when she got him alone. The Thomases now had so much more money than the Grahams that they felt quite guilty about them. "Though after all," Katherine said, "it isn't our fault that you're brighter than Ted Graham!" They were sorry for the Grahams, but it was uncomfortable having to feel sorry and guilty, even without reason; and Katherine couldn't wear her fur coat on the days Mrs. Graham came out with them, because it wasn't tactful. They were glad when the duty drive was over and they could decently keep the car to themselves for at least a week.

They were very pleased with themselves and with one another, and when they looked around at things they were pleased with what they saw. By the end of May, Piccard had succeeded in rising fifty-three thousand feet into the stratosphere, and in June Cupid Complexion Solvent was on the market. But what a state Australia is in, they exclaimed. What a state Austria is in! What a state Germany is in! — Australian stocks falling. Failure of Credit-Anstalt. Depreciation of the mark.

Now profits would begin to come in. "Not much, naturally," he said. "Anyhow to start with. Still it'll help."

He found they were spending a lot more than he'd expected on running expenses, and they'd had to build a garage on the spare plot of garden at the side of the house. "Before long," he said, "they won't think of putting up a house like this without a garage."

They seemed to be spending a good deal; but in the winter, he thought, they wouldn't spend so much and profits would be piling up. "We shall be saving then," he said. "We ought to save a decent bit. We ought to be in a pretty sound position by next year. We ought to be able to think again about young Katherine."

"Oh, well," she said, "perhaps. Yes, perhaps, after all." She smiled. "Or young Robert," she said.

They were putting away the car, closing the new shiny doors of the garage. Suddenly she gripped his arm. "Robert! What should we do with a baby when we drive all day?"

"Oh, well, leave him with a maid, I expect."

"No," she said, "I should hate to do that. He'd catch all the old, wrong ideology we were trying to keep away from him."

Robert laughed. "Well then, take the little beggar along, of course. Give him a motoring sense from his cradle. He'll need it when he grows up."

"It wouldn't be like the Grahams' baby?" she said doubtfully.

"You bet it won't!"

Failure of Banque de Genève, failure of Danat Bank in Germany. They left for their holiday near the end of July, the day after the London Conference opened — "that ought to clear the air" — and drove over to Wales to see Robert's father. Robert was a bit anxious, he thought the old man was breaking up.

There was a line of pylons in sight now from the upper windows of the vicarage and a new petrol station just past the church; but this was really not inconvenient. They decided the place was still quite satisfactorily unspoilt. They made it their headquarters and toured a bit and got back to town by the middle of August. The London Conference had failed and the bank rate had been raised to three and a half and then four per cent. "Things really seem to be looking a bit serious."

The dole was cut, the Labour Cabinet resigned and Snowden brought in his supplementary budget. Robert came back from the factory, looking worried.

"I'm afraid they'll lay-off Graham," he said. "After all he's an extra man, I managed for years without him."

"How awful for them," she said. "What will they do?"

They were sorry for the Grahams. Graham's salary was so much smaller than Robert's that they couldn't possibly have saved anything.

"But they can't make you do double work," she objected.

"Well," he said, "what many firms are doing: they're reducing staff and giving a man one and a half times the pay to do the work of two. So they save half a man's pay, do you see."

"So you'd get half Graham's pay on top of yours? But you'd have to work extra time."

"Well, theoretically. But actually one man could get round the work quite easily. I used to."

"Of course," she said expressionlessly, "Graham's pay's much lower than yours, still..."

"Well it is rather. It would mean roughly about another couple of pounds a week."

"Oh, I see." She tried hard to be expressionless. "But do you think they'll do that?"

"May not."

They tried to concentrate upon how sorry they were for the Grahams.

Robert really felt very badly about it. He would almost rather have known he had no chance of the extra money. Every morning when he got to the factory he was afraid Graham would have heard he was to be laid-off. They were cutting staff here and there among the furnace men and packers. Unless things pulled up pretty sharply it would strike them sooner or later that Graham was superfluous. Graham didn't seem disturbed; he slogged on at his routine work and drew his miserable four pounds at the end of the week and hurried off home to his wife and kid. Robert thought it was lucky none of them seemed to have any imagination. He thought that after all it might not be such a bad thing for Graham if he were laid-off. He'd never make much of a research chemist. He ought to have been a bank clerk. He'd been wrong to get himself tied up so young to a silly little woman like Vi Graham. The best thing he could do, really, would be to start fresh in the Colonics, or somewhere like that.

In the last week of September the bank rate rose to six per cent; the Stock Exchange closed for two days: England went off the gold standard. On the first of October Robert lost his job.

Chapter VII

◇◇

Katherine wouldn't believe it. "They can't possibly mean they want to get rid of you, after all they said."

"It rather looks like it."

"Besides, they'll have to pay you the two pounds a week they owe you for the formula."

"Oh, well," he said.

"Instead of the sum down, I mean."

"Well," he said, "as a matter of fact..."

"Of course you had an agreement, that they'd have to go on paying it for a certain time?"

"As a matter of fact," he said, "I didn't think of it."

Katherine went pink. She thought it was incredibly stupid of Robert, but she didn't want to think that because things were bad enough already. "It's the Grahams," she said angrily. "They must have worked it. Nobody could possibly imagine Ted Graham's work was more valuable than yours.

Of course not." She was never going to see Vi Graham again. After all they'd done.

"Well," he said, "Graham's cheaper of course."

"In any case," she said, trying to see the best of it, "they'll have to pay you the commission on sales of the solvent."

"Doesn't come to much. Still, it's better than nothing, and I'm sure to get something soon."

He went out and cleaned the car to have something to think about, and so that it would be ready for him to drive round and apply for jobs.

Katherine went into the kitchen and began to prepare a meal. She came back to the living-room and turned the wireless on, loud, so that she could hear it in the kitchen. She didn't want to think about how stupid Robert had been, and there was no point in worrying because he would be sure to get another job soon. He ought to get a better job, too, with his experience, and that would teach the Grahams. It wasn't that Robert was stupid, it wasn't that a bit; it was just that he was too bright to have the kind of low cunning of a man like Graham. She took several tins, vegetables, fruit, and galatine in a glass, from a store in the white enamelled cupboard, and prepared a more elaborate meal than usual. When it was ready she looked through the advertisements in the day's papers to find a job for Robert.

Robert came in with his hair ruffled and his cheeks pink under his glasses from cleaning the car.

"There doesn't seem to be much going," she said, putting the paper back in the rack.

He washed his hands and came and sat opposite her in the narrow high-brow dining-room with the plates of shining galatine and tinned pears on rush mats between them. "Nobody'd advertise to-day, couldn't apply Saturday afternoon. We might as well take the car out," he suggested, "now it's clean."

He cleaned the car again on Sunday afternoon and took it out on Monday to apply for a job over in Essex. Katherine knew he couldn't be back until tea-time. She was ready for him in the living-room, with the tea-tray on a low table, and a streak of autumn sunlight on three large chrysanthemums in the smooth grey pottery jar. She rather hoped Robert wouldn't get the job, it was in such a hopeless district they wouldn't know where to live. She heard him drive up and leave the car outside the garage and come in before she had got to the door to meet him.

"No good," he said. "Not worth looking at. Besides," he said with a grin, "they didn't want me."

"I thought not," she said. "It's no good applying to small places, they'll only be afraid of you. What you must look out for is something really big."

"How about writing to some of the big firms," she suggested at the end of a week. "As they don't seem to advertise. Write and give them your qualifications, and tell them you're free."

"Of course," she said, after a fortnight, "when you're out for something big it's no good getting impatient. You can't expect them to sack somebody at once to be able to take you on. It's worthwhile waiting for the right thing."

At the end of three weeks, "I suppose you *are* applying for the small things as well when they turn up? Might as well take something temporary while you're looking round."

At the end of the month she said, "It's really frightfully annoying having to run up debts. Couldn't you borrow something from your father to go on with?"

"Not enough to make much difference."

"And how about the commission Cosmetics Co. are

suppose to pay you? When's that coming in?"

"Well," he said, "there isn't really any agreement about it."

"You must go and see them," she said firmly. "Tell them you'll bring a claim for a sum down if they don't pay up the commission regularly. After all they must be making a lot, you see the stuff everywhere."

Robert went. He felt very uncomfortable, the complexion solvent was a pretty undignified thing to argue about and he was sure he'd get another job soon. He would much rather have heard no more about the complexion solvent but it wouldn't be fair on Kath. He got them to agree to a small commission on profits, paid monthly.

"It won't come to much," he said. "Not much more than about a pound a week. But I'm pretty sure to get that dentifrice job on Thursday."

"After all," she said, "the really important thing is for you to get a worth-while job so long as we can just manage until then."

On Thursday night he said that even if they'd offered it to him it would hardly have been worthwhile.

"The fact is," he said, "this is the worst time. Trade's just about as bad as it's going to be." Bankers on World crisis. Stockbrokers' bankruptcy, theatrical producer's bankruptcy, R.100, total cost a million, to be sold as scrap. Medical library in serious financial difficulties. Deputation of Calcutta businessmen urges Gandhi to end non-co-operation and save Bengal from financial ruin.

"What about the dole? Why can't you get that?"

"Passed the maximum salary, ages back. For non-manual employment, that is."

"I think that's most unfair," she cried. "Why should some manual labourer be able to get it, when you can't. You're of much more value to the community."

"Community doesn't seem to think so."

She thought there was a lot of nonsense talked about the Unemployed. They had the dole, anyhow. They weren't half so badly off as Robert.

"Things ought to look up in the New Year." Aluminium trade revival; growth in car export, Germany's new giant Zeppelin, helium gas; Five-Year Plan a year ahead of time. In the New Year: "The trouble is," he said, "we've got no more in the bank. And what really bothers me," he said, "is what to do about the instalments on things. If we drop them what happens?"

"We can't drop payments," she said definitely. "We should lose all we've spent already."

He lay in a low chair with his legs stretched out over the almost new, plain carpet. Around him were the grey low fat chairs and the scrubbed oak octagonal bookcase and coffee table and the cabinet wireless; he was nervously crumpling in his trouser pocket his last five pounds in notes. "Well," he said doubtfully, "I suppose you can look at it like this. What we've paid already is hire on the stuff, not quite a dead loss. If there's anything we can do without," he said.

Behind the wall to the left there was the refectory table with the raffia mats and beyond that the hatch into the kitchen; glass and enamel fittings and the refrigerator and vacuum cleaner. Upstairs there were the twin beds and the tallboy, and the walls all round and on top the new curved green tiles: none of it paid for. And to the right, outside the front door, there was the new garage and the car. "We can't get rid of the car, very well? It saves travelling expenses."

"Oh no," she said, shocked. "We can't get rid of the car."

"And the furniture," she said, "will be ours in about six months, now."

"We might give up the telephone," she suggested.

"No," he said, "definitely not. It would mean your going out to shop in bad weather."

"There's the vacuum. But I don't quite see..."

"No, of course not. How could you keep all this clean without? Besides, the instalments are so small, comparatively, it wouldn't be worthwhile. There's the wireless, that's actually ours now. Might sell it?"

"But we don't want to sell things," she cried. "It would be so stupid to have to buy them all over again. Suppose you got a job the very next week."

Next week the telephone bill came in, for the December quarter. "I was thinking," he said, "while I'm hanging around I could just as well do the shopping in the car in bad weather."

"But it will be such a nuisance having it installed again. It really doesn't seem worthwhile."

"Oh, all right. After all we needn't pay it yet."

At the end of January he had to borrow from his father to pay the instalments on the house and furniture.

"You'll have to try for jobs in the provinces," Katherine said. She was getting a bit impatient with him. "After all you've got the car to go to interviews in."

"But you know you don't want to live in a provincial town."

"What does that matter," she said angrily because she knew she didn't. "We've got to live somewhere. What do you suppose we're going to do."

Robert said nothing. He picked up the paper from the floor and looked through the advertisement columns for notices of manufacturing chemists in the Midlands and North. He knew it was rough on Kath. She had most of the job of managing food and suchlike.

Katherine said nothing. She knew it wasn't Robert's fault

really. He hadn't enough push, but he couldn't help that and things couldn't go on like this much longer. Something would be sure to turn up quite suddenly, when they weren't expecting it.

Robert went north in the car to apply at a scientific blacking works. He wouldn't be back until supper-time. Katherine went out with a basket to shop at the food shops on the local Parade, because it was cheaper than ordering by telephone from the big stores. She felt very virtuous, walking along the sunny suburban roads with her basket. She thought it must look very incongruous — she carrying a basket — but nobody seemed to think so. Katherine didn't notice this. She carried the basket in a self-conscious, obvious way as if it were a joke. Here's Katherine Thomas pretending to be bourgeois. But by the time it was full of meat and vegetables it was too heavy. She was obliged to let it hang unhumorously at the end of her arm and bump against her leg. After all, she argued, trying to swing the basket and not succeeding, unless *some* intelligent people live in the suburbs, how is one to bring intelligence to the suburbs?

She thought, because it was the least uncomfortable thing to think, that it was amusing to be suburban for a while: *really* suburban, buying at local shops, and never, never for weeks past, going up to an exhibition, or a play, even on a Sunday night, because of the price of tickets and the petrol. The Rights and Lefts, and the other inhabitants of Primrose Green, seemed to go up to the West End quite often. But to musical shows and for the sales of course; Katherine didn't count that; they took the Primrose Green mentality with them. It was amusing to be really suburban because they would so soon have to stop being suburban, she and Robert, and be, or not be, provincial. It wasn't necessary to be provincial, she argued, because one lived in the Provinces. There was at least a small group of intelligent people in most big towns nowadays. Repertory theatres and so on. A nucleus of intelligence. It was fun being suburban for the last time; while she hung some washing out in the back garden she thought of talking to Mrs. Right or Mrs. Left over the fence, but it might be difficult afterwards to shake them off. Besides, she remembered suddenly, she was outraging local custom by hanging washing in the afternoon. Both Mrs. Right and Mrs. Left would by now be well away from the back-yard: most likely at the bridge table or the pictures. She smiled, reflecting with complacency that it was more difficult to be bourgeois than one would think.

She had got a meal ready and was listening for the car. She heard it turn in; from the kitchen window, in the flash of the turning headlights, she could see a strip of wintry flower-bed and the unfinished crazy-paving they had begun last summer cut out of the dark. The headlights went out.

"Well?" she said, running into the hall.

Robert shut the hall door. He was rumpled — tired looking — and he must have left his hat in the car. "Not much good," he said, "too many local applicants. Local university."

"What do you mean?" She stopped short before she got to him and put a hand unconsciously for support and found the dining-room door. "You mean you haven't got it?"

"That's about it."

He went into the living-room and she came after him angrily. "But how can you not have got it? With your experience?"

He dragged a newspaper deliberately from his pocket and threw it on the table. "My dear Kath," he said, coldly, a bit surprised. "Has it occurred to you that there may have been about two hundred applicants in all, and that fifty of them were recent graduates of local or other universities? The choice was among those fifty."

"But that's ridiculous," she cried. "Why should they take a student with no experience, when they could get somebody with *your* record?" He's messed it again, she thought angrily. He can't have told them about the solvent, or how long he was with Cosmetics Co.

"Unfortunately," he said with ironic emphasis, mocking at her and through her at himself, "unfortunately they happen to have a preference for *young* men, with more recent training."

She opened her mouth to say, but you're only thirty. She shut it again. It had not occurred to her before that he was thirty — thirty-one to be exact; yes, he must be thirty-one — or that that meant anything. "What nonsense," she said angrily, instead; and went away to get the supper.

He was a year older than the century and his birthday was in June: yes he'd be thirty-one. She watched him across the refectory table: they had always sat on opposite sides of the table, the end, Robert said, was too patriarchal for him. He was over thirty, and it hadn't meant anything to her until now. It was true he had a tired look; his face had got worried lines lately and there was something unfresh about the skin. How was it she hadn't noticed it? He had always dressed in the same way since they were married, in rather grubby tweeds and woollen pullovers, and he never wore a hat. These clothes and the always rumpled thick hair had given him a sort of perennial undergraduate appearance and youth had left it imperceptibly. Just now, in the old, cheap navy suit he had dug out for interviews, he looked tired and almost middle-aged, and in the hat he must look even worse: the bowler he had left in the car. It was only that he was tired with all this bother, she told herself angrily. But she knew that what these people really thought about was his train-ing, which was ten years out of date. His training was ten years out of date; in those ten years science had been coming on with inconceivable strides, while he was pottering about with face creams in one limited specialised branch. And now both of them depended on his ability to get a job.

"If they'd take married teachers," she said, "I should go back."

"You wouldn't."

"What's the good of talking like that," she said irritably. "We shall have to do something."

They sat through the evening in uneasy silence, afraid of being irritable with one another. Robert sat with the paper across his knees, open at the advertisement pages. He ran down the columns one after another and made marks in the margin. When he had finished a page he began again.

Next day he took the car out after breakfast and spent the day applying for jobs he had marked in the paper. He did this for several days. Katherine was surprised at the num-ber of jobs there seemed to be, but when she looked at one of the papers she saw that he had marked anything, almost anything: advertisements manager, sales representative. "What's the good of this," she said scornfully.

He looked found-out and annoyed. "Well," he said, "I thought one of them might do while I was looking round. May as well see what's going."

She shrugged her shoulders. "You may as well, I suppose."

He took the car out directly after breakfast — it depressed him to stay in the house, with Kath getting glummer every day — and drove round applying for every post he could see advertised. He found that many of the advertisers were busi-ness schools who wanted him to pay to learn things: how to do fashion drawing or write advertisements or sell convincingly. Most of the others required him to invest capital or pay a premium or work for nothing for six months to begin with. And the few who remained turned him down when they heard he had no experience.

After a few days he said, "We shall have to lay up the car for a bit. It's too expensive to run."

"But you'd spend nearly as much in fares, going about."

"Nothing like, really; could walk a lot of it."

Every week-end he ran the car out of the garage and cleaned and polished it and put it back. He liked the feel of it. He liked the feel of its being there, smooth and clean and ready for him the moment he could afford to take it out. At the beginning of March he wanted to sell the wireless to pay the instalment on the car.

Katherine thought that was stupid. "Why the wireless?"

"It's the only thing we can sell. And it costs too much in batteries, anyhow."

"You only lose on selling things," she said. "Why don't you leave the car instalment? They won't say anything if you pay it with next month's."

A few days later, as the last telephone bill had not been paid, the telephone was cut off.

Katherine said, "We shall have to be careful with the electricity and gas. If they cut the light it would be really serious."

She gave up using the vacuum cleaner, because that meant electricity, and they cooked as little as possible although it cost more to buy cooked food, and in the evening they lit one electric bulb and sat in their outdoor clothes in the cold living-room, because the modern, built-in, flush-with-the-wall fire burnt gas.

The place was unnaturally quiet. The wireless was dumb,

without batteries, and the telephone was dead in the hall. When one picked up the receiver nothing happened. In the kitchen the vacuum cleaner was leaning limp against the wall: a small, collapsed dirigible on the tiled floor. The whole place was cold, it was a very cold spring; and an occasional snatch of noise from a distant loud speaker deepened the silence.

They sat close together under the one electric bulb in the living-room, not because they wanted to be near one another but because they needed the light, and pored over the advertisement pages of newspapers.

"We can't go on like this," Katherine said. "I shall go back to teaching."

"How can you?"

"In a private school, I suppose. There must be plenty of small schools which would be glad to get a qualified teacher. The marriage question wouldn't trouble them."

If it hadn't been for Robert she thought, she would still be in a safe job with a steadily increasing salary. Oh well, she thought, biting down her irritation, what's the good,

"Don't do that," he said, "it's a rotten job. We can hang on a bit longer. I'm sure to get something soon."

You won't, she thought, irritated again, and was surprised to find how sure she was of it. After all, she argued with herself, he must find a job some time, he can't go on like this for ever. It's six months now, though. But after all what's that, he had a job for years. Besides nobody stays permanently out of work.

"Well," she said because she didn't want to show that she doubted him, "I could just look round and see what's going. But you'll probably find something long before I shall."

She began to read the educational columns of the papers and to write to agents. She thought that after all he probably would get a job before long, but it wouldn't be a bad idea if they had one apiece, there would be a lot of debts to pay off. Besides, she thought, I can always drop it again. She wrote letters of application.

"Why on earth don't you write to people?" she asked Robert. "You waste so much time and money going round without making appointments."

"No good," he said. "The man on the spot always gets it."

It depressed him too much to stay in the house: he wanted to fiddle with the car all the time and he knew it was no good. He wanted too the feeling of being out, doing something, actually hunting down a job. While he was sitting at home writing letters he felt he was doing nothing: when he was chasing up and down tube escalators and the dusty staircases of City buildings he was working harder than he'd ever worked in his life. And he didn't want to see Kath writing letters of application, he hated the idea of her applying for a job. It made him feel he had let her down.

He took the tube each morning after breakfast, in the cheap, respectable suit he had once worked in and with a hat in his hand, to the City or to some outlying trading estate. For the rest of the day, with the hat on his head, he tramped up and down staircases and in and out of factory offices. Any experience? Wrong sort. Any capital? None. Work on commission?

"I might do that," he said.

"Six months without pay to learn the job and we let you off the premium."

"I couldn't do that," he said. "I couldn't live six months."

"Nope?"

He went up and down stairs to fifth-floor syndicates, and down and up stairs to one-man firms in basements. Able to invest? No. Premium? No. Experience? No.

Nope. Nothing.

The beginning of April he got a notice of two instalments due on the car.

"It'll have to go," he said.

"I thought you were going to sell the wireless. May as well, we can't keep it going."

"Wouldn't cover it. Besides there's the car insurance due. Just a year since we had it."

"And we can't manage that?"

"No," he said roughly, "of course we can't. Where do you think it's coming from."

Katherine shrugged her shoulders. She didn't worry much about the car, there were other things that were worse. "How many instalments have we paid?"

"About half."

"Oh well," she said, "we can count that as hire."

"Yes," he said. "No doubt. Exactly."

He didn't know what he meant except that he was furious. He got out of the house and slammed the door. He didn't give a damn for the value of the car, but he wanted it. He wanted to feel that it was there in the garage and that he'd drive it some day.

The car went.

The car was sold and they got back something on it, about twenty pounds. Robert put it in the bank in Katherine's name, for her to draw on for housekeeping and the furniture instalments.

He felt more tired tramping about the streets, now that the car wasn't in the garage. There seemed less use in going on, but he went on doggedly.

Budget surplus, improvement in trade. "Like to know where. Boosting the National Government, that's all." He went on tramping the wet streets, in his thin cheap ready-made clerk's suit and a hat clamped on his head. Capital, premium, experience? No. "Got a car?"

"No," he said, "I haven't." His fingers were shutting and opening and he knew he mustn't say much or he wouldn't be able to control his voice.

"No, I haven't. I let it go the other day because I couldn't pay the instalments."

"Yeah?"

The business manager was reaching for something across his littered desk. The cigarette between his lips wagged up and down twice. He found the paper he wanted and glanced through it and looked up, surprised to see that Robert was still there. Robert clapped his hat on his head and went. He went out of the office and up some steps on to a cinder track surrounding the factory, and up the track on to a main road. He was a long way out on the road on the south side of the river. There was a gap in the houses where he was, a space filled by factories and advertisement hoardings, and up the road on each side, as far as he could see, the houses went on again. A tram clanged past him, going in the direction of town, but he set out to walk after it. In a minute or two it was out of sight. Where the houses began the road was suburban for a little way, then it turned into a street of shops, then the houses began again, smaller and with smaller gardens. The gardens disappeared and small houses stood up flush with the road, and the shops when they came were small and dingy. As he saw that he had passed from suburb to slum, and was drawing in towards the river, he remembered that Kath's school had been in this district and that she must have lived in one of the side-streets off this very road. He went on for some time, keeping his eye on the street names and after a

179

bit he saw it, Verbena Road. He remembered it. Once or twice he had come with her as far as the corner. But he had never been to the house, she had asked him not to, and he had no curiosity to go and see it now. He went on stolidly on the High Road with his eyes running ahead of him along the pavement. He thought it was a funny thing he'd come here without meaning to. The part where the factory was reminded him of Cosmetics Co. when they started, just such a dump, it might be the same place. Then he had come along here without thinking of anything and found himself at Verbena Road, much the same way as he'd gone home from Cosmetics Co. one evening and met Kath. He'd spent most of his time like that, hadn't he? Walking straight ahead and finding he was somewhere without meaning it. But this time he hadn't got somewhere he'd got nowhere, there wasn't much good in it. Getting the chuck. It wouldn't have mattered so much if he hadn't dragged Kath along with him this time. He stopped on the bridge — his feet were aching — and looked over at the water. He thought for all the good he was to Kath or anyone else he might as well throw himself in. He knew he didn't mean to do it; he knew that he wasn't even seriously considering the possibility of doing it. He couldn't imagine himself wanting to do it. He couldn't imagine the minds of people who did it. Except those who were hunted by fear: one could see that. But the depressed and the tired of life and the too bored to live. No backbone, he thought.

The thought bucked him up, he felt full of backbone. His tired feet stretched and contracted tentatively in his shoes. He took out the advertisement sheet and studied it and felt the coppers in his pocket. Bus fare, or snack? It was two o'clock and he had not eaten since breakfast, but he decided it would be better to save his feet. He crossed the bridge, walked on until he came to a fare stage and took a twopenny ticket on a bus going in the direction of the City.

The League Financial Committee sits at Geneva: financial plight of Europe: six million unemployed are registered in Germany, three hundred thousand in France and two million in Great Britain. In the West End plays are coming off after unprecedentedly short runs; managers play for safety in revivals of Shaw and Shakespeare. Shipyards are standing silent around the coasts of Great Britain. The impact of the Kreuger crash is reverberating through Europe — Berne, Stock-holm, Italy — and across the Atlantic. The foreign trade of the world is down by three billion pounds. Robert comes briskly down a staircase in the City and hurries out along the pavement and then slows down, because there is no longer any reason to hurry or to look brisk. He has applied to all the firms marked on the grubby, folded piece of paper in his pocket. There is nothing to do but go home, walking as much of the way as possible, and sit opposite Kath under the one electric bulb and watch her trying not to be impatient with him until they can decently go to bed. As he comes along the street where business premises are closing there is nothing particular to show him that the world is falling in. A postman is clearing in a leisurely way a box at the corner, a whistling errand boy zigzags by on a bicycle, a dray with two horses rattles past eastward to stable for the night. Lights are turned on in the windows of a bank where a night watchman is beginning his vigil, and because it is evening more men than usual, and in more of a hurry, are bolting in succession from the doors of office buildings and around corners to the tube. They look very much like Robert. None of them looks at Robert or would notice him if he did. None of them knows that Robert's feet are sore in his shoes from looking for a job: in any case their own feet are probably just as sore from running errands or standing behind a desk all day. None of them, thought Robert, knows that the world is falling in.

Robert knew the world was falling in because he read the papers: he had taken to reading the papers in public libraries, for economy, to see the advertisements. On some mornings he would stop at the Primrose Green library on his way to the tube: but the building was too new and small; there were few readers and wide gaps between the desks and he felt self-conscious. Feeling the eye of the librarian upon him, he would hurry through a paper and jot down an address or two, and hurry out, as if he were on his way to business and had dropped in for an odd bit of information: sometimes he would find that the addresses he had jotted down in this way were illegible or incomplete. More often he waited until he got up to town, and entered some big stuffy borough library where he felt anonymous and safe. He was content to take his turn at the crowded paper-stands among the down-and-outs and nondescripts each at his favourite stand, poring and shuffling. He liked the warm shuffling quietness of the big reading-rooms and the anonymous unvoiced companionship. These men were not a regiment like the city workers whose uniform he wore though their ranks were closed to him; these were the individualists, who expected nothing and got it. There were a few who rushed feverishly through the advertisement columns and hurried out; their feet could be heard slapping the stone steps while the swing door closed behind them in diminishing thuds. But most were in no hurry: lived probably on a pension or the dole or a tiny income, defeated or content. Robert stayed for an hour or more reading the papers: he knew that the bottom was falling out of the world. It's nothing but a great machine he thought, run down, and why try to start it up again? He could feel the warm dirty elbow of his neighbour's coat turning a page: these, he thought, they don't bother: they're the slack the machine's thrown out, the slum left at the bottom. But they don't worry. And now the machine's run down.

For about five minutes he thought he would give it up. He had a few shillings a week coming in from Cupid Complexion Solvent: many of these fellows haven't even that, he thought, but they don't try to live in houses too big for them. He was beginning to hate the house. The house reminded him of Kath and he jerked up guiltily. The man had gone from the stand beside him, many of them had gone: drifted out imperceptibly for the opening of the pubs. Ten to twelve. Robert made sure he had the list of addresses in his pocket, picked out the nearest address and memorised it, hurried through the swing door and down the steps.

As he took a ticket at the tube he thought of Kath again. He thought poor old Kath, she was sitting back there in the house with none too much to eat and no wonder it got on her nerves. He owed it to her to get a job: even if the machine was running down he owed it to her to get back into the machine. As he sat down tired in the tube and was swayed from side to side he thought it would make all the difference, his getting a job. He thought how pleased she'd be, and everything would be jolly, as it was before. He thought they'd had some jolly times with the car. He'd get the car back and Kath would be herself again. Poor old Kath she was a good sort just as she'd always been, but the way they were living was too much for anyone's nerves. He'd get rid of that blasted house with its gadgets that didn't work, and when he'd got rid of that he'd find Kath again. He thought like that they'd cheat the machine. What he didn't see was that the wheels were turning between them.

Robert came out of the tube at Aldwych where his ticket expired, and walked the rest of the way to his destination, a warehouse near the docks. Over hoardings at the side of the road he could see the smokeless funnels of boats, docked by tariff and world depression. A famous Eastern steamship line had passed its dividend for the first time within living memory. In Naples an international circus was bankrupt and stranded, unable to sell, move away, or feed its animals. Millions were being lost in rubber. A South American Oilfields company was wound up. Chile went off the gold standard, seven million acres of cotton plantation were auctioned in Mississippi to pay planters' taxes. Factories were closed down across America — "smokeless chimneys and paralysed industry" — New York Opera lost a hundred thousand in one season, transatlantic shipping companies cancelled sailings, vessels were lying idle along Southampton Water, a little way out of London, in a south-western suburb, Katherine was applying for a post in a private school.

The school was very select and it was called Blankston House School. If it had been called Blankston College it would have been smaller, and the Head shabbier. The Head was tall and drooping with vague faded blue eyes and an overblown, faded face. She let Katherine wait for some minutes in the drawing-room with the grand piano and chintz-covered settees and the French window open on to a lawn. While she crossed the room the faded vague eyes seemed to be focusing ready to peer. They failed, slipped past, came back.

"I understand you're married?" she said. "May I ask why you wish to take a post?"

"My husband lost his employment some months ago."

"And what is his profession?"

"Research chemist."

"Ah, very interesting. And you have no children?" The eyes appraised coldly.

"No," Katherine said. She longed to add, Have you?

"Here," said the Head, looking around fondly, "we aim at giving our girls an education in the highest sense. Mere learning," she said, giving Katherine an accusing stare, "we do not think of so much account as the development of character. Now your experience…" Suddenly she looked at Katherine as if she were seeing her for the first time. "I couldn't possibly take somebody with council school experience," she said sharply. "It wouldn't be fair to our girls. I can't think what the agents were thinking about to send you."

She led the way to the door, suave again and conversational. "Our aim is to bring up our girls as gentlewomen."

"I see," said Katherine angrily. She thought of saying, "I taught at a council school because my father was killed in the War. He was a master at Harchester." But because they had got to the door and she saw it opening on to the carpeted hall and because she knew urgently what she must say and was angry at the necessity, she said, angrily and abruptly, "Would you mind letting me have my fare?"

The Head started and stiffened. She turned back to a bureau and bending over it began ostentatiously to look through a pile of papers.

"Let me see, you come from, ah, Primrose Green?"

"One and six return," Katherine said harshly.

The Head took a shilling and a sixpence from a purse and laid them delicately on the extreme, polished edge of the bureau. She bent again to make a note in a book.

Katherine picked up the coins, "*Thank* you," and went.

When she got outside she was furious that she had not said more: How dared she ask me all those questions when she knew she didn't mean to offer me the job.

She broke her journey at Shepherd's Bush, where she could buy some vegetables cheap at the street market, and then was annoyed because this would mean walking some way in the tidy shoes she kept for interviews.

The vegetables were wrapped in newspaper; in places their wet green rotted the paper and broke through. She took off her gloves and put them in her hand-bag and held the vegetables away from her with both hands. At Primrose Green she walked from the tube station, to save a penny, with the wet parcel held away from her skirt, making her arm ache. When she stopped at the gate there was a man in a cap shuffling behind her, a down-and-out, begging.

"I been to the War, lady."

His eyes were pale and bleary and his voice was cracked and the hand he had half put out was shaking. She knew it was with hunger and exhaustion, but she was too angry to let herself know it. Drink, she thought stubbornly. Half of them are frauds.

"That's over long ago," she said coldly, looking away, easing the weight of the parcel on the gate-post while she felt for the latch. She didn't know why the look of the man made her so angry.

"I wish I 'adn't come back. I do indeed, lady."

She shut the gate behind her and went on to the door and shut it.

By the time Robert came in she had rolled the vegetables, wet and muddy, on to the kitchen table and thrown away the newspaper and changed into her old clothes and the down-at-heel shoes.

"Well?" she said, knowing it was hardly worthwhile to ask him.

"Nothing, I've been all round."

"What's the good," she said angrily, "you'll never get a job that way, you're only wasting time and money going round like that. Why don't you pick out the things you're qualified for."

"There aren't any. Only now and then."

"Well, why can't you get on and invent something more. That's the only way you ever made any money. And you messed up that, so that you only get half of it. Why can't you invent some more complexion stuff, and go and sell it?"

"With no laboratory?" he said. "So likely."

They were both tired and angry. He thought bitterly that she had been resting all day, pottering round the house, while he was looking for a job to keep them; and she was angry at his not thinking she might be tired too, but she didn't want him to know she had applied for a job and failed to get it.

After supper he looked round the room and hated it. "I'm going to get rid of this place," he said. "We can't afford to live here."

"Oh? And how do you think we can afford to take another one?"

"I don't care. I hate the place."

"And I suppose you don't think I hate it too?"

They looked at one another. They knew they could either go on or stop, but that if they were going to stop it would have to be now.

Katherine said, grudgingly, "How long is it before we own the house?"

"About fourteen years."

"What! Nonsense."

"Well, it was nine hundred and we paid fifty deposit and

we're paying for the rest at twenty-three shillings a week..."

"You mean your father is," she reminded him, and was glad to see him wince.

"...that makes it about fourteen years and we've been here just over two."

"But we can't stay here for twelve years," she said, really frightened.

"It doesn't look as if we could."

He felt in his pocket for a cigarette but didn't find one. He remembered he'd smoked the last, chucked away the packet in the tube. The discovery took the bite out of his sarcasm.

"Well, look here," he said, deflated. "What are we going to do?"

"I can't think. Except that I must get a job."

The more apologetic he looked the more her mood hardened. She couldn't forget how stupid he had been to mess things up with the Cosmetics Co.: he ought at least to have had his sum down. And she was sure he was missing chances now through stupidity.

"I wish you wouldn't," he said. "Must you?"

"It rather looks like it, doesn't it?"

She wrote to all the educational agents, and almost every day after Robert had gone out she put on her tidy clothes and comparatively new shoes and went out to interview a headmistress. The shoes began to look less new. She went to "girls' colleges" in the suburbs, and finishing schools and secretarial schools, co-educational schools, kindergartens. Practically all the Heads were anxious that she should thoroughly understand and admire the aims of their schools. We believe in character building, we believe in free discipline, we believe in education on a health basis. Practically all of them asked searching personal questions before revealing that the post was already filled or that in any case she would not have suited them. At a very modern school in a distant suburb she was asked to admire the whole building, from roof garden to swimming pool; the headmaster of a nondescript, co-educational "academy" pressed for her view on the present generation of children.

"Well," she said, "that depends."

"What d'you think of 'em?" he repeated with a fixed stare. "This lot born since the War?"

"Oh," said Katherine, grateful for the clue. "I should say they're rather highly strung, on the whole."

"Highly strung, eh?" He laughed. He slapped the desk in front of him. "If you ask me they're a dotty lot!"

"A dotty lot," he muttered several times. He looked up suddenly. "You'd do, but as a matter of fact I've got someone coming already. Leave your name will you, and I'll keep you in mind if they don't suit."

Katherine thought she had got the next job: general culture classes in a secretarial college. "Just a little literature and that kind of thing," said the principal. She was a large, soft woman with wet, prune-like eyes. "Shelley, you know, and Lord Dryden."

"Oh, yes," said Katherine, but too quickly.

The prune-like eyes fell upon her suspiciously. Something wrong, what was it? Those poets. It sounded right, and yet... Of course! The eyes hardened with hatred. "Well," said the principal curtly, "I will write and let you know."

Some of them said they couldn't feel justified in taking on a married teacher, in these days of unemployment, and some said the council school experience would never do, but most of them said they would write.

May was the month in which Doumer was murdered in

Paris; Germany voted four million marks for construction of Pocket Battleship C, successor to the *Deutschland*, the Siberian broadcasting station was launching a campaign of military instruction for all Soviet citizens in Eastern Siberia; the Japanese army was demanding supreme political power; the French luxury liner *Georges Philippar* was destroyed by fire in the Gulf of Aden on her maiden voyage from the Far East; Robert got a final notice from the Primrose Green and District Electric Lighting Company.

He turned the slip over in his hand, wondering how to break the news to Kath.

"So they're going to cut the light," she said, coming into the room.

She had seen the envelope an hour ago, meeting the post for letters that never came.

He said doubtfully, "What about the twenty we got for the car? I suppose..."

"It's gone. What do you expect. Most of it went on the furniture."

"Looks as if you'd have to take that job," he said, rueful and unwilling. "For a bit. Till things clear up."

She laughed harshly. "You needn't count on that. There aren't any jobs. None that I'm qualified for, anyway."

"Oh, nonsense," he said. "Nonsense, my dear Kath. Look at the experience you've had."

"Yes," she said, dangerously. "Council school experience. Very useful. Just see what any school will say when you offer them that."

Because he was worried he didn't notice her tone. "Well how about trying," he suggested. "Experience must be worth something."

She shouted suddenly, "How do *you* know whether I've

tried or not. If you think I'm not sick of having that council school thrown back at me. '*We* try to bring up our girls as *gentlewomen*.' And having to take their filthy money for the fare, and ask for it, generally.

"And how about the experience *you've got?*" she said on a new wave of anger. "You don't seem to be doing much with that. If you can't get a job I don't see why I should be expected to."

He got up from the table and went into the hall for his hat. "I see," he said. "I'm sorry." She heard him go out.

Unreasonably he was less depressed instead of more now he knew that Kath too had failed to get a job. Poor old Kath he thought, feeling superior and protective, on his way to the station. It was hard on her being dependent on him like that. He'd have to be careful not to let her down. He spent less time than usual in reading the papers after he had copied his addresses for the day, and set off more briskly with the list in his pocket.

As he came home in the evening, his feet tight in his shoes, he began to think about Kath again. Poor old girl, he'd have to cheer her up as well as he could. He hadn't thought that she might have been round looking for a job, just as he had.

Katherine was in an unresponsive mood. She had not been out because she had received no notice of a post to be applied for. She had spent the day in thinking how unjust everything was and wondering whether to apply for what the agents called private work, in other words a post as daily governess. Most of these positions were badly paid, involved heavy travelling expenses and would prevent her careful shopping in the cheapest markets, and laborious cooking, which made it possible for them to live. If she were to come back late in the evening and open expensive tins for supper the profits of the day would be gone. She had also thought over the increasing shabbiness of her clothes and the impossibility of replacing them. The one thing that had not crossed her mind was any notion of herself as dependent upon Robert. She had dismissed him as ineffectual.

Just before he came in she had gone upstairs to brush her clothes for an interview the next morning. It seemed necessary to apply in a tailor-made but by now her winter things were too hot. She got out a last summer's suit, the only one that seemed at all possible, and spread it on her bed and looked at it. It had not been meant to look business-like, nor to last. It was lucky that she had bought anything at all in a dark colour last year. The thin crêpe-like material was creased and sagging. She sat on the bed in a sudden wave of hopelessness. What on earth am I going to do. She heard Robert come in but he was neither a solution nor a problem; merely one more irritating factor in an impossible situation.

She went downstairs. Through the open door of the living-room she could see him loafing with his hands in his pockets, looking out at the drive. She didn't say Well, questioningly: by this time she had given it up, the answer was so obvious. Without saying anything she went into the kitchen and took the meat for supper from where she had left it to cool on the windowsill: the refrigerator was out of action this summer because it used electricity.

At supper she said sourly, "How about that electric bill? What are you going to do about it?"

"I don't know."

"Well, you'd better do something, we can't have the light cut off. It's no good leaving it as you did the car and the telephone."

Robert looked round. "I hate the place," he said. "I'm going to get rid of it."

"Well, we can't do that now, so you'd better do something practical about the light. Why don't you sell the wireless, may as well, for all the good it is."

"All right," he said.

In his tired mind the problem was disposed of. He was looking at Kath, poor old girl, turned down because she'd been a council school-teacher. He hadn't seen her like that before, as an ex-school-teacher. Six or seven years she'd taught: after all she wasn't so young, then. Must be plenty of youngsters coming on, taking the jobs, just as it was with him. He tried to see her as she would seem to a possible employer; he couldn't quite. But he thought she looked a bit fagged. He thought she looked older than a year ago. He thought after all she wasn't so young. He thought she was an ex-school-marm who couldn't get a job. Just that. Funny. Poor old Kath, it was a shame.

When he was going out the next morning she called after him sharply, "How about that wireless? Are you going to see to it, or shall I?"

"Oh," he said. He had forgotten about it. "You do it if you like."

On her way back from the interview she got a dealer to call in and buy the wireless, and late in the afternoon she went out again with the money, to pay the electricity bill.

In June, when the financial conference of the League was sitting at Lausanne and a Czechoslovakian brewer ruined by the depression had drowned himself in a vat of beer, Katherine got a job for September at a pound a week, at a private school in a north-eastern suburb, and a couple of days later they heard that Robert's father had died.

Robert said he must go to the funeral, he said he couldn't afford the fare, he said he didn't know what to do.

"Of course you must go," Katherine said impatiently. "You'll have to be on the spot and see that things are settled up properly. We shall have to sell something."

The vacuum cleaner was theirs by this time, Robert's father had paid the instalments. They sold it and Robert took a ticket to North Wales by motor-coach because it was the cheapest way.

When the funeral was over and he had got things sorted out, he found there would be enough to pay for the funeral and settle up debts and leave about thirty pounds over. He wandered up the lane to where a channel of mountain water that had run quietly beside the road cut suddenly through a bank and fell flush into a rocky stream a hundred feet below.

He wished he hadn't to think about how little there was left.

He lit a cigarette which he had found in the vicarage. He was still wearing his shoddy town suit and Katherine had sewed a mourning band around its arm. He listened to the swish of the water and watched the light changing on its bend where it curved to the drop; the lane felt pleasantly cool and damp and there were some long, smooth ferns, very green and quiet. The machine doesn't reach here, he thought. When he listened hard he could hear over the water-splash a tinny hammering in the garage down in the village, and on a crest at the head of the valley one high pylon and one low, dipping into the hollow, and a section of wires stretched between them cut the horizon crookedly from hill to hill.

But he knew that these things didn't matter. He could hear the great northern sweep of the wheels, through South Wales and the potteries to Lancashire and north to Newcastle, passing him by, above the crest at the end of the valley. I should like to stay here, he thought, why not; and then he remembered Kath. Or London and Birmingham and Stoke and Durham. Or a wheel so great that its passing segment was not far from a straight line: Cardiff and past to Manchester and Glasgow and over the Pole, down the great, stricken length of America. He remembered: the machine's stopped, anyhow. But it hadn't.

Four Powers' Conference, Disarmament Conference, Financial Conference, Imperial Economic Conference, Coming World Financial Conference: Katherine said, "Now we've got to look at this straight. Once those thirty pounds have gone there'll be nobody to pay the instalments on the house and furniture, and the pound a week I'm going to get won't do it."

They were sitting at the refectory table, over the supper plates. He looked at the stone-stained walls and the raffia mats, the smooth, superior oak that seemed to be sneering at them. "We'll get rid of the lot," he said, "I hate it."

"Don't be silly, we've almost paid for the furniture, haven't we? But we can't afford to live here, it will take half that pound a week in travelling expenses. If we use that thirty pounds we can pay up things that are owing. But if we let the furniture go..."

"All right," he said. "Have it your own way."

August was hot and dusty. Nazis and Communists were fighting in Germany, Chinese and Japanese were fighting in Manchuria, economic distress was widespread in Japan, the "missing link" had been discovered in Africa, Mussolini, in the *Popolo d'Italia*, stated: "Fascism in view of general human nature and progress does not believe in the possibility or utility of peace." With the thirty pounds Robert's father had left they paid off the remaining instalments on the furniture and settled their bills. They gave up the house at Primrose Green, forfeiting the deposit, and took a two-roomed flat at

Holloway, North, at fifteen shillings a week. In September Katherine began to teach at the Blankenhall College for Girls and Little Boys: Miss Podbin.

The flat was in a "converted" house, but the conversion had reached only as far as the back room: a fair-sized room which with a gas-cooker and sink introduced into one corner had become a kitchen. The doors of the two rooms opened separately on to a landing of the public staircase; so that in passing from one room to another there was danger of running into the neighbours on the third floor above, the Ups, or of being seen by those on the first floor below, the Downs, on their way to the bathroom on the half-landing between. The bathroom was common to all four floors. Both Mr. Up and Mr. Down went to business. So far Mrs. Down had stared in hostile silence and Mrs. Up had said it was a nice day. Katherine frigidly agreed. The Ups were common; the Downs were genteel.

The rooms were high, with plaster moulding around the cornice and large plaster fireplaces, and the plain modern furniture looked ridiculous. The front room was much larger than the living-room at Primrose Green; the grey carpet left an uncovered stretch of boards, wider at the ends than at the sides, before the chocolate skirting began and purplish-brown mottled wallpaper. The paper was reasonably new and there was no likelihood of its being changed for some years. There were two straight windows side by side, each with a high, narrow sill, and the grey pottery jar looked ridiculous on either.

The more Katherine saw how ridiculous the whole place looked, the more determined she became not to get rid of the furniture or change anything or admit that Primrose Green had been better: it was middleclass and suburban, she said, and they were lucky to have got out of it; now at least they were up against reality. She stared haughtily at Mrs. Down on the stairs, and condescendingly at Mrs. Up, and sent Robert down to the area with the dustbin, to empty it, in the evening, after dark.

The more she hated the place and the rusty inefficient stove and the smell of drains from the sink, the more angry she was with Robert, and the more carelessly contemptuous she was of him, treating him as if he couldn't help it, and the more she was determined to see the thing through: feeling she had to pick him up and prod him and find him a job and sit him in it, and push him up ahead of her to lift them both up again: but first of all she had to make sure of her own job.

She wondered why she didn't leave him. She wondered it one day, putting on her hat in front of the small cracked hidden-away mirror in the tiny staff cloakroom of Blankenhall College: the room was a cross between a cupboard and a conservatory and was entered from the garden: it was cold and stuffy and crammed three deep with coats and smelt as if somebody had a cold in the head.

Katherine looked at herself for a second or two in the mirror. She always looked better in this mirror; in these generally decayed surroundings she felt she looked young and almost charming. She hadn't thought much about it before, but now she was glad to look like that. She gave herself an encouraging glance as she bent her knees to look and put on her hat, and decided that she supposed it must be force of habit that made her stick to Robert after the mess he'd made of things — poor old Robert — but that she felt fairly convinced that in time she'd pull them both out of this mess.

Poor old Robert, she thought in the tube, but as soon as she saw him she was angry again.

He was limp and lazy and she hated him without warmth. "Why don't you try the French firms that are opening factories over here?"

"They aren't."

"The papers say so. Since the tariffs."

"One or two may be, but they've got their own formulas." His legs were aching, he sat suddenly in one of the dumpy chairs and slumped back in it, with his pushed-out heel wrinkling the carpet.

"Tried?" she said shortly, going away from him into the kitchen.

"Yes, I have," he said. He jumped up and winced at his legs' aching and went angrily after her. "What do you imagine I've been doing every day for the last twelve months, eh?"

He knew the "eh" was melodramatic and quite without effect. He knew it before he came up with her, sneering at him, twiddling a frying pan over the stove. His anger went and left him rag-like and vulnerable. "I don't see what else I can do," he said.

She twiddled the frying pan with the sizzling fat in it and said nothing. The diminishing lump of fat shot round and round over the black floor of the pan, leaving a trail of bubbling, yellowish-white liquid; dwindled to a whitish bubble on a yellow pool. Robert stood at her elbow as if he had been told to wait. He didn't care where he was. He had forgotten he was standing there. The pan was covered at the bottom. Katherine set it down on the gas-burner and reached for eggs and broke them into the bubbling fat.

"I don't want any," Robert said, as she reached for a third egg. He felt weak and nauseated by her jeer and the smell of the fat in the pan.

"Nonsense," she said, and broke the egg and another.

When she had done and the eggs were popping and siz-zling she turned away to the sink and Robert was left standing alone where her elbow had been. He looked ridiculous, as if he had been holding on to her and she had walked away. "Why don't you get on and invent something," she said and smiled privately. "That's the only way you can seem to make anything."

"Easy without a laboratory," he said bitterly. He went back to the living-room, bitter, but hunger drove out the bit-terness and left him full of pity for himself. When she had called him and they had eaten the eggs he forgot self-pity and bitterness and was himself again, abased.

Kath was earning, Kath was keeping them; Complexion Solvent wasn't bringing in much now, not more than a few shillings a week. Kath was out at eight and back at six, doing the work of the flat. The thought of it drove him out early — out when she was out — and sent him tramping the streets farther and more at random. He took to applying for labour-ers' jobs, though he knew they went to men from the labour exchanges. He stood in queues for hours for jobs he knew he wouldn't get and tramped along streets of small shops with his eyes dragging the windows for Wanted cards, Apply Within.

He knew he had to get a job, because of Kath. Kath couldn't go on, he couldn't go on letting Kath. He plodded along with his eyes on the windows, hair-cut and small tai-lors, Apprentice wanted, Smart Lad to learn. He knew there was a job somewhere, and he had to find it. He turned a cor-ner and came face to face across the street with a slab of house-high hoardings, Bovo for Bonny Bairns, and a grin-ning crane-top in a gap between roofs. He knew suddenly with certainty that he would never get a job. He stopped short and read it over, Bovo for Bonny Bairns. It meant nothing to him and the crane meant nothing, and it meant nothing that a dingy house or two had been pulled down and hoardings were up house-high along the site. But when he had first seen the five-foot blue letters on the red ground, and the slanting crane-head and a yard or so of tiles on the next roof, he had known he would never get a job.

He jerked away from the corner, across the road from the hoarding, and went on, shoulders up and head down; he knew there was a job somewhere and he meant to get it.

London was full of hunger-marchers. He came upon them scattered about Hyde Park, declamatory at Marble Arch, and in a shouting police-churned mob in Parliament Square. He hovered on the edge of the crowd and nobody took any notice of him, he might have been one of them. The only difference was, he thought, that they had the dole and he hadn't. The black-coated worker, he thought, and dug his fists deep into the pockets of his old tweed. He laughed to think they would call him a capitalist — three to four shillings a week dividend from Cupid Cosmetics Co. — but nobody even looked round to see what he was laughing at.

"Nonsense," Katherine said and twiddled the kippers in the pan. "Nobody'd call you a capitalist, how could they."

"And yet they'd be right," he said, with that vague, absent look that made her want to smack him. "Why should I draw even four shillings a week without working for it. They'd be right."

She lifted the pan and smacked it down so that the kippers jumped. "As if you hadn't worked for it before. And as if you hadn't let Cosmetics Co. swindle you out of more than half. As if you wouldn't be well off now..."

"Yet on the other hand," he said, as if she had said nothing, "they draw the dole and I don't, and why not? Because I'm not a manual labourer. Why make an unfair distinction?

The trouble is," he said plaintively, "one can see both sides. Whereas the proletariat can see only one."

She slapped the kippers furiously on to plates. "The trouble with you is you can't see further than your nose." She felt tears form in her eyes, from tiredness and anger. "And as for your being a capitalist," she said, "you might try a bit of that for a change. It mightn't be such a bad idea."

She was too tired of it all to be angry with him for long. She had given him up; she knew he wasn't any good. She took a tram and then a tube and from the tube station on foot cut into a block of suburb, long empty pavements under dripping bushes. This was a long-established suburb, no mushroom growth like Primrose Green. The houses were dark red and gabled, set back behind their laurels and monkey puzzlers, above varnished gates. The gate of Blankenhall Girls' College: Miss Podbin, was varnished yellow and squeaked. It squeaked every day in the same way and the drive squished wetly. Katherine slunk round the corner of the house, where the drive grew narrower and squishier and turned into a path, to the stuffy staff cloakroom, and in at the back door, and upstairs to her Middle Form in what had been a bedroom. The bedroom fireplace remained, facing the desks, and beside it, immediately behind Katherine's chair, a locked door shut off the Principal's sitting-room. At times, quite regularly during Katherine's first weeks at the College, odd creaks and breathings would come from behind this door; later they came only at odd moments and seemed to retire, satisfied. Miss Podbin was gracious.

Miss Podbin had a sallow complexion and a head too small for her body. She wore a woollen cardigan, open, over a cloth frock. All her resident staff wore sloppy woollen cardigans dragged down at the pockets over cloth frocks and their eyes followed Miss Podbin with an abject adulation which would have been exaggerated in the slaves of an Eastern tyrant. Most of them were middle-aged and all were indifferently qualified; what but her pleasure stood between them and destitution?

Katherine despised the servile staff and went as seldom as possible into the staff-room, a narrow, draughty room full of tables, into which it seemed impossible to crowd another person. The staff-room faced Miss Podbin's private office, the door of which usually stood ajar. Katherine despised the staff for their servility, and Miss Podbin for her slyness and smooth tyranny, and the girls because they were well fed and genteel and slow.

Their brains moved slowly, so slowly: clogged with breakfast foods and hot milk night-caps and meat and potatoes in stuffy dining-rooms behind the laurels and monkey puzzlers. The boarders — there were a few boarders — surely could not be stuffed to the same extent, but they were just as slow. Their food, though there was less of it, might be more clogging; and they were always fidgeting and scratching their chilblains. Katherine had given up trying to keep back to their brains, trying to make them keep pace. Her mind broke away and rushed ahead on its own business while her mouth spoke mechanically; was there to prompt, and away again, out of sight: prancing on and back and on, like a young dog off the lead.

Wilberforce Street; why had she never noticed how quick the children were? She had never had to wait for an answer. Hungry and ragged and quick: the proletariat. Oh yes, there was no doubt about it. Though shuffling and boorish and giggly, some of them. Most of them. You had to admit that. Still. Oh, the revolution will come all right, she thought, no doubt of it. But not in time to do *us* much good.

No, she thought — without remembering that she had not thought about it for two or three years — not much use thinking about *that*.

She thought of old Halliburton and her talk about the revolution. — Where was old Halliburton now? At the school most likely, the same as ever. — A lot of good *that* would be. Not for two or three generations afterwards, until things had settled down. Katherine didn't want that. She wanted security and comfort and a Life Worth Living. She wanted Robert to get a sound, decent, progressive job.

She wondered whether she were wrong to lose hope in Robert, to let him see she was fed up. He had to get a job, there was nothing else to be done, there was no other way out. There was Miss Podbin's, with the elderly, servile staff, servile from fear; and back along the tube, a little way to the south-west, there was the horrible flat: the drains that smelt and the holes in the floorboards and the carpets that didn't fit; and further on again, in the City — he ought to be in the City — there was Robert. There was nothing for it but Robert, there must be Robert, there was Robert.

There was Robert. Robert was there. Robert was going to get a job. Robert was loafing with his hands in his pockets through a broken-down houseboat-tramcar-railway-carriage hamlet straggled along a Thames backwater on the Essex flats. His shoulders were up and his head was down and he was zigzagging roughly in the direction of London.

He wished he lived in one of these places. A shirt had been hung to dry in front of a brazier or stove, snug red: it was all he could see through the squat door. The barge stood on mud; a narrow, rotten-looking plank reached from its deck and lay a good way over on the grass verge, ready to rise and slant when the barge floated with the tide. Turf had been lifted and the earth scratched in a rough square, round about where the end of the gangway came; a few late plants, straggling chrysanthemums, were still in flower; a cockled tin or two, bright coloured with torn paper, peeped between the brown withered stems. He wished he lived here — one of these — no rent to pay or none worth reckoning. No worries, time to think. Eat without bother and chuck out the tin, and wash his shirt over the side when the tide came up. Shut up tight and snug, door slammed against the night marshes, with an oil lamp and the brazier snug-hot, shirt steaming dry overhead, and he might even have — yes, by god, he'd have a dog for company. Oh, and Kath.

He swerved from the track winding past the barges, worn uneven and shiny in the coarse, tumpy grass; back over the grass on to the main road. He had to get back and look for a job, he had to get back to Kath. He heard a train whistle somewhere close and wondered how near he was to a station. If he'd taken a train straight off from the trading estate down the line he'd have been back in the City an hour ago, two hours. Having another look round. He fetched some coins, five coppers and a shilling, from the bottom of a pocket and spread them with a balancing movement of the hand until they lay separate on his palm. If he took a train now he'd have no more fares for the week, and this was Thursday. Have to ask Kath. He knew she would give it to him; he knew how she would look as she did it; he knew it was no good getting back to the City. He slid the coins back into his pocket and clenched his hand and left it there on top of them: hands in pockets he started off at a steady tramp along the main road, meaning to cut up north later on and be back before Kath and clear things up a bit before she got in for supper.

The hunger march was breaking up; knots of marchers were setting off back along the high roads to the west and north: some had gone back already by train or motor-coach but some were taking the chance of a tramp and luck on the way: tramping out dogged and sturdy, in the water-tight boots collected by the organisers of the inward march, on the chance of a stroke of luck.

From the marshes on the east Robert was coming in, dogged and hungry, his head was down and his fists were clenched in the pockets of his seedy suit on top of his one-and-five-pence. His feet were sore from walking and the damp that had come in where the boot soles were worn through under the tread and lapped up around the polished uppers. He was thinking it was no use his going on into the City, his luck was out, there was no luck for him there. It was no use his applying for a job in the state he was in, looking like a down-and-out. He thought, A workman could get a job in the clothes I'm in, but I shouldn't stand a chance of getting further than the office mat. He thought dumbly that wasn't equality. There were more thoughts at the back of his mind but he was too tired to think them. When he got home to the rooms at Holloway he took off his boots and his wet socks and put on some very old felt-soled slippers. Then he remembered he would have to put his boots on again later to take the dust-bin down to the area. He pottered around in the slippers, moving his toes to feel the comfort of the felt, and got out the supper plates. He found the liver and bacon in its paper in the cupboard and put it out by the stove, with the frying pan, to be ready for Kath.

Katherine came in tired and threw her books on the bed. "Well?" she said and took off her hat. He knew she meant had he got the job he had been to apply for, but she had given up asking him for weeks and the sudden question made him nervous.

"Oh," he said, "I got in early so I put the stuff out for supper, by the stove." With a quick self-preservative gesture he forgot what she had meant.

She shrugged her shoulders and went over wearily and began to fry the liver and bacon. Hopeless, she thought but she couldn't let herself think of it yet. When she had put the liver in the pan she hung his socks to dry on a towel-horse near the stove.

The gas-ring took the chill off the kitchen and the food was hot and Robert's feet were warm in their slippers. He hitched his chair back and crossed his legs. "They're putting up another council block down the road."

"So I saw."

"Now that's a very peculiar thing," he said, "if you look at it. I suppose those flats will have three or four rooms and a bath and a decent kitchen, and the rents will be half of what we pay here. And you and I couldn't take one of them if we wanted to. Now why not?"

Katherine shrugged her shoulders.

"Because theoretically, theoretically mind you, we belong to the capitalist class. Although I've been out of a job for over a year. And the family that gets one of those flats may be earning four or five pounds a week between them. Now it's a very remarkable thing," he said, the hot food expansive in him, "that not only would the Council indignantly deny us any right to benefit from the rates, but the fellow in the council house earning his four pounds still *feels* that we are better off than he is. Still resents us. Now why do you think that is?"

"*I* don't know," she said irritably. "You're very conversational to-night." She got up and began to clear the plates. She rebuked herself: "I suppose you haven't been talking all day."

"Sorry." The momentary feeling of comfort left him; he cursed himself for forgetting Kath was tired. He wondered vaguely how it was this work tired her more than the council school: she used to be ready enough to argue anything at the end of a day, liked it. He cursed himself because she'd had to take that rotten job. He helped her to clear and wash up and then he put on his wet boots and lugged the dust-bin down to the area. When he came up again he took the boots off and began to polish them.

"Got an interview to-morrow?"

"Nothing definite, but I'll try a few places."

"Better let me press your suit."

She sighed over the table, holding the heavy iron suspended, trying to raise the nap on the shiny spots. Hopeless. That's what's so disheartening.

I suppose that's it, she thought. Everything's so tiring nowadays because it's going nowhere.

She turned the drying socks on the towel-horse and picked up one of the boots he was cleaning. "You ought to get these mended. You'll only let the holes get bigger."

"Doesn't matter," he said. "Once there's a hole at all you might as well walk in your socks."

They started out together in the morning. From the entrance to the tube she watched him walking away, upright and brisk in his pressed suit, in the brightly polished boots with the sodden soles on the damp pavement, and the buses bumping past with a ting, two a minute. She wondered how long he'd keep it up. Walking off briskly down the hill, with a look of energy and confidence; the morning energy of boiled egg and tea. She heard the rumble of a tube train going out, and jumped, and hurried into the lift.

Robert swung on down the road, less confident now Kath had gone, into the free library, and copied down addresses on an envelope and took a penny bus ticket at a fare stage on the way to the West End. He ran up a few flights of stairs and slouched down again and tramped to his next address, in the City, because it was mid-day and if he stopped walking he would feel hungry.

He climbed the stairs in the City and slunk down them and began to tramp, dogged and heavy, without any particular notion where to go, shivering in the fog. His head was down again now and his feet were wet; the shine had come off his boots. He slunk on doggedly through the November fogs, but in December it rained a lot and he took to spending more time in reading-rooms staring aimlessly at the papers. Now and then he would jot down an address and dash out into the slush and tramp and climb some stairs; then he would give it up and turn into the next library and shuffle the news pages aimlessly until he thought of Kath and rushed down the advertisement columns and out into the slush. He knew it was no good. All that winter he had known it was no good, but by January there was no fight left in him. They were fighting in the streets in Germany: three political murders in the early hours of January first; forty trucks of Italian arms entered Hungary; Stalin proclaimed powerful air defence of U.S.S.R.; communal rioting in Bombay; China was preparing for war against Japan, Mexico buying cruisers and fighting aeroplanes from Spain, Colombia and Peru mobilising; an explosion had led to the discovery of a bomb factory in Catalonia; in Dublin they were fighting over the Free State elections. Robert was standing at a street corner off the Strand with his back to an eating-house; his feet were in the slush and the polish was off his boots and his hands were in his pockets.

He looked round at the streaked card in the eating-house window: Cut from the joint and two veg. 9*d*. He felt the coppers under his fingers and took a step back towards the shop and collided with a passer-by. The jolt sent him back to the edge of the pavement and he stood there, uncertain, fingering the pennies. Can't blow ninepence in the middle of the week. He stood for some time in the slush without thinking and began to shiver. No good getting a cold. He moved again, hesitating, but a man striding past in a hurry brushed him back to the curb. Find a coffee stall, cheaper. He went on standing there. Or a bus home, twopenny bus on the way home. Waste to spend twopence on a bus. Cheaper than food. Food cheaper at home.

He stepped off the pavement, but the traffic drove him back. While he waited to cross he thought of Kath, sweating at a job, up north somewhere in the country. Couldn't go home middle day. Go home like a hog and wolf up all the food in the house.

He was jostled into the roadway and stepped back just in time; a taxi-driver leant round and swore at him.

Better to eat here and go on looking for a job.

Isn't any job. Cheaper to eat at home.

Wolfing like a hog.

He stood staring at the traffic going by.

Suddenly he jerked up. Must make a decision. Hesitating, decision, indecisive — won't do to be indecisive. He turned and pushed roughly to the door of the eating-house and swung it open. As the smell of food rushed out he slammed the door again and leant against the wall, shivering.

Enough to make you sick. Better with a cup of coffee.

He began to walk slowly eastward through back streets, trying to keep his legs from shaking and to get away from the smell of food. The steam from each kitchen grill he passed along the pavement sent a hot gust of nausea through him, up and down, and left him shaking, cold. London was full of food. Expensive, dainty food in the West End, back behind him; and heaped-up abundant food in the big stores and the big popular restaurants, and coarse greasy food in the eating-houses and pubs he sagged away from, out in front of a dray, and was driven back with curses. Food toyed with and shovelled in and torn ravenously and hoarded, prized, gloated over. Fish-and-chips and fat chops and the weekly imported joint cut in slivers in suburban boarding-houses. And buses, trams, trains: stormed, fought over, black with fight and hurry, for the minute saved, for the evening meal, for food!

The crowd jostled him back against the barred door of an office; when he was past them, past the stop, the street seemed empty. He shuffled on along an almost empty pavement with water squishing between his socks and the sodden leather of his soles. He thought of Covent Garden and Smithfield and Billingsgate and the meat trains grinding in in early morning; and farmers getting up to milk before daylight, and fishing fleets putting out in the dark in rough weather; and cans and crates, and the trains, trains and lorries and carts, grinding in to the centre, and the swift outward eddies in lorries and drays and vans, and heaped-up counters and slabs and fat women with shopping baskets, and soapy heaped potatoes and knives and forks, and the crowd pelting homewards. And then he thought of the sewers, and laughed.

An elderly negro in navvy's overalls stood still and stared at him. None of the other people took any notice. Fat women and skinny children were hurrying by with papers of fish-and-chips and pints from the pub. Flash boys and girls were swaggering arm in arm down the middle of the pavement. The negro's face gaped with its mouth open against a lit-up shop: Frying to-night.

Robert laughed again. He shot into a side-turning and went on quickly and then slowly between rows of dark, shut houses. He must be near the river, where the sewers run out. Near the docks. Part of a ship's funnel stood up, blunt, ahead of him, over a line of squat black roofs. He took several turnings and came to a narrow lane between warehouses, and a place where a hoarding was broken down over the water in a gap between high, blank walls. Two or three planks of the hoarding were loose and swayed outwards, overhanging a waste patch of ground. They swung when he pushed at them. He leant against the wood and looked through the gap at a triangular patch of river. It was black and thick, with a pale swirl on it here and there.

He saw the negro's face again and thought of sugar plantations and rice fields; and grain, and the great meat plains of the Argentine; navvies sweating in docks, and food boats chugging up the river into London Pool. Drays and vans and the shout of market porters; and hotels and restaurants and pubs and eating-houses and coffee-stalls, and the dark, underground city of drains, bigger and bigger drains. Back, down the river.

He clambered through the gap in the palings and sat on a thrown-down packing case on the waste ground. He could see where the ground ended over the water, because the water was darker and had pale streaks on it.

He thought it was time he went home to supper. The thought of supper, an anticipated smell of kippers, made him retch again. He thought he'd go in a few minutes. Kath would wonder where he was.

Poor old Kath. He'd have to go back and she'd know he hadn't got a job again. He ought to try for a job at the docks. God knew he'd take a job at the docks if he could get it. Unloading food, fuel for the machine. Food. Kath frying kippers.

Fuel, that's it. To keep the machine going. London: nothing but a big machine.

London be damned, he thought angrily, it's the whole civilised world. And where isn't it civilised, by now. Civilised enough for that: dig out food and pump it in, send it round the pipes of the whole machine. Chinese coolie eating rice; just enough rice to grow more rice. Rice boat chugging into London docks. Rice pudding for Manchester cotton operatives. Cheap Manchester cotton for Chinese coolie: civilisation for coolie to encourage him to grow more rice to feed civilisation.

The heavy step of a policeman moved steadily along the outside of the hoarding and turned a corner. Robert sat up straight and shivered. His hands were burning now. It's all very well, he thought, I've got to hurry.

He stared in front of him for a moment and wondered what he had to hurry about, and slumped again.

He wasn't part of the machine: it didn't want him, it wouldn't have him. Waste product. Couldn't use him. That was why he didn't eat, because he wasn't part of the machine. No, he wasn't part of the machine because he didn't eat. No.

Well he wasn't part of the machine, that was it. He could hear civilisation rumbling in the distance, going on without him. Flying Hamburger does ninety-one miles per hour, unsocial elements given ten days to quit Russian towns, six-hundred-mile oil pipe laid across Persian desert, Kingsford-Smith flies Tasman Sea in fourteen hours fifteen minutes, French architect visualises bomb-proof cities of the future. And here he was sitting on a soap-box on a patch of waste ground, he'd better be quick about it.

About what?

He sat up again, taut and sweating with urgency. When he stood his legs felt weak, but never mind that, get on with it. Of course, he must have known all the time what he had to hurry for, or he wouldn't have come here: hurry up and get into the water and finish it because it isn't fair on poor old Kath.

He walked along the dark ground to the edge over the water. His legs were shaking but that was from sitting so long. He wasn't afraid, it only took a minute or two, it was easy like this, slipping into the dark.

A yard from the edge his foot caught a hidden brick and he stumbled; the water came up, dark, leapt up; well, he'd wanted hadn't he... But by then he had thrown himself round and was full length on the earth, clutching at tufts of grass with his nails.

He lay for some time face down, the earth smelt sour and wet. He dared not get up because he didn't know how near the edge was. He raised himself on his hands, but when he tried to stand, the thought of the water turned him sick. He lay down again. After a time he crawled carefully on hands and knees over the unseen ground to where a distant street-lamp made a faintly lighter streak of the gap in the hoarding. He stood up, clutching at the broken wood, and climbed through. Then, because his knees were shaking, he got down on the cobbles in the lane and sat, without thought. He knew he would never do it now.

Presently a light was flashed on him.

"All right," he said, scrambling up, "I'm going, I didn't feel well."

The policeman looked him over suspiciously but let him go. In a spot-light from the following torch he stumbled around the corner and up an unlit side-street towards the lamps of East India Dock Road. He felt the coppers in his pocket and hoped the buses were still running, he knew he couldn't walk much farther and he had to get home to Kath.

"I didn't feel well," he said dully.

She looked him up and down, stared suspiciously at the earth stains on the knees of his trousers: "But where have you been? Why didn't you come home before?"

He shook his head.

"You've got flu," she said. "That's what's the matter with you."

When Katherine had gone out he lay and looked at the wallpaper. It was purplish-brown and mottled and stopped at a chocolate-brown picture rail. In several places above the rail the plaster was stained yellow in loops, where rain had oozed in and dried. In the top far corner, near the window, frieze and ceiling were splashed brown. The ceiling had cracks in it.

After a time he swung his legs on to the floor and sat up: his head swam and he lay down again. He lay and looked at the wallpaper. He knew he couldn't get up. He knew it was no good anyhow.

He knew he was no good if he got up. He might as well lie here with the stained plaster and the picture rail and the purple paper and the chocolate corner of the wall-cupboard and the door shut on to the stairs. The world was going on without him, he might as well stay here because he wasn't any use when he was up: he hadn't even been able to finish it.

New two-million-pound highway between the City and Royal Docks was to save trade a million pounds daily; Russia was outlining a second Five-Year Plan: capital was flowing into Palestine; gold was booming in South Africa; United States banker saw revival ahead; Katherine, stuffing on her hat in the cloakroom of the Blankenhall Girls' College, was wondering what on earth she was going to do if Robert had to have a doctor. She worried all the way back in the tube: there was less chance than ever now of his getting a job. Suppose he were going to be ill for a long time. Then she began to worry about Robert and wondered how he had managed, alone all day.

"You ought to see a doctor."

"What's the use," he said. "We can't afford it."

"I know."

She wanted to be nice to him but she was tired and worried. It worried her that he would try to get up before he was fit. She snapped, "You may as well stay there, you know."

Yes, he knew. He wasn't any use when he was up.

He lay there and felt sorry for himself, and then for Kath, and then for both of them together. Then he thought they weren't very much together nowadays, in the way they had been. Then he began to wonder how far they had ever been together. He wondered why she stuck to him as she did: he was no use to her or anyone else.

At the end of a week he got up and found Kath had had his boots mended.

"You oughtn't to have done that."

"What's the use of your getting your feet wet again."

He sat on the edge of the bed and looked at the boots, playing with the laces. When she had gone out he lay down again because he felt so weak, and so sorry Kath had had to pay for mending his boots.

Next day he went to the public library and hung about,

listlessly turning the advertisement sheets. He knew it was no good applying; he was no good to anybody, he couldn't even finish it.

He took to hanging about at street corners and thinking things out. He thought he was thinking things out. He thought the world was a machine, he could almost hear the wheels turning, but it had thrown him out all right. He thought the machine was running down anyhow. — Two-hundred-and-fifty-thousand-pound road scheme postponed, German budget forty-million deficit, Soviet budget four-hundred-and-fifty-million deficit, French budget eighty-eight-million deficit, thirty-million-pound public work held up would have given employment to three hundred thousand. — Civilisation was going broke, it couldn't go on much longer.

He tried to tell Kath about it in the evening, but she was tired and snappy, they couldn't talk as they used to. He went home early now because she told him to — "What's the good of hanging about getting a cold?" — but it irritated her to find him loafing around when she came in, when she had a pile of exercises to correct. "Haven't you got anything to do? Why don't you *do* something."

The last week in January Cupid Cosmetics Co. Ltd. closed down, and the sales of Cupid Complexion Solvent stopped.

He began to stay out again, to be out of her way. He couldn't afford the pub, but he hung around in libraries long after the lights were put on. The perpetual speechless shuffle of feet and pages, broken only by a cough now and then, was soothing, it was company. Like him, most of these men had been thrown out of the machine, nothing to do but drag through the day to the evening pint and pipe. He could almost hear their minds shuffling with their feet, dull and unresentful, mildly revolving, filling out the day.

He thought, dully and without resentment, of the things he had lost for want of money. A home and a child and even Kath. Kath wasn't the same: thin and irritable and thought of nothing beyond her job, and yet she hated it. Well, and what about himself? Kath hadn't got much of a bargain. All she'd got was a good-for-nothing loafer, a down-and-out. No good to anybody, couldn't even finish it. They might always have been like that, he a coward and she not really caring about anything, but they hadn't known it. That was what the machine had done to them, shown them one another. Each had seen the other as something the machine didn't want. And now it had caught up Kath again and tired her out, so that she couldn't think of anything but food and rent. It didn't make much difference whether the machine caught you up or threw you out; it came to the same in the end.

Cunarder 534 standing abandoned at Clydebank, collision in air at thirteen thousand feet, five thousand two hundred and forty-five flu deaths in four weeks, motor factory explosion in Paris, boy kills great-aunt in imitating film bandit, gasometer explosion at Neuenkirchen, eighty-one killed in Shanghai rubber factory explosion, cage crashes seven thousand feet in Johannesburg mine and kills fourteen ("No damage was done to the shaft and the output of the mine has not been affected"), yellow fever spreading by plane from West Africa, eleven million unemployed in U.S.A.

Hitler becomes Chancellor, burning of Reichstag, rise of Nazi power, Hitler wants four years; Japan building ships, ferro-concrete buildings and aeroplane factories at top speed, Japan fears world war over Manchuria, Japan leaves the League; Pacific base for United States fleet, bomb in post for Roosevelt; armoured cars in streets in Irish Free State:

Canon at Church conference, "Man is an exploded fallacy."

George Bernard Shaw, "Indians ought to give up romantic notions of liberty." Hitler, "We are on the road to victory." Chancellor of the Exchequer, "As prosperity comes again we shall not be able to employ the same number of people we did ten years ago, because of the introduction of new mechanical devices." Lord Irwin, "The machine to-day is dominating the man." Lloyd George, "Mankind is nearing an abyss."

Ten million pound Century of Progress Exhibition at Chicago: rays from Arcturus, travelling two hundred and forty trillion miles, are used to light up exhibition.

"*Standard*, sir?"

"No," he said. "I haven't any money."

The man looked at him, tone changed, pally. "Out of work?"

He nodded. "Bad times for everybody."

"Ah, it is bad times. It is that. Things aren't what they were. I used to be making my five and six pound a week.

"Munitions, that's what it was. That was the job. That *was* a job for you.

"Paper, sir?

"What we want's a nice war."

As summer came round, the heat made Katherine more irritable. She came from the stuffy class-room into the hot tube and out into the dusty, noisy street. The dust and noise made her shut the windows and the air inside became heavier and hotter. She held her head over a pile of smudged, careless exercises but her thoughts jumped off, exasperated, to Robert, who stayed out later and later in the hot evenings to avoid getting on her nerves. Things seemed more hopeless than ever, she knew he wasn't even trying to get a job. It was hardly worthwhile going on.

And for months now, ever since Cosmetics Co. stopped paying, in January, they'd only had five shillings a week for food. Just five shillings clear after the rent: lucky she'd stood out for her fares from Podbin. Bread and butter and tea for breakfast, and dinner at school (and Robert with a few coppers in his pocket and goodness knows what he got with them) and kippers or eggs for supper. Sometimes sausages at the week-ends; but nothing was quite so cheap as kippers. When you got them in the street. It meant going round to one of the street markets late in the evening, to pick things up cheap for the next day. To start with she'd taken Robert with her, but he got on her nerves so, standing and staring round, always looking the wrong way when she wanted the basket, that she'd rather be by herself, it was less trouble than having him there.

When she could she saved a penny to buy a paper; looked through the advertisements herself, in the tube, and ticked off things he ought to apply for. She sponged and pressed his suit and saw him clean his boots and start out. He always came back and told her he had failed but she never knew whether he had really been.

Cotton Industry Conference London, World Power Conference Stockholm (wireless set for each delegate), International Labour Conference Geneva, World Economic Conference;

Five hundred thousand pounds' worth of timber from Russia, Japanese textiles make a bid for world market, two thousand workless on the march in France, posts found in England for German Law professors;

Socialist ban in Germany, Nationalist Party dissolved, Nazi control of Church "no room for other parties," Nazi campaign for larger families; reported anti-Nazi pact Austria and Vatican, Austrian war on Nazis, thirty thousand cheer Dollfuss; Soviet fortifications in Far East, Soviet warns Germany; thirty-two new warships for U.S.A.;

Thunderstorm filmed, flight over Everest, new planet discovered, new gland extract for growth, artificial thunder and lightning made in Paris.

With the school holidays the flat got more and more on Katherine's nerves. Robert went out after breakfast — "Why don't you get out and *look* for something?" — and soon after the street was hot and dusty and thick dust coated the windows and the air inside was hot and thick. No school dinner in the holidays, but she didn't feel like eating. Might make a cup of tea later on. She set to work with nervous ferocity, sweating in the heat: sweeping and scrubbing and scouring and cleaning windows again and again, putting her hatred of the place into the banging broom.

"But why do you bother with all this," Robert would say when he found her pale and fagged. "The place is quite clean, you did it two days ago." But she only snapped at him. "It's always dirty, however much you do it."

She hated the place not so much because it was dirty and the drain smelt and mice came out of unstoppable holes in the back room, three or four at a time even while they were eating, as because the carpet didn't fit and the width of uneven, badly varnished boards made the grey, plain carpet ridiculous. She hated the place because the furniture looked ridiculous and was getting grubby, and because of the mottled walls and brown paint and because there was no chance of getting away and because it seemed as if Robert didn't care.

He went out and hung about and she didn't know what he did do, but it couldn't be much because she knew he had no money. So far as she could see he was just hanging about and not even caring.

He hung about on the shady side of streets and under the trees in public gardens. It was very hot and he didn't bother to think much. The world didn't want him, it seemed to get on all right without him.

Blue shirts in Dublin, Nazi arrests in Tyrol, Japan's fifty per cent increase in exports, air raid feats over Tokyo, South African pied crow takes to using wire for nests and builds on electric pylons, Italian air armada reaches Chicago, medical advice by wireless to mid-Atlantic, Liverpool air-port opened.

When the heat went on into September Kath's nagging got worse and worse.

"Why don't you *try* to get something. Things are beginning to look up. Other people are doing things."

Chemical workers demand higher pay for shorter week; grid scheme completed, twenty-six thousand pylons in Great Britain; Persian contract for Lancashire, two hundred and fifty thousand pounds' worth of textile machinery; one thousand taken on at wireless factory; fifty-seven thousand more at work.

"Look here," she said, and held the paper out to him: Manufacturers of high-class toilet products reconstructing. The firm had an address in the West End. "You've *got* to make these people give you a job."

"What's the good. It'll be like all the rest."

"Except that this happens to be your job and you've got about ten years' experience and invented some stuff of your own. I can't think why you can't push yourself better. I wish I…"

"Oh, all right," he said. He knew it was no good; but he let her press his suit and send him off.

Ten thousand new houses in Liverpool, Finnish electrical order for Britain, two hundred brass bands at New York Prosperity Parade, and Robert on his way with his boots shined to apply for a job.

What's the good, he thought. They'll do their reconstructing all right, without *me*. He put his hands in his pockets and his right hand knocked against the twopence Kath had given him for a bus: "Better not get there late or in a mess." Oh well. He found a fare-stage and waited. May as well see. Things are looking up a bit.

Things are looking up. Rail traffic is expanding, eight hundred thousand pounds advance in seven weeks; the coal trade improves and more orders are coming in for iron and steel. Robert Thomas gets his job, shipping is better, the Soviets reorganise textile industry: mills in Turkestan and Central Russia, France builds a new luxury liner to replace the *Atlantique*, sky-scraper for St. James's Square to cost three hundred and fifty thousand...

Chapter VIII

The wheels came round and picked up Robert. Twenty-eight miners killed in Monmouthshire cage crash; Battersea power station hand in contact with sixty-six thousand volts; eight killed at level crossing in Burgundy; Italian air ace trapped in blazing monoplane; eight dead in Balkan air crash; five Soviet air chiefs killed; Indian airman crashes; express rammed from rear and fourteen killed in U.S.A.; man's body carried six miles on buffers of train to London terminus; Robert at a street corner, not bothering much, giving it up, waiting for evening, waiting to go home to supper. Heart restarted eleven times in London hospital; man lives with half a brain, no change detectable; German doctor cures disease by wireless; Russia grows cabbages thirty times the size of normal; new species created by X-rays, "Man will in a large measure be able to control his own destiny"; Robert with his shabby suit sponged and pressed, with his boots shined and his hair cut and a hat on, stalking down to the City, because Kath has sent him, to apply for a job. Famous oaks, three hundred years old, felled for sale; Eskimos and Australian aborigines killed by civilisation; four chamois in air crash on way to London Zoo; physician warns against stress of modern life counteracting improved health services; another tube death, pits for tube platforms; robot house coming; combine harvester cheaper than man-power; "Robot tyranny," Sir Giles Scott; Robert in a new suit bought on credit, checking formulas with five other chemists, surrounded by brand-new apparatus in a big new factory out in Hertfordshire, with machinery pounding like mad on the other side of the wall.

"Is it really the same firm then? Cosmetics Co. again?"

"Well, practically. Reconstructed a good bit. That's why they've gone farther out I suppose, wanted room to build."

Coming from the tube station he found it in almost open country, a big white modern building towering in the fields, with sprawled across the front a huge neon sign waiting for night: KUPID KOSMETICS KO. After he had been there once or twice he noticed that all the land around was being marked out in sites for small houses for employees.

Katherine said, "We'll be able to move now.

"But not out there," she said quickly. "We don't want to live out again. What we want is a flat in a decent modern block, somewhere central.

"The journey's nothing," she said. "It's nothing to being stuck out in a suburb where you can never go to anything without running for the last train. And of course it'll be easier still when we get a car."

He didn't mind where they lived, so long as they moved from where they were. He went with Kath now and then at the week-end to look at blocks of flats but he was glad when she went on looking by herself on the days she got home before him.

Katherine was nicer to him now. She had given notice to the school and would leave at Christmas. She sat at her desk in the Middle Form room of the Blankenhall Girls' College with half a dozen rows of pale meaty faces in front of her and a draught trickling round her feet from under the locked door into Miss Podbin's sitting-room; but outside, past the wet, yellow trees and down the railway line, at half a dozen points on a band she had drawn tight around the heart of London, there were concrete blocks and all-electric flats and roof gardens and dining-alcoves, and there was strange, new, tantalising furniture made of steel tubing.

She and Robert came into London by different lines, he from the north and she from the north-east, and converged upon the chilly rooms at Holloway. Now that they were going to leave, the rooms had become almost amusing; they told one another it was funny to think they'd lived there for over a year, and they'd never have thought they could do it, and it wasn't such a bad thing because now they knew what it was like, and it would be fun to look back upon.

Kath was brighter than she'd been for a long time. She'd had a time poor kid. He was glad she'd found a place she liked. He went to see it with her one Saturday afternoon, just off Edgware Road, and he wondered how they were going to fit in: two tiny rooms and kitchen and bath — you could have cut the whole lot out of the front room at Holloway. Fitted into a box. But he was glad Kath had got something she liked, she deserved it poor kid. And he was glad he hadn't got to look any further himself: he was feeling tired, feeling the strain of the new job.

The strain of a job after hanging around idle for so long,

he told himself. But this was a different job altogether from the old one. More noise and more bustle. Different altogether.

The laboratory he worked in was a long, light room with an almost continuous belt of window giving on to a concrete yard. There were benches with sinks along the walls and hot-water pipes under the benches. No smoky coke stoves here. Robert wondered what had happened to Rodney. And Graham. Funny he'd never run up against Graham. Wonder if Graham's looking for a job. Wonder if Graham got one of those jobs.

Five other chemists worked with him at the long benches and Mr. Livingsby, the Chief, had a room of his own off the end of the lab. Livingsby did the interesting part of the work, and only he, and sometimes May who had the bench nearest his door and acted as his assistant when he wanted one, knew the full formulas before they had been put on the market. Out in the lab there was plenty of routine work and checking up, not much time here to potter and look out of the window. All of them except old Ball were younger than Robert, but the least experienced was getting more a week than he had got at the other factory.

"It's the noise," he told Katherine. "The job's good enough. It's only the noise."

"I should think you were used to that by this time."

"It was nothing like this before," he said. "You can't imagine it."

Behind the high white façade with the neon sign the factory cut back into the fields in parallel one-storied blocks, separated by a few feet of concrete paving. Offices and executive, laboratory, machinery, back to back, and the rooms where they put up the stuff into boxes. The flying cupids had gone from the lids, replaced by a geometrical design of circles in silver and purple and a huge, metallic, intersecting K. The noise of the machines came in a continuous rattle and roar from the open doors at the ends of the blocks; all day heavy motor-vans were passing over the concrete out-side the laboratory windows to and from the packing sheds at the end and every few minutes a sharp ting of a telephone bell from the executive or one of the departments punctured like a pin the dull, fat roar of vans and machinery. Robert would be conscious of the sharp ting, maddeningly repeated if Livingsby were out or busy, through the glass partition at the end of the laboratory; of a grating click as Livingsby or May jerked off the receiver, and then of the roar, back again, drowning the voice; roaring, of course, all the time, outside the window; not even stopping, naturally, when the bell tinged.

"It's getting on my nerves," he said.

Katherine said, "I expect you'll get used to it. One gets used to anything. After all, the other men work there, don't they. They don't seem to mind. I should think you ought to be used to it by this time."

He wondered how old Ball put up with it. Ball couldn't be so very old or he wouldn't be there. Or was he related to somebody in the firm? He couldn't be so very old but his hair was quite grey and you wouldn't have thought he could stand that racket. Ball never gave any sign either of liking or disliking his job. When it was over for the day he went off by himself with a few short good nights and lit his pipe as soon as he was outside the gate. Robert never knew where he lived. He and Robert had the only two pipes in the laboratory, all the younger men smoked cigarettes.

Robert wondered whether he was getting old himself. He couldn't stand the racket; he didn't know how he was going to stand it.

Katherine said impatiently, "After all, I got used to living in this place. You couldn't have much worse than that to get used to."

She really didn't want to be impatient with him.

But how like him, she thought, to make a fuss about a job when he did get one. After a year, too. And even then, if it hadn't been for me... She took him over with her in a bus to see the flat again — to take his mind off things — to see where the furniture would go.

"It'll look quite nice in here," she said. His head was aching like mad, he wondered if it were eye-strain, but he was glad Kath had got what she wanted at last, she'd waited long enough, poor old Kath. There was no dining-alcove in this flat, the rooms were quite square; she was measuring the space under the window for the dining-table.

"It'll look all right," he said.

She got up from the floor. "I expect the old furniture will have to do, to start with. We can't afford any yet. I expect it'll look quite nice really."

"Why," he said, surprised, "what's wrong with it?"

"We ought to have modern furniture in here."

"But I thought that was what we'd got!"

"Five years ago," she grunted. "Steel wasn't in then."

"Steel?" Funny idea, wanting steel furniture. Hadn't he been somewhere...? He wondered where it was he'd seen furniture that looked like steel. Somebody's house, not a shop.

"Well," he said, "I daresay we can manage it later." He wanted Kath to have what she wanted, she deserved it poor old girl. She always had the managing to do, and he hoped she'd manage, in the end, to get what she wanted. He was glad she was spending money already, smartening herself up: she'd lost some of the tired look she used to have. She'd had a new shingle and her hair waved and she must have been buying some clothes. He wanted her to have a decent time now and he wanted to have a decent time himself, with Kath; but he hadn't reckoned with the noise.

After they moved, at the New Year, he was getting it at night as well as by day. Although the flat was in a side-street a block away from the main road, he could hear the traffic in a continuous rumble from the time he got home until well into the night, and when he dropped off for a few hours and woke it was there again. He would lie awake and listen to the buses coming near in a confused rumble, loud and separate past the end of the street and rumbling again and the next coming up. He lay and listened to them until it was time to take a bus and then a tube and rattle out through the fields to the factory, to the thumping roar of the machinery and heavy lorries crunching past the window and the sharp puncturing ting of the telephone. He rocked back in the tube, with a sharp rattle over dark fields and a dull rumble in the tunnel, and a bus grunted and chugged him to the end of the street; and in the flat he would try to read, to dance music from the wireless Kath had got and wireless programmes from up and down and each side through the new, thin walls, and lie and listen to the traffic growing sparser and more hurried as it grew late, and turn restlessly to an occasional grinding lorry, and wake to find the rumble there again and a clatter of early delivery vans, and hurry out to catch his bus.

The noise was getting on his nerves. He knew he was getting irritable and grumpy, grumpier than old Ball who worked all day without a word to anybody and stumped off home alone with his pipe. He would hear himself snapping at young Chapman who worked next to him, when Chapman made some ordinary remark: just then a lorry would go by and it would be too much effort to listen, to pick out the words and answer them. At first he tried to hear or pretended to hear, nodding and grunting non-committally in answer, but after a few weeks he gave it up and pretended not to know that Chapman was speaking. Chapman got tired of it and left him alone. Robert wondered how it was the younger fellows seemed not to mind the noise, not to notice it. Brought up to it, he supposed, and the next generation wouldn't be able to do without: deaf in a silence. It worried him that he should be snappy, it made him feel old. It worried him having to lunch in the crowded noisy cafeteria attached to the factory: there was nowhere else to eat, without going back into town. It worried him that he was irritable with Kath in the evenings.

"Can't we have that wireless off?"

"Why?"

She knew why, but it irritated her and the irritation made her ask though she knew that his answer would irritate her more. His tiredness and the fuss he made about noise were constant small nagging annoyances. His strained look, and the wrinkles he was getting between the eyes — eye-strain. Why can't he get it seen to — were a sort of reproach. She didn't want him to be tired all the time, just because they were living decently for once; she didn't want his tiredness to be the price of it, she didn't want to think he was tired. If he was tired, she didn't want to know about it.

"You can have it on all day," he muttered, apologetic.

She switched off the wireless ungraciously and they sat without speaking, Robert poring over his paper.

"Trade seems to be improving," he said presently, for something to say. "There seems to be more money about."

"About time," she said.

British trade revival, new industries springing up; one

hundred thousand for Codex Sinaiticus; big Empire air scheme under consideration; South African digger refuses seventy-five thousand for two diamonds; Bankers on World Trade, steady improvement; Robert out in Herts with the thumping machines and the lorries grinding past the window, wrinkling his face from nine till six over specimens of tooth-paste, in a row of white overalled men and drawing better pay than most of them because of his experience, drawing his pay and taking it back to Kath.

The wireless was off and Katherine hadn't said anything for a good time. Robert was looking around at the new duck's-egg-blue walls and the bright new pillar-box-red woodwork.

"We could almost afford to have a child now," he said suddenly.

"What on earth?" What surprised her most was that she had never thought he might want to. She hadn't any arguments ready. "The flat's too small," she said to gain time.

"Oh yes, I suppose it is."

She thought, in sudden huddled fright: not likely. Just when things are a bit better. Just when we're getting clear. Just now when I've been through all that having it all upset. Back again.... She really quite hated him for wanting it, for not caring; for wanting to saddle her with that after all she'd been through....

"If we lived a bit farther out," he said.

Yes, she hated him, for the note in his voice that wanted it: the note that said he'd been done out of something, even if he didn't know it. As if she hadn't been done out of most things, practically everything she ought to have had, until now. And even now he was only earning just enough to keep the two of them decently. "Anyhow," she said hard and cold, "we can't afford it."

"Yet people do manage, somehow." Poor old Kath, she always had to think of the ways and means. It was always her job to manage on what he could make, it would be hard luck on her if they had to move again to a cheaper place. He supposed it was an expensive business having a child. The working classes seemed to think nothing of it, they got it all for nothing: the medical business and education and the lot, but it was different with people like him and Kath, they had to pay for everything they had. It would be rough on Kath, all those years of managing and making ends meet, and yet it did seem hard luck.

— No compulsory sterilisation: departmental committee pronounces against sterilisation of mental defectives. —

Perhaps if they waited a bit things might get better or Kath might change her mind. It did seem hard luck, and if Kath felt she wanted it too... "People do seem to manage," he said. "If you wanted it..."

She hated him for saying it again, for trying to put her in a trap. That was it, a trap. She could see it closing in around her, huge and impalpable, made up of small disgusting objects: babies' diapers and slobbering mouths and washing lines in suburban gardens, and down-at-heel shoes tramping dusty roads to save a penny, and shopping baskets and the smell of sour milk. She struggled for breath, pushing it: I won't have it, I won't, I won't go under, why should I.

"Likely I should want it. Likely I should want to live in some hole and slave and never have a minute to myself and think of nothing but how to save money and how to get to the end of the week. Do you think I haven't had enough of that? So likely," she said, hot and breathing at him.

"No," he said. "No, you're right," he said dully. "I may be able to make more another day."

She turned and switched on the wireless. She hated him now because she had let herself go. As fear died away her anger turned cold and settled into a hard resentment. He didn't care how empty her life was. He'd like to take even what she *had* got.

"Christ!" he said in sudden fury. "Can't we have that wireless off?"

She switched it off in the middle of a bar and picked up a book and stared at it stonily until she heard him go out of the room. She left the wireless off, ostentatiously, for the rest of the evening. When he came back they sat with the silence between them blaring at them. The flat was a small, dead cell in the big comb of cells each with its noise. They sat at the bottom of it and avoided looking at one another. After supper he said, "I don't know how it is, I always have a headache nowadays."

"Eye-strain probably. You ought to have glasses."

"I had some once, but I don't know where they are."

She said nothing, contemptuously. On Saturday she made him see an oculist and get fitted out with shell rims, but he still had a headache.

British Industries Fair a turning point in British Trade. Cunard-White Star Merger: No. 534[1], on the stocks at Clydebank since 1931, is to be completed. Trade agreement signed with Russia. Observations made in the Caroline Islands of an eclipse of the sun cost two thousand four hundred and seventeen pounds a minute. Ten million are workless in America; two thousand hunger marchers reach London; Chancellor says British Trade is "firmly on the upgrade": Robert jumps

---

1 Cunard liner 534, later named The Queen Mary

on to a bus, and the bus takes him to the tube and the tube takes him to the factory: his hair is cut and sleek under his hat, and his suit is new and clean and well pressed; he puts on his white starched overalls and his shell-rimmed glasses and gets to work among the clean, shining retorts, in a row with Anderson and Ball and May and Chapman and White. He is in the middle of the row: White and Anderson and Thomas, and Chapman and Ball and May: in a row, in clean white overalls, with blank scrubbed faces, with the pounding, grinding, pinging noises of machinery and lorries and telephone bells, and the sharp sudden small hiss of a burner near and large, large as a lorry through the window, penetrating their smooth clean faces and scratching at their brains.

Göring at work in Germany, Austria rallying to Dollfuss, Russia arming in the Far East, Japan recruiting, eighty thousand unemployed peasants as munition workers, ships and planes for U.S.A., Shaw on the next war; the thing was getting on Robert's nerves, it was as much as he could do to get through the day. He got out into the quiet road and lit a pipe, he was ahead of the others. Anderson pushed past him from behind and broke into a run up the road and charged an empty, waiting bus. Robert moved on smartly to the station, he could hear the others coming. Chapman and May were close behind him talking about football; old Ball had gone off by himself, he walked home from his work, nobody knew where he lived. Robert hurried on to keep ahead of the other two, or White might catch him up and want to talk. As he got to the top of the tube steps the factory syren began to sound, in five minutes the road would be full and running. A train was coming in. Robert ran down the steps and grabbed on to a door and squeezed himself in before the train had stopped moving. Chapman and May passed the window without seeing him. The train stopped and stood still and waited. Robert sat taut in a sweat of impatience and clutched his hat on his knees. If it waited another three minutes the crowd would be out, another two minutes. The train moved on. He threw the hat on the rack, his muscles relaxed, the train rocked him from side to side.

Britain's new disarmament plan, France objects to rearmament of Germany. Arms talks, Eden in Berlin, three-year plan for French air force. Peace Defence Congress in Brussels, fleet of German planes for war service. The tube rocked him to the bus and the bus jolted him to the flat, he found Kath in a fluster to get supper out of the way because the Jenkinses were coming in for bridge.

Robert had a racking head, he hated bridge and he hated Jenkins. The Jenkinses lived on the ground floor of the block and Kath had picked them up or they had picked up Kath. Mrs. Jenkins was a dashing young woman with sleek hair and a long cigarette-holder and bright hard eyes and a bright hard smooth manner of overpowering efficiency. She spent a good deal of time going to dress-shows and fed Jenkins on food from the cooked-meat departments of the big stores. Robert thought Jenkins was a silly young fool, with his sleeked-down hair and shell-rimmed glasses: but when presently he caught sight of himself in the chromium plating above the let-in electric fire he looked a bit older than Jenkins but not very different.

He had a splitting head. He was rude to the Jenkinses and after they had gone Katherine sulked. He didn't care whether she sulked, he didn't care about anything so long as he could get some sleep before morning. The bus ground him to the tube and the tube joggled him to the factory and the factory pounded and bumped and thumped at him and threw him out into the tube and the Jenkinses came in more and more often in the evenings. Kath made him buy a dinner jacket, and they had dinner now instead of supper so that they could ask the Jenkinses to dinner.

Barricades in Paris streets, police charge fifty thousand in the Place de la Concorde, Gardes Mobiles fire on mob, over three thousand wounded. Riots and looting in Marseilles. Austrian revolt, troops occupy Vienna, armoured cars in streets, Karl Marx House shelled into surrender. Riots in Kashmir, ten dead in Washington prison mutiny, taxi strike riots on Broadway. Women riot in Madrid, stolen taxis transport arms in Barcelona, Germany carries out naval manoeuvres in Danish waters, Russian dockyards in the Arctic. Black Sea and Far East work day and night, Japan fortifies Manchuria. New York psychologist asserts that, according to the present rate of increase, insanity will be universal by the year 2139.

Robert wondered whether he was going mad. He couldn't stop worrying about things. The papers were full of riots and fighting and threats of war and they made noises round him as bad as the rattle of the tube and the grinding of bus gears and Mrs. Jenkins' loud, efficient laugh. While he was waiting for the bus outside the public-house by Paddington he thought he couldn't stand it any longer. He turned into the bar and had a small whisky. He had only had a drink a few times before in his life — until, lately, Katherine had bought a cocktail shaker so that he could shake cocktails for the Jenkinses — and the small whisky made things look a good deal better.

Two-hundred-and-fifty-thousand-pound rail scheme is completed in Ulster; Britain plans air routes around Africa; Arabian kings make peace by wireless; a twenty mile roadway is constructed in eight weeks with rock drills and concrete breakers among the mountains of the North-West Frontier; a London–Shanghai telephone line is opened; the first regular transatlantic air service is organised by a German line to South America; Katherine is shop-gazing in the West End: her eyes harden over the things she can't afford but ought to have and her mind hardens against Robert.

I ought to have a new bridge coat, we ought to have a cocktail cabinet, it's ridiculous, I ought to get a manicure before to-night, we ought to have oysters while they're in season, of course we ought to have a car.

We ought to, she thought. He ought to be able to afford it. I ought to have it in the afternoons, we ought to be able to go out of town at the week-ends.

Everything was owing to her, because she had lived for a horrible year at Holloway, and because she'd had a horrible time ever since she married Robert, and because before that... We ought to have some decent modern furniture. We ought to have a black carpet and chromium furniture and long curtains of oiled silk. It would look awful in those little rooms. We ought to have a better flat.

That isn't a new block, it must have been up for years.

We ought to get into one of the new blocks. They're putting them up all over the place, in Mayfair, too. Well and why not, we ought to be able to afford it. He ought to work up and get a better job.

Katherine has wandered into Berkeley Square. Rita Jenkins got that black hat in Berkeley Square. I ought to get some decent clothes. First transatlantic air mail plane reaches Brazil; thirty-four million telephones are in use, encircling the world; gland transfer is legalised in Italy, Berlin plans a new stratosphere flight; up in Herts, a world away, Robert is bending over a sizzling burner, he can feel his forehead twitching with that nervous tic he has got lately and that Kath keeps telling him about.

He straightens up and rubs his forehead with the back of his hand but as soon as he stops the tic starts again. It is there in the tube and the bus and when he's got home and is dressing for bridge with the Timsons. Kath picked them up at the Jenkinses. It makes Kath tell him about it sharply.

"You ought to do something about that."

"It's only tiredness, I expect."

She looks at him, puzzled and annoyed, but mostly annoyed. "I can't think why. You oughtn't to be tired like that."

It annoyed her that he was tired. Why should he be tired. He only worked till six. He had plenty of relaxation in the evenings.

A spectator is crushed to death in a cup-tie crowd; the Soviet balloonists crash from a height of thirteen miles; a French mail-plane crashes in Africa; eight are killed in a mine accident at Johannesburg, ten killed in collision of Spanish football special, over fifty thousand killed and a million injured in eight years on the roads of Great Britain; Robert stoops over his work, a lorry swerves and changes gear outside the window, his face twitches, he can feel it, he doesn't care, Kath isn't there to tell him off about it. When he thinks about it he can see the rims of his glasses, he tries to push the glasses further on so that he can't see the rims; he finds he can always see them; now he has once seen them he can't stop seeing them: he is conscious of seeing everything through the small round portholes of his glasses, as if he were seeing it through the end of a tunnel; he can always see the frame edging the picture. It gets on his nerves, always seeing the rims: he blinks, and the blink becomes a habit; he frowns, and stretches his brow and frowns, trying to drag the frame further on.

Six lochs dammed and Ben Nevis tunnelled to feed a hundred thousand h.p. power station; the water hyacinth of Bengal waterways collected into dumps and used to produce power spirit; aged wood-carver's suicide by gas-poisoning; sixty sheep roasted alive in a lorry in the Lake District; horse electrocuted on live rail: Robert took the tube and the bus, his face was working like mad, he knew he must try to stop it before Kath saw him. His bus crawled along Praed Street behind a van: a horse van from one of the yards behind the station. After a bit the bus pulled around and the horse, lunging for foothold on the slippery road, dropped back alongside Robert. In a moment, snorting at the bus fumes, it had dropped back out of sight. No place for animals, thought Robert; oughtn't to be allowed.

No place for horse-flesh, he thought, his forehead working madly. The bus took the corner and plunge into Edgware Road. No place for flesh. No place for flesh and blood, and skin that feels and branching nerve-ends on the move like twigs in a wind. Iron and steel and heavy wheels grinding and bright clean blood on a dirty pavement, that day, pushing in bright trickles through the dirt.

He took the length of the bus in a stride, and off, and ran alongside, and caught his balance, his face working like mad; he let go the bus rail and turned back sharply along the pavement. His nerves were all to bits and he'd better not let Kath see him like that. When he got in she was in the bedroom, dressing for bridge with the Moseleys. Kath had picked up the Moseleys at the Timsons'. — "We ought to know more people; we ought to go out more." — He went into the sitting-room and mixed himself a stiffish drink from the tray on the sideboard. — "We ought to have a cocktail cabinet."

The drink did him good: he was able to think about things

philosophically in spite of the Moseleys' being there. His brain was quite clear. He was surprised at how clear his brain was. The Moseleys didn't want to talk to him: Mrs. Moseley was keen on the game and Moseley was telling Kath about a week-end cottage they'd bought, down in Dorset — "*We* ought to have something like that." His brain was quite clear and calm, thinking things out. Flesh, he thought, flesh used to be the standard. The unit. One man-power, the speed a man could walk. Never was meant to go faster than he could walk. Addles his brain. Or jogging along on a horse: flesh again. "And then you'd have to have a car," Mrs. Moseley was saying, "it wouldn't be much good without a car." All this dashing round in cars and expresses and planes: body getting there before the brain can adjust itself, shock to the nervous system. Meant to move as fast as his legs can carry him.

The drink he had had wore off and he didn't like to get up and take another. And fighting, he thought. Going out to battle, man against man, man on his horse, and may the best man win. What a piece of work is man! Who said that.

Man! Men. Flesh debased. Crammed into drab, tight clothes and loaded on machines, packed and pushed and shoved and rattled, tipped out, herded to work. Crammed into steel hats and gas-masks and mown down by machine guns. Men! Man-power. Power for the big rattling booming hustling machines. The whole big world-machine of it. Countless millions of wheels grinding and producing and killing. Who for? Not for the capitalists. Big Bosses, the Kings of Industry: chained to desks, chained to time, chained to their bank accounts: mounds of uneasy, sweating flesh in fifty guinea suits. For their wives then? Like Kath. Wanting everything. Chained to the things they haven't got yet, the things other wives have got. Chained to the things they've got, the urgency of going one better. Chained to fear: the fear of losing what they've got, of not getting more, for not having the right thing, of not doing the right things, of not going to the right places. The fear of growing old. Chained to their ready-made, machine-made, mass production — their machine-turning, exclusive pleasures.

For nothing, for nobody. One huge, senseless machine. Men making it and it making men: little machine-made, swarming men, in tight black suits, running in and out between the huge wheels, feeding the machine.

How about waste products? In the hospitals and asylums. Better look out, thought Robert. He could feel the nerves twitching in his face. He gave Moseley a drink and took a drink himself. He took a few drinks now before people came, and a good few after they'd gone. On the evenings Kath went out, to the Jenkinses' or Timsons' or Moseleys' or Francises' or Wilsons', he took to letting her go alone and sitting with a book or paper on his knee beside the gagged wireless, and having a few drinks to put him right.

Even on fine spring evenings like this he sat with the window shut to keep out the traffic noises. He got up and measured himself a half-glass and held up the bottle to the light, and telephoned for another bottle while Kath was out: they delivered up to nine, it was eight-thirty, she wouldn't be back before twelve. He waited in a sweat of impatience for the bell to ring, because it was going to ring and he couldn't settle down: he couldn't sit down quietly with his half-glass, or the full glass left in the bottle, knowing that the bell was going to ping in the kitchen, that he would have to go out to the door and take in the bottle and say good evening and fumble for change. If only he could get a stretch of time to himself he'd be able to get a grip on himself and straighten things out.

241

Ammonia Works accident in the Midlands, Youth demonstration in Berlin, Moscow's Underground in course of construction, Japan and China, Disarmament Conference two years old, Fascists at Plymouth; factory explosion in Fife, German newspaper campaign, strike violence in Bombay, bombs in Austria, gangster too young for the police court, machinery on the farm.

When the boy had been, with the whisky, he was able to settle down with the glass and a half by his chair and the unopened bottle in the sideboard cupboard. He wouldn't want it to-night. It was the feeling that Kath might turn nasty when he wanted to order more. He sat and emptied the half-glass. He wouldn't put on the wireless; he didn't want dance music and he didn't want to know what was going on: Germany marching and arming, and the *International*, and rasping, un-intelligible talks in Italian. He was glad the thing couldn't get Japan. He disturbed himself again to take the unopened bottle from the sideboard cupboard and remove the tinfoil and draw the cork and put the bottle back in the cupboard. Kath wouldn't notice it was newly opened. He took the trouble to go into the kitchen and drop the tinfoil under the lid of the dustbin. On second thoughts he took the bottle from the cupboard again and put it by his chair, plenty of time to stick it back before midnight. No reason why I shouldn't have a drink, but no good making unpleasantness. When he had sat again he saw that he now had two bottles by him. He emptied the remainder of the old bottle into his glass and took the bottle to the kitchen and put it in the dust-bin.

Although the wireless was shut off he had an impression that the noises were going on, just the same, inside: he only had to take out a stopper to let them loose, blaring

GERTRUDE EILEEN TREVELYAN

and marching and arguing. Funny his sitting here by himself shut into a blue and red room like a box and holding things off. Sitting here alone and Kath so near, over at the Francises, that she could almost have seen him from where she was, at the bridge-table, if there'd been nothing in the way. Funny that: the Jenkinses downstairs with people in, dancing; and people in the other flats, talking or playing cards or going to bed; and Kath along in Baker Street at the Francises', and some band sawing away at the B.B.C studios, and people still out in the streets catching buses and in restaurants eating meals, and he keeping them all off with a brick wall and a few plaster partitions and the turn of a screw on the wireless. He poured himself another drink. If he took a few Kath wouldn't notice it was a new bottle.

Funny thing, that. London going on all round him and didn't know it, didn't know he was there. Lot it would care if it did. And outside that, all those other countries going on. Hitler and Dollfuss and what's the Russian fellow, Stalin. Nobody minds his name. Communism anyway. And Mussolini, and Spain, and the French worked up about Germany. And further out still, he thought, warming up: all those cold countries, and Russia going ahead in the Arctic, and China-and-Japan, and Russia, be at war before anybody knows it; and what comes after that, Australia, and Africa, and up through South America and the States. Taking in the world, pretty well. Yes, he thought, there isn't much left out; circle of sea pretty-well if you went round outside that, Arctic and Pacific and along the Antarctic and up the Pacific. Funny thing that, now. Draw a circle, pretty-well, to take in the lot.

He took another drink, he felt a mild sort of excitement: he had discovered that if he drew circles of different radii from the point where he himself was sitting, more or less all the important places in the world would come along their circumferences. Now that's a damn funny thing.

It puzzled him for a minute. He took a drink and sipped it thoughtfully. But he didn't see where he could be wrong. And what about the air? How about the stratosphere? And those shooting stars. He, Robert Thomas, sitting here with a glass in his hand and the universe laid around him in concentric circles: streets and traffic and flats and hotels tucked tight with people sleeping and eating and hurrying to work, and great power-houses and furnaces and enormous clanging factories and warehouses and wharves, and workers scurrying like ants, and whole peoples in arms, crammed into factories, tearing up the wilderness, rearing huge power stations and arms factories among the forests, and hostile industrious nations swarming: more factories and more arms: more, bigger, faster. Racing cars and planes and bombers and tanks and speed boats and luxury yachts and submarines and great floating cities; and balloons thirteen miles up in the stratosphere, and the spied-on planets and chained light of far distant stars, and vague, golden nebulae for ever falling through space. He could see, now, that there was a purpose in it. But the purpose kept getting away from him, he couldn't say what it was.

Vast, empty space, and the packed, busy solar system, stratosphere and air and ice-fields and oceans and throbbing plains, and the huge teeming factory of Europe, and London with the traffic dimmed and lights turned down, and Robert Thomas sitting with his glass at the bottom of a box, and Kath taking the lid off and saying, what she say? and walking away, contemptuous, and the bedroom door shutting with a snap.

Covent Garden going home and charwomen setting out to work, Tom Smith yawning and cursing the alarum in

Celestin Road, Brixton, Ted Brown cursing and catching the bus at Peckham Rye, Syd Jones scratching his head in the tube at Uxbridge, Robert Thomas, with a mouth like cotton-wool dragging in at the gates of Kupid Kosmetics Ko., Kupidtown, Herts, Bill Robinson cranking up a lorry at Epping…

Robert wondered what it was he'd hit upon that was so bright, the night before. Something to do with a meaning to this infernal din. Industrialism and so on. Something like a pattern to the whole lot. It had struck him as bright at the time but he couldn't for the life of him think what it was. He had an awful head, he hoped he didn't look shaky. When a lorry changed gear suddenly in the yard it made him drop a test-tube and it broke to bits in the white enamel sink. Nobody seemed to have noticed. Luckily young Anderson had gone out for a minute, and old Ball was snuffling over his own work. Rotten luck the cafeteria wasn't licensed, get one on the way back. Better not, Kath might spot it. Kath was in an awful wack. She wouldn't notice if he had just one, at the pub, before he got there. What the hell was he working for, anyway, if he couldn't get a drink when he wanted one. He had a rotten head.

The one he had at the pub made him feel better, it made him sorry for Kath. Poor old girl no wonder she sulked, coming in and finding him soaked like that. She said nothing about it, she hadn't said anything, she was just sitting and looking at him over her book across the small sitting-room. She hadn't asked anybody in for to-night, or else she'd put them off.

She never said anything about it. For a night or two he sat and stared at her miserably over his paper, and after that the Jenkinses came back, and the Moseleys and the Timsons and the Francises. When she went out in the evening he went with her, and he never dared to have more than one before at the pub.

It was a bore for Katherine having to take Robert with her everywhere, looking glum and twitching his face. Trying to make a martyr of himself. He hadn't the slightest glimmer of social sense. None. He didn't even *want* to meet people. He hadn't even the sense to see that it would help him on in his job. Of course she ought to have a chance of getting to know his Directors' wives. There must be heaps of ways: people who know people... Give him a bit of a pull. But she couldn't even get out of him what the Directors' names were. Oh well, old Stein, he supposed. Came along in his Rolls for the audits and when anything went wrong. Likely his wife was going to call on one of the chemists' wives.

"But there must be plenty of other people, under him," she said impatiently. "Managers and sub-managers. Who's the head of your department? He's probably married."

"Old Livingsby? Shouldn't think so."

She could have smacked him. She could have smacked him for looking so glum and stupid in the Wilsons' drawing-room: just mooning around, with nothing to say. Alec Wilson had been at business all day, just as much as he had, but he knew how to enjoy himself in the evenings.

When Robert was there she was quite glad to get away and get home. She was glad to wake in the morning, before it got hot, and hear the traffic starting in the street under the open window. She was glad it was day again and Robert would be going off to business, giving her a chance to get things done.

As soon as he was gone she turned on the wireless, loud, so that she could hear it in the other rooms — he wouldn't have it on at breakfast; made such a ridiculous fuss — and ran the vacuum cleaner over the carpets. The grey carpet didn't go too badly really with the blue and red paint, but it didn't go too well. Getting worn, too. And the grey furniture. She'd have to think out a scheme. Black mightn't be bad. Or red leather.

Robert had left his pipe on the book-table, and his book face downwards on the arm of a chair. She dropped the pipe into a black glass vase where it wouldn't show — serve him right if he couldn't find it — snatched up the book contemptuously and pushed it into the writing-table drawer. Not even as if he read anything worth reading. Ridiculous detective stuff. You'd think somebody who calls himself cultured...

She dusted the shelves of the book-table. Shaw, and Moore, and a Conrad or two, in nice editions. And one or two slim, austerely bound Moderns. You couldn't say this was the room of somebody who wasn't cultured. When she had run a duster over the chromium fire-surround — and nobody could say she minded work, in decent conditions; it was that filthy kitchen that had got her down — she went back to the bedroom to massage her face and get dressed.

As soon as she was dressed she settled at the telephone in the hall and rang around to the shops to give her orders and to Rita Jenkins to find out if it was all right for that evening and Meta Francis to remind her of the post-impressionist lecture at five o'clock. Of course there'd be dozens of interesting people there. And Roy Francis was art critic for Provincial Periodicals: Meta would be sure to know everybody.

She got back just before Robert, hot and tired but glad she'd been, in time to dress for the Jenkinses. She'd be able to tell Rita about the lecture and Rex Ingham: how lucky she'd spotted him from his photograph and Meta had been able to catch him on the way out. She mustn't lose the Inghams' address: Hampstead, somewhere. Not that it was much good talking to Rita about things like that. Poor dear Rita wasn't the least bit intellectual, though luckily she had the sense to know it. You couldn't ask Rita to meet the Inghams, for instance.

Robert came in as she was putting their cold supper on the kitchen table, so that the sitting-room would be tidy for Rita and Ted. She sent him off in a hurry to get cleaned up. Really, he looked too squalid for words. She thought it was decent of Ted Jenkins to take the trouble to talk to him as he did. Robert was the limit. He was just as grumpy when he came home in the evening as he was in the morning, when he bolted his breakfast and went off almost without a word. She was quite glad to have him out of the way.

Professor lectures on the physiological cost of noise in industry, trade on the up-grade, steel buildings to be cheaper, pit explosion in Lancashire, wreck of German express, gasometer explodes in Hong-Kong.

The heat was getting him down. With the heat, they had to open the laboratory windows and all day the lorries seemed to be driving over his head. When he had had one at the pub he couldn't resist having another. After that he had one or two more. He'd only had one or two, hadn't he?

British warning to Germany, dictatorship in Latvia, Goebbels sees Pilsudski, Hitler sees Mussolini, new disarmament move at Geneva, bombs by post in Paris, Fascists at Newcastle.

He hadn't had quite enough to make things look better, or else he'd had too much. He started to walk home to get rid of his headache but the more he was jostled in the street the worse he felt. He got on a bus and was angry at the way it threw him about. He was late for dinner already: he hoped to god Kath wasn't going to get in a wack because he didn't feel like standing for it. And if she was going out, he wasn't. He'd have a quiet evening for once to himself. He reached, with relief, the comparative quiet and coolness of the staircase and let himself into the flat and found the Timsons there, ready for bridge.

"We didn't wait dinner," Katherine said, heading him towards the kitchen, "but there's something for you if you want it. Or will you wait till later?"

He edged around her into the sitting-room. Clarice Timson with her silly, fixed smile was perched on an arm of his chair, he could see her around Timson's big stomach. Timson was twiddling a glass in one beefy hand and holding out the other.

Robert looked at him. "You get out," he said, slowly and distinctly.

Timson's smirk faded. Behind him, Clarice gave a gasp.

"Robert," Katherine whispered furiously. She caught his arm and tried to pull him out into the hall.

He jerked away from her and went further in. "Get out. Both of you. Had enough. Can't get peazen-quiet in my own home. Peashen-quiet," he said, leaning heavily on the back of a chair.

Clarice stopped looking frightened and began to giggle. Timson's meaty hand slapped him on the back, "That's all right, old boy. That's all right."

Suddenly Robert turned round, pushed past Katherine in the doorway and shut himself into the bedroom. He felt horribly ill. He heard Kath say, in the hall, "No, please don't. No, of course not." He heard the sitting-room door shut and voices cooing wordlessly behind it and then a laugh. The bridge table creaked as they put it up. Playing dummy. He felt horribly sick.

He wondered why he'd made such a fool of himself as to shut himself away in here. If he'd stayed there they would have had to go, or pretend not to notice. He could still feel Timson's patronising slap when he'd realised Robert was lit-up. Think all the more of him probably for being drunk. *That* kind of gross brute. Robert felt sick with himself.

He thought he was going to be sick. He lay down on the bed. He could still hear their voices cooing and gurgling in the next room. Then he woke up and saw Kath in her dressing-gown, creaming her face in front of the glass.

She came across and looked at him, contemptuously. "If you get drunk again," she said, "I shall leave you." Then she went out.

He lay there thinking he ought to get up, he couldn't let her sleep on the sofa in the sitting-room. The light was still on and he saw he hadn't undressed. He half got up but felt so sick he lay down again. He went to sleep.

Neither of them said anything at breakfast. Robert didn't eat anything. When he had gone out Katherine put on the wireless and pottered about, seriously wondering whether she should leave him. Robert was an old stick-in-the-mud, he didn't want to do any of the things other people did and he didn't look like getting any further in his job. In spite of all she'd done to help him. And now if he was going to do this... Neither of them had the slightest feeling left for the other, had they? Well then. She didn't think he was likely to drink so much again, she'd told him off fairly well, but last night seemed a good reason for breaking. She'd have to think about it.

To a wireless transmission of gramophone record from Paris she went round the room, energetically flicking dust off the furniture, collecting last night's glasses and the shaker, turning them into the kitchen for the morning Help to wash. She stood the bottles back in the sideboard cupboard: we really ought to get that cocktail cabinet. She rubbed the chromium-plating around the electric fire and the highly polished wood of the wireless. If we do get some new furniture in here it won't look so bad.

Shall I leave him? I'll have to see.

She went into the bedroom and made up her face; sounds of washing-up were coming from the kitchen. Not so bad as when I used to do that. The things I've put up with, on Robert's account. And now look at him.

The flats of the block backed on to a courtyard, from the bedroom window she could see across the court the Jenkinses' daily woman shaking out their bear-skin mat. We ought to have one of those, she thought mechanically. She wondered whether it would be safe to ask the Jenkinses in for a game in the evening or whether she'd better have Rita alone in the afternoon while the men were at work. He'll be all right, she thought, shrugging impatiently. She snapped the cap on her lipstick and shot it into a drawer, and laughed to herself rather ruefully as she realised she had slid to a decision. I expect I'll have to put up with him a bit longer, it looks like it.

He wondered what sort of a wack Kath would be in to-night. He wondered whether he'd get there and find she'd left him, left a note on the pin-cushion. She wouldn't do that, there was nothing melodramatic about Kath: more likely have just gone and said nothing. He wondered if he'd mind if she did go, they hadn't got much to say to one another nowadays, hadn't had for a long time. It wouldn't make much difference. But as he got near the flat he found he was hurrying for fear she'd gone, for fear he'd find the place empty. He didn't want Kath to go. He didn't know what he'd do without old Kath. Of course she hadn't gone: there was nothing melodramatic like that about Kath.

He almost wished there were. In a way he'd rather she'd made a fuss and flown at him than been quiet like that, saying nothing about it. Not sulking exactly, just not mentioning it. Waiting? Going to say something to-morrow?

She said nothing, she seemed to have forgotten it.

Poor old girl, he thought, I haven't treated her too well. She hasn't had too good a time.

He came straight home in the hot evenings. He felt done-in. He took aspirins for his headache. When she told him they ought to start getting a car on instalments before the holidays, he got it.

They kept to the main roads because side lanes would be bad for the car. They were going to the Land's End because Katherine wanted to see it; the Moseleys were touring and thought they might come around that way, and the Inghams had taken a cottage near St. Ives. There seemed to be a great many cars about, more than there had been two years before, and more hikers, and more men and girls in shorts on bicycles. Robert's eye was on the road, he hadn't much time to look at scenery. TEAS and petrol pumps and khaki shorts. Over Bodmin moor a line of pylons caught his eye; it must have followed them down, but it showed more in the open, treeless country. At the Land's End they parked in a big enclosure full of cars. They walked down past the hotels on to the narrowing headland and parched grass. "Don't go too near the edge," Robert said anxiously. From where they were standing they couldn't see much in the way of cliffs. There were a number of people picnicking and standing about. "So that's Land's End," Katherine said. "I call it over-rated." She bought some postcards and posted them to the Jenkinses and Timsons and Francises.

They got into the car again and started back.

GERTRUDE EILEEN TREVELYAN

They went round by St. Ives, to see if the Inghams were still there. The line of pylons met them again, riding the crest of a carn; cut down towards them across the moor, across the site of a British village, their iron legs straddling a prehistoric burial ground, one foot on a gorse-grown Roman road. Queer thing, Robert thought. Men with clubs in huts — round huts they had, where these circles are — one with a roof somewhere — Romans marching — all roads lead to Rome — what happened down here after that? Tin mines, and nothing — mostly nothing — then these things planted in the bog and me driving under them in a car.

"Bit inappropriate," he said jerking his head at the pylons.

Neolithic man and Robert Thomas.

"Hm. Wonder if the Inghams will be there."

Robert thought, funny thing time. Meant to do something about it, one time. He wondered what had happened to that thing he'd been going to write. Made a lot of notes. Must be somewhere about.

Fortified hill tops and huddled huts and high sun altars; Phoenicians mining for tin, carving huge Asiatic faces on the tall cliffs; Roman legions cutting roads; coal mining and clay mining; medieval Christianity in the fertile valleys, saints and holy wells, and the high moors left to sun and fog; rackrent farms and fishing villages, discovery by artists and invasion by the arty, and Tom, Dick and Harry in their baby cars, and TEAS and campers; and consternation in the camps, shorts and long faces, and a warm solid Cornish voice in the yard of Penzance Station, "Dollfuss is murdered."

Robert was back at the factory. The war hadn't come as everybody thought it would. Brooklands speed records. German plebiscite. Heil Hitler. May hadn't come back from his holiday, it was rumoured he was ill, he'd been very queer before he left. Robert was put in to take his place, Chief's assistant, Robert had had more experience than most of them. Stork entangled in high tension wires stops Warsaw broadcast, whole valley in Lake district is flooded to provide water for Sheffield, ancient manor submerged: fertile quiet fields sodden, turned to slime, under mud, stone walls green-slimed, crumbled, water gushing from a tap over a greasy sink in a foetid oil-clothed scullery; belt system introduced into railway works throws out thirteen hundred men. May wasn't coming back, they said he had had a breakdown. Robert got his job permanently, and a rise.

Robert didn't like to think of May's breakdown. He thought he must have been near having one himself, back in the spring. He found May's job easier than his own, although the work was more exacting. He did most of the Chief's work while the Chief was out at conferences or meetings of departments, but he was able to work in the Chief's private room partitioned off at the end of the laboratory. It was a long time since he had been alone. He could still feel, or thought he could, the pounding of the machines, and the lorries still changed gear outside the window, but his face twitched less often when there was nobody to see it twitch, and the telephone bell didn't irritate him so much when he could answer it himself. At the end of the day he slumped in the tube and let it rock him back to town. Launch of the *Queen Mary*, two hundred and sixty-five killed at Gresford; broadcast during parachute descent, New York–California plane meets shower of meteors; Communists and Fascists in Paris street battle, Fascists at Manchester; Soviet's new giant industry, German reprisals after plebiscite; Russia joins League, armed Soviet plane in Manchuria. He didn't much care. His nerve was dulled. He thought the holiday must have done him good. He sat back slack and let the tube rock him back to Kath.

Katherine said, "Now you're earning more we ought to have a better flat."

"Flat?" he said. He had got used to it. He had got used to sitting inside himself in the evenings, in the crampy room. The crampiness of it had got on his nerves at first but lately he'd got used to it, he'd found a way of sitting inside himself. He remembered he used to crave for space, some chance of getting alone and thinking things out. Still, about time they did get a bigger flat. Settled down. More of a family flat.

"Not a bad idea," he said. "You look round."

He was glad to leave it to Kath. He had enough to do. He was glad she didn't bother him to look at flats on Saturdays and Sundays. He went to the factory and came back and took a hand at bridge and sat with the paper on his knee and dozed, and drove out to a road-house with Kath and the Jenkinses or the Francises, and took a hand at bridge and went to the factory on Monday morning; he was glad Kath was doing the looking round.

London to Dublin airline, world's largest telescope in America, news pictures by wireless from Australia in twenty-five minutes; London to Istanbul motor road, air mail to Australia, American chemists make artificial blood; Katherine, in the snow, was looking round Westminster and Chelsea and Kensington and Knightsbridge, but she had her eye on Mayfair.

The tube pushed Robert out to the factory and dragged him back to bridge. Four-forty miles per hour air speed, pedestrian crossings for London, new oil engine on roads; explosion in Bourbon factory, bombing plane crashes in Belgium, East End tramcar collision. And pushed him out and dragged him back. Oil-well set fire to in Germany, bomb for King Carol on railway, bomb thrown at president of Cuba, Communists sentenced at Dortmund, Duce: "This century is ours." Fascists fight at Tufnell Park. And pushed and dragged. Naval talks in London, Japanese outline proposals, proposals rejected by Washington; Germany launches the *Deutschland*, Italy laying two battleships, thirty-five thousand-ton cruisers, Belgium's fortified frontiers, Britain's gun-turrets on bombers, Alexander is murdered at Marseilles....

The King of Italy in the royal yacht, October 1934, cruises in the eastern Mediterranean, goes ashore at Port Said and Aden and makes a tour of Italian possessions in the Red Sea.

Robert wasn't bothering so much about things: he began to think about them. "Queer that assassination," he said, "The Yugoslavian chap, so soon after Dollfuss. Only two strong men in eastern Europe. And then Albert of Belgium, back in the spring."

"That was an accident," Katherine said.

"All who stood for peace," he said, taking no notice.

Katherine said, "When we move we ought to get rid of this old furniture and get something fresh."

"All right," he said, "you see to it."

National Housing Committee's scheme for a million new houses, oriental music banned in Turkey, fish trapped in New York bathtubs, seadromes proposed as air ports for transatlantic air service, London's most modern building: walls of cork and glass. Kath, in the fog, looking round furniture show-rooms and discussing deferred terms.

Spy executions secret in Germany, American marchers shot down by machine guns, deserting sailor's family banished from Russia; German meat shops closed by Nazis, Fascist education rests on book and rifle, bombs in Arizona for Asiatic settlers;

Forty-two warships for U.S.A., French troops ready for the Saar, Japan's air bases in Pacific; German air speed-up,

British air push;

German robot aeroplane, Soviet troops fortify Far East....

More speed in the air, latest World Atlas includes the stratosphere, longest escalator in the world in course of construction at Leicester Square, excavator can dig three thousand six hundred cubic feet in nine minutes, scientists succeed in weighing atoms, Katherine at the back of a crowd in the Mall stands for four hours and peers round backs of people peering round backs to see the procession for the Royal wedding.

"It'll be the Jubilee next year," she said, "we ought to have seats."

She hadn't managed Mayfair quite. She found a block not far from Marble Arch — not quite on the Park, but so that you could think it was. She told. Robert it was a good address, "You ought to have a good address

"Bayswater."

"Not really," she said, quite annoyed.

The block had an entrance hall of chromium and black tiles and a commissionaire and a lift: it was all very new and shiny. The flat had two small rooms, one leading out of the other: you couldn't get to the bedroom except through the sitting-room or to the bathroom except through the sitting-room and bedroom; the kitchenette was tucked into a corner behind the hall-door. But that was Kath's look-out. Good job.

"We shan't want to cook," she said, "there's a restaurant in the basement."

When he looked at the place he could feel the anger rushing up hot to his head. "What's the good of spending more to be cooped up like this? You said you were getting something bigger."

"Not bigger: better. Where we are now is an old block. Not pre-war of course, but quite ten years old."

"How's this any better?"

"Don't be silly. Can't you see it's only been up a few months?"

"What do you want it bigger for," she said. "It only makes work.

"Unless you want a regular service flat," she said, with a harsh sideways look. "That's what we *ought* to have."

His anger went and left him depressed and tired. He didn't much care what they had so long as Kath was satisfied: so long as he could have the place quiet to himself now and then, when she went out. He didn't get much chance of that when they first moved in. Kath had the place full every night, she had to show it to everyone she knew.

The floors and walls were all made of polished wood, and the cupboards and wireless and cocktail cabinet and writing bureau and as much of the furniture as possible was built-in, flush with the wall. When it was all shut you would have said there was nothing in the room but the chairs of steel tubing Kath had put there, and one skin rug on the floor and the steel-legged table for breakfast in the dining alcove with steel stools to sit on.

Robert had a feeling there was something wrong about that metal furniture in that room: it didn't look right, even if you liked that kind of thing. It wasn't so new as all that, either; he could remember years ago...

All at once he remembered where he had seen steel furniture before. That was it, What-was-her-name. He stared for a moment, puzzled, and then he put back his head and laughed. Sheila!

That was it, that night he was tight, that Bond Street flat; when this sort of thing first came in, before you saw it in the shops. Poor old Kath, she thought she was modern, she'd gone one ahead of Rita Jenkins. She'd wanted this stuff for years. She didn't know Robert had seen it back in — when was it: 1928? — in Sheila's flat. She'd throw a fit if she knew about him that night. She didn't even know steel was dead, five years back. What was Sheila sitting on by now? Cork, or banana skins.

He grinned. The thought of Sheila made him feel young. Hadn't felt so young for years. He wondered if that dancing place was still going. Wondered if he'd find her there if he went along. Or someone else.

Kath came under the archway from the bedroom, she was dressed for the evening. "Aren't you going to get ready? They'll be here in twenty minutes."

He got up with a start and went through into the bathroom.

It amused him to see Kath showing off the flat: careless about it but hoping they would notice it all: showing off her steel furniture, five years out of date. Poor old Kath, slipped up over the steel tubes. For a bit he played with the idea of going along sometime to look for that dancing place, but it was so unquestionably certain that he never would that before the evening was half through he was tired of the pretence. In another half-hour he had even stopped being amused at Kath.

League force for the Saar, Franco-Soviet commercial agreement, Italo-Abyssinian relations strained — Where's Abyssinia? — Abyssinian losses at Wal-Wal, Italian Government seizes securities, Mussolini on importance of fighting. Göring professes friendship with Britain, Memel trial begins at Kovno, executions by the Soviets, Japan renounces Washington treaty, Italy wants French land in Africa, Abyssinia complains to League....

Proficiency in rifle shooting to be compulsory for all students, men and women, of German universities, Land Year for every German child, "Blood and soil." Italian boy Fascists to carry rifles, "Book and rifle." Blood and mud.

"When I think," said Grant, shuffling the cards and cutting to his wife, "of what the world will be like for the next generation, I can't be too glad we've no child of our own."

Robert didn't mind Grant so much. Kath had got hold of the Grants since they moved to Bayswater. Mrs. Grant was a big, showy woman who went about a lot and belonged to clubs and played golf. Grant was a decent chap.

Robert said, "You're right."

He'd thought like that once himself. Maybe there was something in it. Maybe Kath was right, after all: but he couldn't help feeling she was right for the wrong reason.

Italy looks forward with confidence to the New Year: "the Fascist state firmly entrenched": projected Franco-Italian pact. Hitler, at the opening of the third Nazi year, recapitulates his work: "an unparalleled mobilisation of human forces"; on January 4th calls a secret meeting of leaders. Ramsay MacDonald acclaims "the nation's return to health"; a mounting home market; brighter peace prospects, advance without revolution.

Two thousand five hundred miners strike at York. Prisoners mutiny at Glasgow. Wild scenes in the Commons: strangers' gallery is cleared by the police.

Germany prepares for the Saar plebiscite. Germany triumphs in Saar plebiscite. Germany is looking for expansion to the East. German troops are massed near Memel. Lithuania is uneasy. Russia seeks to revive Eastern Locarno pact: All-Union Congress of Soviets is warned of "immediate danger of war." Japan is looking for expansion in China. Italy is looking for expansion in Africa: increased anxiety in Abyssinia: gun trained on Union Jack at Wal-Wal.

Robert would twist round in his steel-framed chair and switch off the wireless: the set built into the scrubbed oak panelling. It got on his nerves: the news, and the foreign stations jabbering nineteen to the dozen in languages he couldn't understand, and dance tunes and occasional bursts of military music.

New French destroyer breaks world speed record; Swiss Socialist Party adopts a policy of national defence; profits for Krupps, annual report shows fifty-six per cent increase in business chiefly from home trade. Vienna sentries equipped with gas-masks. Nazis murder German exile in Prague. Eve of Bulgarian military dictatorship. Soviet air fleet increased by three hundred and thirty per cent in four years. Firearms seized in Calcutta. New defence works for Singapore. Japanese and Chinese fight near the Great Wall. United States place uninhabited Pacific islands under control of naval authorities. Revolution in Uruguay. Martial law in Louisiana. Mechanised infantry and anti-tank platoon for the British Army.

Within eight days three extinct volcanoes become active in India, South Africa and Italy.

"Now why do you suppose that is?" said Grant.

"Couldn't say."

"I thought you scientific fellows knew all about it." Katherine piped up in her high, society voice, "Robert used to be keen on science and that kind of thing. But he seems to have got tired of it, I don't know why."

French armies concentrated on the Saar frontier and German armies concentrated on Memel. Russia fortifying the Far East against Japan, Japanese boats in American waters. America afraid of Japan and Japan afraid of Russia and Russia afraid of Germany and Germany pretending to be afraid of France: Italian troops massing in Eritrea and Abyssinia arming in fear of Italy and South American republics arming against one another. Small black tight-ranked ant-like armies marching on the smooth empty surface of the globe, and the globe rumbling and seething inside like a huge shut furnace, shooting out a tongue of fire now and then through a crack. Robert turns in his steely skeleton chair and twiggles the knob of the wireless. Blah-blah-blah-vous-venez-d'entendre, blah-blah-blah il-duce-blah-blah, tum-TUM-tum-tum-TUM-blah-blah-Moscow, b'rum-b'rum-b'rum-Heil-Hitler! Tum-ti-tum-ti-tum-TUM, LIT-tle man you've HAD a busy day.

He took to listening to wireless talks on astronomy. He took to reading again on the nights Kath was out playing bridge without him: sitting with his one glass of whisky by the shut-off wireless, reading Jeans and Wells. He would sit up reading after Kath had gone to bed on the other side of the archway, in the bedroom that was more like an alcove. He would sit up for a bit in his wooden box, by the let-in, disguised, almost invisible electric radiator, with the green oiled-silk curtains drawn at his back. He read *An Experiment with Time*, and wondered whether that was the kind of thing he'd meant to do, once, when he'd thought of doing something about Time. He thought not. When he came to think about it he didn't know quite what he *had* meant to do. He didn't know even now just what it was that had hung at the back of his mind for so long and seemed so well worth catching on to. It was a pity in a way he hadn't been able to catch it. He wondered what had happened to his notes. Took a lot of notes. Kath must have chucked them out or they'd got lost in one of the moves. Something like that. It couldn't be helped. It wouldn't have been much use. He would have liked to do it: he would have liked to have done it: he would have liked to have worked out some scheme to make a bit of sense out of things. He had thought once he'd seen some meaning in the way things were, but then he'd lost it. He would have liked to do something, just to have done it. He hadn't done much. If he had done it it wouldn't have been much use, but he would have liked to have done it.

He lifted his chair back to where Kath liked it, crossways between the radiator and the window, and took his empty glass to the kitchenette and put it tidily on the slab, and carefully put out the lights and tiptoed past the end of the bed in the dark and switched on the light in the bathroom.

Machine solves mathematical problems; synthetic diamonds made in London; electric waves speed up the growth of crops in Russia; motor roads cross the desert to Mecca; Indian pilgrims travel in motor buses; the Olympic Games will be held at Tokyo in 1940.

"1940? We shall all be blown to blazes before 1940."

Bust of Hitler carved from two and a half tons of basalt lava will take some months to complete, Colossus of Rome — Mussolini two hundred and thirteen foot high in bronze — to be ready in two years, Italy mobilises, rebellion in Greece, fighting in Bucharest, machine guns in Vienna streets, Göring sees Pilsudski.

Germany builds submarine without batteries, America spends two million pounds on air base scheme: "twenty-five thousand of the hundred thousand Japanese in California are capable of going under arms to-morrow"; Italy "can mobilise thirty-seven classes with a total strength of from seven to eight millions"; " the Red Army has all that is necessary for victory if she is attacked," six thousand five hundred million roubles assigned to the army for 1935; German birthrate up; gas-warfare: "if a single drop fell on the clothing the entire skin of the victim would be burnt off in a few seconds." Italian troops embark. A London evening paper: "we can with clear conscience fold our hands and await the news on the wireless."

Scrawled in chalk on a wall in Kilburn: MIND BRITAINS BUSINESS.

Relief cut, protest in South Wales, dole riot in Sheffield, relief office stormed by unemployed in Cumberland, more disturbances in the Midlands, Means Test demonstration in Hyde Park.

Full Jubilee programme.

Big stores' higher profits; rail dividend up; six million eight hundred and eighty-eight thousand radio licences in force, town council installs gramophones for funerals, eight hundred and fifty-seven million phone calls in London last year, fool-proof air taxi for eighty pounds.

Belfast to Croydon in two hours, London to Amsterdam in sixty-two minutes, Europe to South America in two days, world's largest airship on the floor of the Pacific:

"Blown up," he said. "The thing will have to stop. The whole damn machine's going so fast it'll blow itself up."

To Newcastle by train in two hundred and thirty-seven minutes, by air to Zurich in four hours, Rome to Paris in three hours. Blue Bird does two-seventy m.p.h., Sohn flies twelve thousand feet under his own power at Daytona Beach, stratosphere flight Los Angeles to Ohio, parachutist dies at thirty thousand feet Copenhagen, phone talks with Tokyo, Blue Bird does two-eight-one m.p.h., suicide from air liner.

Plane suicide at Basle, Hamburg gasworks spend a quarter of a million to prevent gas suicides, carload of opium for Paris, thousand drug arrests in New York, plane suicide at Toronto, three million with nervous breakdown in Great Britain, suicide for fear of poison gas, insomnia the curse of modern life.

Berlin air-raid trials, Hitler's hoarseness prevents Simon's visit, Germany introduces conscription, Eden in Moscow, Moscow toasts the King, eleven hundred Soviet arrests due to German conscription, Italy's call to arms, another twenty-two million eight hundred and fifty for French air force, Hitler's photograph for Simon; pit riot at Wrexham, Cumberland shepherd electrocuted, ten ton bell for 1936 Olympic games cast in Berlin, seven hundred million eggs a year from China, talking films for Africa, British West Indians pledge themselves to fight against Mussolini, Hauptmann's New York home to become museum, explosion at Southampton oil depot heard twenty miles away....

It was only when he was drunk that he had seen any meaning in it.

Southampton explosion said to have been caused by a small bubble of sulphuretted hydrogen formed on the roof of a tank. The advancing Sahara threatens two hundred square miles of West Africa.

"Nature," he said, "that's it. Nature taking revenge. Like those buried continents." The damned machine blowing itself up and nature covering the wreckage, tidily, with sea and sand.

He had read somewhere that the universe was slowing down. That life on the earth flared up, as it were, in belts of a few million years between the ice ages. Protozoa, like jelly-fishes, in swamps; and then the protozoa frozen out, only a few holding on, adapting to conditions: the world getting warm again and reptiles where the protozoa had been. A few thousand centuries of basking reptiles. Then ice again, and only a few intelligent reptiles compromising with the new conditions, lumbering out on legs from the freezing swamps. Mammoths.

That was Wells, that about the ice ages, Not the part

about slowing down. Wells didn't believe in slowing down, he believed in progress. No such thing as progress. Look at the world now. Only civilisations coming up and falling back. "Modern man may have existed a million years ago in Africa." If that was so the negroes had had their day. They weren't a young race coming up. An old race, exhausted. Remnants of the first civilisation, back before Egypt. Might account for the Atlantis legend? If that was so there wouldn't be anything in what people said about a black rising, black against white, universal rallying to Abyssinia. If that were the case most of the races had had their day. Japan to come up: Japanese World Empire. That was about all. Then it would be about time for another ice age. Even Wells admitted that: another ice age coming. And after that what would crawl up out of the melting ice? Not man. This was the age of man. And not super-men. Why should it be? Man isn't a super-reptile.

Something quite different. Adapted to new conditions of life on earth.

Because the resources of the earth were being used up: coal, oil, and finally water: water being used for power. Power being gradually drained from the earth, used up for speed and armaments and an increasing number of trivial, unnecessary purposes. Every housewife putting on an electric iron in her kitchen using up a bit of power from the earth's centre. Like a lunatic on a tree, sawing off the branch he sits on. The world living on its capital.

The world gradually losing its heat, losing its vitality, turning more slowly, running down. The machine running down. Humanity blowing itself up; one civilisation after another blowing itself up and another coming on, building on the ruins, using up power, hurrying on the end. Not making much difference. A few million years or so.

Because the earth was growing colder in any case. Once there'd been tropical forests and swamps as far north as Scotland. Colder after each ice age. Whatever came next, after man, would have a much smaller world to people.

Man would stand a better chance in a way than the protozoa and the reptiles and the mammoths. He would be more adaptable. As the ice crept down he would build cold-resisting houses and heat them up, hotter and hotter, by electric power and hardly go out except in electrically heated cars. He would tend to huddle along the equator and wait for better times. Probably a fair number of him would survive, but by the time the cold had passed he would have ceased to be man. He would have learned to breathe very little or not at all in his heated burrows, and he would have had no use for legs. He would only need a long fore-finger for pressing buttons. Or a pair of small flippers like a penguin's would be enough, to roll him into his heated, padded car which would shoot along the corridors of gigantic indoor flat-towns. With the limited space of the habitable world he would seldom need to reproduce. He might grow an enormous brain or none at all. But in one respect he would be worse off than the mammoths or the reptiles or even the protozoa: he would not have adapted himself to the natural conditions of his world. Man, by his intelligence, would have given his successor artificial means of life, and as the earth's supply of power dwindled these rolling, button-pressing penguins would die out. And a good job too.

And a few small, decayed, over-looked forms of life would crawl for a time in the thinning belt of pine-trees on the equator and in turn be frozen out, and the earth would revolve always more slowly, for vast ages, quite empty in space, and pieces would break off, and the whole lump of dead matter, without sufficient speed to hold it in suspension, would fall through space and go on falling.

But at this moment, as if no such thing were ever going to happen, Robert with his glass of whisky and Katherine patting her permanent wave and Jenkins dealing the cards and Rita Jenkins being sweet and catty about the curtains and Ted Tims selling papers in the Haymarket and Tom Tod cranking up his lorry on the Great West Road and Miss Prim conferring with the Vicar about the Sunday School Jubilee celebrations at Little Toddleton, and ten Nazi guards chasing a Jew down a street in Berlin and an Abyssinian chief sharpening his sword outside his mud hut and waving it at the sky because he has been told that that way Mussolini will come, and Mussolini and Hitler and the leader-writer of the *Evening Shriek*, are turning over in space at the rate of 365.2563 revolutions a year and not one of them except Robert seems to think it strange.

Katherine hadn't quite dropped the Jenkinses. She said they were restful. She liked to have them in for a quiet evening now and then when she wasn't doing anything with the Grants or the Kleins — Klein was Roy Francis' chief at Provincial Periodicals — or the Kalmanns. The Kalmanns were friends of the Kleins'. Mr. Kalmann was something quite big in the City, a Company Promoter. If Robert hadn't been so mopey and stupid when Katherine took him to the Kalmanns', Kalmann might have promoted Robert.

It was restful sometimes to have a quiet evening and be able to wear her older frocks — unless she had a *very* new one to show Rita — and listen to poor Rita's chatter. Poor Rita was almost the only one of Katherine's friends now who wasn't intellectual. Marian Grant belonged to discussion groups on housing and birth-control at the Ladies' Coliseum Club, and Lucie Klein was keen on *avant-garde* films, and the

Inghams, of course, were Art, and Hetta Kalmann was terribly keen on German-Jewish refugees.

The Kalmanns had a large house in St. John's Wood. They gave dance recitals for Jewish refugee dancers and exhibitions for Jewish refugee painters and afternoon receptions for haggard, underfed and usually female ex-German university professors. Everybody who was anybody came to the Kalmanns' receptions. Evangeline Todd — the Honourable Evangeline Todd — and Mrs. John Applepen. John Applepen was a Parliamentary Private Secretary.

The Kleins had a big house too, in Bloomsbury, and entertained a lot. They knew the Levys, who ran an Art Cinema Society and lived at Golders Green, and the Levys knew Ben Rothsberg, who managed a big chain of commercial cinemas and lived at Regent's Park. And the Applepens had a flat in Westminster. The Todds lived in Curzon Street, but they never asked Katherine to anything.

Speed planes for French frontier, submarines for Germany, Russia develops the Arctic Circle, Fascism in Japan, United States manoeuvres in the Pacific, Italy builds "air city," Rumania orders arms, Russia's air force, fireworks factory explosion in Bombay.

A hundred and fifty thousand seats for Jubilee.

Two million German citizens in uniform, German aeroplane manufactures, German plane down in Italy, Italy charges Abyssinia with preparing for war, gas-masks for French babies, air raid shelter directions.

Jubilee procession to be enlarged, Jubilee medals. Empire and Jubilee. Jubilee medals dumped from abroad.

Paris air defence plans, Germany's three thousand seven hundred military aerodromes, German expelled from Russia, Abyssinia's new note to League.

Jubilee seats, Jubilee drives, flood-lighting for Jubilee; 109,410 fewer unemployed, new factories, increasing output, seven thousand children to see royal drive.

Secret German battleships, Göring on Germany's secret air force, France claims bigger air force than Germany's, Britain's answer to Germany, first "gravest debate on foreign affairs since 1914."

Seventeen hundred bonfires, twenty-six thousand to guard royal route, Empire comes to London, 131,593 fewer unemployed, Britain's electricity record, new era for steel trade, rail speed-up, more work all round, Jubilee seats, Jubilee drives, Jubilee mugs, Jubilee decorations, Jubilee crowds, bunting gazing in the rain, traffic jams in West End, vast crowds in streets all-night vigil of thousands on route of procession.

From their seats in a third-floor window they could see almost the whole length of Fleet Street, he and Kath. Kath had made him take seats and he wasn't sorry, it was something to see. Something to have seen. Kath was a bit annoyed he'd taken these seats in Fleet Street, the Kleins were in the Mall and the Kalmanns had a first-floor in Piccadilly, but this was good enough for him. Leaning out they could see the yellow sanded ribbon of road stretching in both directions and the crowds on the opposite pavement and the huge packed newspaper buildings facing them, all window. Every few minutes, as the sun grew stronger, somebody in the crowd fainted and was fetched out, carried along the road and back through the crowd again, up a side-street, out of sight. The crowd was a long way below them, black and packed, like packed, black beetles. A woman in a red hat was trying to climb on top of a letter-box and sit on it with a newspaper under her: each time she had nearly got her knees on the round, red, slippery top she slipped back or the newspaper slipped. Suddenly the crowd began to laugh, away to the left towards Temple Bar, and the laugh ran along the pavements like fire along a dry forest trail. The dog was small and yellow. Dog got loose. He ran like mad down the middle of the sanded empty roadway between the packed crowds and the laughter ran alongside him like fire along a row of hay ricks. His tongue was hanging out and however fast he ran the laughter ran faster: it was behind and alongside and in front, waiting for him. He ran past and on, and the laughter ran past and on, to the right, towards St. Paul's; and round his panting, panic-driven body there was all England building bonfires, and the North Sea and Belgium and France and the English Channel, and beyond that there was the Atlantic and Iceland and Norway and Sweden and Germany — Hitler addressing two hundred and seventy thousand members of the Youth Movement in the Lustgarten, Berlin — and Spain and the Atlantic, and further still Greenland and the Arctic Ocean and Russia — May Day military parade in the Red Square, three thousand planes and three thousand tanks — and Arabia and Egypt and the Sahara and Atlantic, and the Arctic Circle and Siberia and Manchuria and China and India and the Congo and Brazil and the Middle West and Alaska, and the North Pacific and New Guinea and the Indian Ocean and Cape Colony and the Argentine and the South Pacific, and the whole lot was whizzing round on its axis in such a way that the dog and the crowd and the troops and St. Paul's and the first distant royal carriage starting along Constitution Hill were all rushing headlong or sidelong upon the Steppes and would be occupying space now covered by the Rocky Mountains within the next twelve hours. The dog was much more afraid of the crowd's laughter, and the crowd was much more interested in the plumed head-dresses of foreign

diplomats and in minor members of the Royal Family sliding by in closed cars.

A band was playing *Pack Up Your Troubles*, and part of
the crowd, the part that was old enough to remember the
words — not more than half, not even that — was joining
in the chorus. The band changed to *Colonel Bogey*, played
it through and stopped. People at the back of the crowd,
against the walls, were getting on to tiptoe, the troops lining
the pavements stood to attention; the roadway was empty.
Be here any time now.

"What's that?" said Robert. A splash of red had caught
his eye, across the street to the right. From where he was sitting he could only see the end of something red, like a ban-
ner, and a word or syllable in white block letters: WORK...
Something that hadn't been there before. "What's..." he
began, leaning forward, but Katherine jogged his elbow. She
hadn't seen anything. She was too busy holding on to her
hat and wondering whether those really were the Timsons in
that window opposite.

Here they come!

Far up the street to the left he could see the carriage
with the King and Queen. They came at a good pace down
the middle of the yellow sanded road and the cheering ran
alongside them like fire along thatch. They came by and the
cheering came by and had passed, and he was leaning far out
watching the carriage draw away with the cheering up the
long narrow sunny track towards St. Paul's.

He was leaning from a balcony, looking down on a wet,
dark crowd packed behind a barrier which was drawn across
the end of Sussex Gardens. From the balcony he could see
on both sides of the barrier. Behind it the crowd was black
and packed solid over the road, between drawn-up cars and

the big, leafless trees. On the other side was the long, narrow vista of Oxford and Cambridge Terrace, empty road and packed, black pavements: he could see the purple pennons drooping from a stand on the corner, and presently the Earl Marshal on foot, alone, between the shining dripping umbrellas that filled the pavements, coming down the long straight empty street in the rain.

Katherine thought John Applepen might have asked them to a window in Whitehall. Finally they'd taken this first-floor balcony with the Jenkinses, near Paddington: because Robert said he couldn't pay more and Katherine said she wouldn't be any higher than the first floor, this time. Robert would rather have been farther up. It was too near the crowd. He could almost feel them shoving and shuffling, tightening around him. Although he knew he could go back into the house if he wanted to, each time the crowd swayed — swaying under its own weight — up against the shut gate of the garden under the balcony, he felt trapped, as if he were down there: as if they'd be over him, if the gate went.

A narrow ledge ran along the barrier, half-way up, and the first row of the crowd had their hands on the ledge, ready to jump up when something happened. Every few minutes a policeman in a shiny black mackintosh cape edged his feet along the ledge, the hands went down in front of his boots and sprang up again behind and the crowd laughed. The sound of the bands came from a distance and the first row was up, clinging to the top; the policeman was driving them off and people were laughing, farther back. While the first troops were passing in the wet, empty road, the policeman was pushing along, clearing the ledge, and the crowd was springing up behind him like trodden, wiry grass.

The garden gate was down. They were through; swarming

up over the black, wintry flowerbeds. The crowd was swaying and pressing in a solid mass under the balcony and across the road; the line of railings was lost in the crowd. People were running, farther back, down the street, closing up the gaps.

As the dark, white-flecked block of bluejackets came into sight far up the terrace, around the corner from Edgware Road, the crowd was up on the barrier like bees swarming, four or five deep, second and third rows clinging to the front, and fourth and fifth, holding on for a minute and giving a shout or a gasp or a giggle and dropping off. The slow, steady tramp of the sailors came nearer and the white, drawn ropes, stiff as ramrods. The police on the barrier pushed at the crowd and somebody called Blackguards and somebody called Hush, and there was a burst of laughter when somebody clambered out of reach of the police and somebody fell off. People at the windows were hissing Hush.

"Hush," hissed Katherine indignantly. She was wondering whether the rain would make the dye run on to her face from the new black hat. The first line of bluejackets was wheeling at the corner.

He hadn't expected it to be like that. He hadn't thought about it. If he had been asked he would most likely have said it would be a big, tomb-like business, gilt, with purple hangings, what-would-they-call-it, a catafalque. Something high; the centre-piece of the procession. He hadn't expected an ordinary coffin. He hadn't expected anything; but when the coffin, plain and small and drawn with perfect ease, drawn like nothing, low down on the gun-carriage, rounded the corner, he was surprised at its smallness. Such a small coffin. The size of a man. The coffin of a quite ordinary man, who had lived and grown tired and died; but because he had been a king (and because there was only one crowned head to every 153 million, 846 thousand odd of the world's inhabitants) five million people were pushing and struggling in the streets of London, or paying out guineas for seats, or crushing one another to exhaustion and even to death in Hyde Park, and breaking police cordons and storming barriers and giving way unwillingly behind the linked rifles and straining muscles of guardsmen, to catch one glimpse of the heads of the gun-team. The real thing, that was it, that was what got them. The real thing, for once: not a picture. Because by now — potted, canned, congealed, synthetic, "cultured" — hardly anything was real. The real, living gun-team — men who had got up that morning and shined their boots and had breakfast and were digesting it — and the real, solid, wooden coffin. Like frenzied film-fans mobbing a star. Gaping wonder of the many at the one, the single, the unique; at the actual, fleshly being, or had-being, of something that had existed for them only in mechanical representations: on the screen, the wireless. Synthetic foods, canned education, "cultured" emotions, potted lives. Soon, he was thinking, they wouldn't be able to have this kind of thing anymore. All ceremonies would have to take place in private, be followed only on the wireless or films. Television, that's how they'd do it. As crowds get bigger still, he thought. Mechanised humanity had grown too big, it was too much for any individual to cope with. The concerted, concentrated, centri-focused attention of a huge, mechanised crowd would be enough to kill its object, just as well with cheers or idle curiosity as with rage and boos. He looked around him at the crowd, below and alongside. Machine-made man, even now: man miraculously multiplied since the growth of machines. Multiplied and transported until in his numbers he became a menace to any single fleshly thing his wonder fastened on. Like that dog: tongue-hanging, panicked lope between the packed pavements. Just look at them here. What was once the population of a country, herding into a few streets, packed and dangerously swaying. All of them, really, honestly sorry the king was dead; but that didn't prevent their laughing down the police and scuffling and trampling. And nearly all of them, too, taken separately — that was the funny part of it — peaceable, unassuming people: but menacing in numbers, with the blind, mindless sway of crowds. Quiet, peace-loving, law-respecting Tom Smith, without a word to say for himself at the office and always polite to the bus conductor, breaking down somebody's gate and trampling somebody's flowerbeds, just because Charlie Jones and Ted Brown (whom he doesn't know) are doing the same thing at the same time. And Mrs. Robinson, who's so mild she doesn't like to complain to the butcher about the meat. Football crowds — man pushed to death on railings — and racing crowds and sales crowds, snatching, and election crowds, and scuffling, angry, demonstrating crowds. Karl Schmidt and Ivan Petrovitch and Giovanni Rossi, fond of their homes and fond of a quiet, companionable drink of an evening: multiply them by the hundred thousand, and there they are marching and shouting in the Lustgarten, the Red Square, the Piazza Venezia; marching on Lithuania, on Manchuria, on Abyssinia. Marching and shouting and menacing, swayed and swaying, pushing, crushing, hunting down. Behind the small, plain coffin sliding out of sight between the dripping trees.

Banked, blank faces white and small among black clothes and odd, dipping, black umbrellas. Tom Smith and Ted Brown and Charlie Jones. And Violet Jones and Maud Brown and Gladys Smith. Each, whether he sits in an office or stands in a shop or runs with papers in the street or unloads food at the dock or carts it or sells it or buys it or eats it, or goes to the pictures or the dogs, or presses a lift button or punches a bell or screws a nut on each of an infinite series of identical objects, a centre of countless concentric circles spreading out and out, a cog on the circumference of countless intersecting, interlocking wheels. All the wheels turning and grinding and gathering speed: one vast, intricate machine, speeding up, quicker and quicker, running on man-power, running with loudening roar and grind through space to nothing.

What man had come to. It was a pity man had come to that.

It was a pity they'd all come to this. Come to think of it. Kath with her tight, metallic waves — Henna application. Why? — and massaged smile, and her varnished hands dealing out the cards. Poor old Kath running to keep up, running after the tantalising, flicking tail of modernity, in and out of beauty salons and smart highbrow lectures, panting and hard and bitter. And himself. He could see himself in one of the frameless mirror panels in the oak wall. Tired and twitching and with ridiculous shell-rimmed spectacles and getting thin on top and groomed slick, in a dinner jacket. Odd thing that: he could only see himself from the outside, and he knew Kath through and through. He was fond of old Kath. But he hadn't loved her for a long time now, and she didn't love him, yet he hadn't left her; not out of virtue or as a matter of principle but because it would have disturbed his routine. And he hadn't even been unfaithful to her, since they'd been married. He would have had to make an opportunity, and it had never seemed worthwhile.

He had given up his work — his own work, his real work — to make money for a home and a youngster; and he'd given up the youngster to please Kath; and he'd lost Kath to money and modernity, to the machine; and Kath had taken the home with her. There wasn't much the machine hadn't had from him. He'd thought once it was the want of money that did it, but he had plenty of money now and it was just the same. There'd been a time when he used to believe in things, and in Kath, and in himself, and now he didn't believe in anything. He'd dropped himself, some-where, long ago.

It was true he hadn't been worth much. He hadn't been able to do a lot. And if he had it wouldn't have been worth doing, most likely. It wasn't of great importance. It was a bit of a pity, but it didn't matter much.

Katherine was saying, with her loud, hard laugh, "Rob-ert's got some theory the world's running down. Or blowing up. I forget which."

Mrs. Grant chuckled hoarsely but Grant gave him a shrewd look. Robert's mouth twitched painfully at them, into a smile. "It doesn't much matter," he said.

He'd get a bit older, and so would Kath. She'd want a bit more henna and a bit more massage, and when the Italians won, as they obviously would, she'd take up Abyssinians instead of German Jews and then she'd take up something else. In time Livingsby would retire and Robert might get his job, he'd be a little bit older and a bit more tired and he'd have a little less hair and he'd care a little bit less that he'd never done any of the things he'd wanted to, and they'd be able to have a newer flat, and a newer and a newer flat, and Kath would want a plane instead of a car. There'd be regular air services to New York and stratosphere races for aviators, and he'd be a bit older and pretty bald and Kath would have a transformation, and then there'd be regular stratosphere services and the record breakers would be higher up still, in rockets, and Kath would want a stratosphere cruise in the summer instead of a trip by air.

And then he'd be dead, and so would Kath. Even Kath would be dead. And there'd be regular services by rocket to New York, and the aviators would be god-knows-where, but it wouldn't make much difference.

He said, "It doesn't make much difference."

Marian Grant chuckled, "I don't know. I think on the whole I'd rather run down than blow up, wouldn't you, George?"

Grant said, turning to Robert, "There may be something..."

Katherine said, "Don't be silly, Robert. Get Marian a drink."

Robert got up and slid back the panel of the cocktail cabinet and mixed the drinks. Above the syphon fizz he could hear the smooth burr of the service lift outside: a waiter from the restaurant in the basement fetching down the dinner trays. The telephone rang and he answered it. For Kath. He brought the filled glasses, carefully, to the table.

"Evie Applepen," she said coming back, pleased, taking up the cards. "She wants us to dine to-morrow. They're having some of the foreign attachés who came over for the funeral."

"I thought we were going somewhere."

"Oh, nowhere. Only to the Inghams'. Sylvia won't mind." She pushed the pack across at him, impatiently.

He picked it up and began to deal.

When the Grants had gone and Katherine was in bed he went round the flat, turning off wireless and radiator and drawing the oiled-silk curtains upon the late swish of traffic below in the street; putting out the lights. He tiptoed through in the dark to the light, white bathroom and undressed; set the alarm for eight o'clock and arranged his shaving things straight and handy on the glass shelf. In a path of light from the bathroom door he pushed open one of the white, sliding wall-cupboards and got out his clothes and folded them neatly over a chair to save time in the morning.

The Eclipse of Gertrude Trevelyan

by Brad Bigelow

<><><><><><><><><><><><><><><><><><><><><><><><><><><><><><><><><><><><><><><><><>

Gertrude Eileen Trevelyan's life is a cautionary tale. She may have come closer than any writer of her time to fulfilling Virginia Woolf's vision from *A Room of One's Own* (1929). Give a talented young woman writer 'a room of her own and five hundred a year, let her speak her mind and leave out half that she now puts in,' Woolf predicted, 'and she will write a better book one of these days. She will be a poet.' In Trevelyan's case, she found her room at 107 Lansdowne Road in Kensington in 1931, had at least five hundred a year thanks to her father's modest fortune, and put the two to good use, producing eight novels of striking originality in the space of as many years. She had a small circle of friends, avoided the limelight, reviewed no books, neither taught nor edited, made no trips abroad or otherwise diverted her time and energy from the task of writing. This allowed her to take great risks in style, structure and approach, exploring the theme of metamorphosis in works of imaginative intensity unequalled by any novelist of her time aside from Woolf herself. Then a German bomb hit her flat and she and her books were forgotten — demonstrating that talent alone isn't enough to sustain a literary reputation.

Ironically, Trevelyan's career began with instant worldwide celebrity. 'First Woman Winner of Newdigate Prize' announced a headline in *The Times* of Wednesday, June 8, 1927. In her last year as an undergraduate at Lady Margaret Hall, Oxford, Trevelyan won the Newdigate Prize for English verse for her poem 'Julia, Daughter of Claudius'. Although the prize amounted to a modest £21, the novelty of its award to a woman led papers throughout the English-speaking world — from Kenosha, Wisconsin to Auckland, New Zealand — to print the story with similar headlines in the following weeks. When she died in early 1941, the few papers that printed an obituary cited the Newdigate Prize as her primary achievement.

Many articles about Trevelyan's prize drew attention to her family connections. It was true, as stated, that she was related to the historian George Macaulay Trevelyan and a line of Baronets and Cabinet ministers. These were not close relations, however. Her grandfather — the historian's great uncle — was a vicar who had been removed after speaking out against Church reforms and spent the rest of his life as a 'Priest without care of souls'. Her father's career was even less distinguished. Having inherited a comfortable legacy, Edward Trevelyan spent his time riding and managing his garden. He married in his forties; Gertrude, born in Bath in 1903, was their only child. She remained close to her parents all her life.

There was also nothing exceptional about Gertrude Trevelyan's childhood. She attended the Princess Helena College in Ealing as a boarder, winning the school's essay prize two years in a row but graduating without distinction. She went up to Oxford without a scholarship, entering Lady Margaret Hall in the fall of 1923. There, she avoided as many activities as possible, enabling her to maintain 'a position of total obscurity', as she later wrote with some pride.

After the worldwide notoriety of the Newdigate Prize, Trevelyan returned to this position. She moved to London, published a few poems, and wrote some forgettable articles for minor magazines. After living in a series of women's hotels, she moved to the flat in Kensington in 1931. And here, Gertrude Trevelyan's biography effectively stops. Until her death in 1941, there is almost no record of her life outside the reviews of her novels.

The unremarkable facts of Trevelyan's life offer a stark contrast to the originality and intensity of her novels — none more powerfully than with her debut, *Appius and Virginia* (1932). She published the book as G. E. Trevelyan, which protected her identity so well that several reviewers thought the author was a man. On the surface, *Appius and Virginia* appears to be more novelty than novel: a 40-year-old spinster buys an infant orangutan and takes him to a cottage in a remote country village where for the next eight years she attempts to raise him as a human. Some compared the book to John Collier's 1930 novel, *His Monkey Wife*, in which a schoolteacher marries a literate chimpanzee. Phyllis. Bentley, writing in *The New Statesman*, felt, however, that Appius 'emerges triumphantly from the comparison.' She found *Appius* a tragic figure. 'One lays down the book grieving oddly over this half-man and feeling that in some sense he is symbolic of human destinies.' Bentley understood that this book was much more than just an exotic oddity.

Trevelyan's aim, in fact, to show the impossibility of genuine communication and understanding between species. Virginia Hutton undertakes the experiment to transform the ape into a human: 'I believe that if a young ape were taken at birth and brought up completely in human surroundings,' she writes in her diary, 'exactly like a child, it would grow up like a child — would, in fact, *become* a child.' As her experiment plays out, Virginia is able to produce from Appius behaviours that convince her that the orangutan is becoming not merely human but, potentially, super-human:

> He would bring to his learning an untired brain and a completely untouched stock of mental energy. His physical strength, too, would be greater than that of an ordinary man, and this, because he had learnt to think, would be transformed into brain power. He had boundless possibilities. He would be tireless. He would be able to do more in ten years than any man had achieved in a lifetime.

Virginia lives in a fantasy of her own creation, however. Appius's responses are not demonstrations of his cognitive development but merely of his ability to reproduce the actions which Virginia has trained him to perform through repetition and positive and negative stimuli. The real transformation is not the ape's but the woman's.

Virginia eventually admits that what she had been seeking all along was not an intellectual achievement but something more basic: 'I only wanted you to be human and talk to me. And I thought perhaps you'd grow to be fond of me, too, if I'd always looked after you when you were small.' But she is looking for a connection across an uncrossable divide. Virginia's 'words had no meaning' for Appius; instead, 'her tone exasperated him, goading him into movement.... In a moment he was upon her and she was falling backwards, screaming weakly.'

Trevelyan's aim was so ambitious that many reviewers failed to grasp it. In *The Daily Mail*, the veteran James Agate dismissed the book as 'pretentious puling twaddle... saved from being disgusting only by its frantic silliness.' L.P. Hartley in *The Sketch* found it 'absorbing but horrible, and almost entirely devoid of beauty.' American reviewers tended to take the book literally: 'an absorbing study in the education and environmental adjustments of a young ape,' said *The New York Times*' reviewer.

Leonora Eyles, who remained Trevelyan's most steadfast supporter among critics, applauded the novelist's ambition. 'It must have required considerable courage to conceive *Appius and Virginia* and to carry out the conception so carefully', she wrote in the *Times Literary Supplement*. She warned, however, that 'Miss G. E. Trevelyan demands equal courage from her readers.' Eyles recognized how the nature of the relationship between Virginia and Appius shifts in the course of the story: 'So by degrees she forgets his subhuman origin and her own scientific project and demands of him the affection of a son.' For Eyles, though, Appius's lot remains throughout that of a victim, meekly accepting what he understands only as 'incomprehensible and indigestible scraps of information from his loving torturer.' Indeed, some today will find *Appius and Virginia* a prescient account of the perils inherent in playing with the boundaries between humans and the animal world.

Trevelyan's third novel, *As It Was in the Beginning* (1934), was another bold experiment, this time into the use of stream of consciousness narrative. The book takes place entirely in the mind of Millicent, Lady Chesborough, widow of Lord Harold, as she lies in a nursing home, dying from the effects of a stroke. Nurses come in and go out, always adjusting her sheets, lifting her numb left arm as they do. As Millicent floats in and out of consciousness, she revisits moments from her life, rerunning these memories as one sometimes gets a bit of a song caught in mind.

Trevelyan manages deftly to weave two opposing lines of transformation. One — externally apparent through the actions taking place in Millicent's room — is the approach of death. The other, shown solely through Millicent's thoughts, takes her back through her life, from her final foolish affair with a handsome but untrustworthy young man through her unhappy marriage to her girlhood, infancy, and, in her last moments, to birth. Millicent struggles for a sense of self, feeling herself 'there, but not in the body: watching it from the outside and feeling responsible for it, without having it firmly in hand. Having to creep back in to pull the strings.' Trevelyan builds a powerful sense of a woman whose life was a constant struggle to define her identity — a struggle she often lost — until, at the end, she fades into nothingness.

War Without a Hero (1935), which followed, is in some ways even more claustrophobic in mood than *As It Was in the Beginning*. Its story is implausible: a sophisticated socialite takes a room with a fisherman's family on a remote Channel Isle to ride out the initial storm over her divorce. She takes pity on family's blind son, marries him to wrest the young man from his domineering mother and arranges for surgery in London to restore his sight. When the couple return to the island, however, she herself falls into a battle of wills with the mother and loses, transforming slowly into a grey, hopeless scullery maid as her husband, now able to see, changes from a timid recluse into a bold philanderer. As a novel, *War*

Without a Hero is an unconvincing failure. As a psychological horror story, however, it's as powerful as a vortex.

In contrast, *Two Thousand Million Man-Power* (1937) takes the lives of its two leading characters — Katherine, a schoolteacher, and Robert, a chemist (as in scientist, not pharmacist) — and sets them against a backdrop of national and international events. Trevelyan makes frequent use of a motif resembling the 'Newsreel' feature in John Dos Passos' *U.S.A.*, the last volume of which appeared the year before *Two Thousand Million Man-Power* was published. Trevelyan peppers her text with snatches of news of the world, using the technique almost like the chorus in a Greek tragedy. Thus, when Katherine suggests she and Robert have a child because 'We could afford it now' and 'Things are improving everywhere,' the news provides the evidence:

> The successful trials of R.100 were completed. A Dutch scientist was working out a scheme for the production of artificial rain. A Beam wireless service was opened between England and Japan. A pilot flew over six thousand miles of African jungle to carry anti-hydrophobia serum to a missionary. Agricultural machines in France were grading and marking eggs at the rate of a hundred and twenty a minute. Escalators were speeding up, the biggest building in the Empire was in course of construction at Olympia, Katherine and Robert were in their white-enamelled kitchen one Sunday afternoon, washing the tea-things in instantaneous hot water and hanging them to dry in an electrically heated rack.

Robert and Katherine see themselves as superior to most of their neighbors and co-workers — at least at first. They meet in a League of Nations debate (Katherine envisions the League's headquarters as a glowing 'Temple of Justice' on the shores of Lake Geneva). Having been dissuaded by his father from pursuing an academic career, Robert works in the laboratory of the Cupid Cosmetics Company Ltd. but labors away in his room at night, trying to discover 'the precise mathematical formula for the nature of Time.' Katherine disdains the mundane worries of her fellow teachers (rumors the London City Council will let married teachers go) and lovingly darns Robert's socks at night, knowing he's engaged in an effort of profound significance.

As they become more deeply involved, though, that business of married teachers becomes more relevant. Katherine cannot bring a man to her room. Robert's landlady keeps close track of the frequency and duration of Katherine's visits. They spend endless hours walking up and down along the Thames. Trevelyan shows a keen awareness of how public and private mores and spaces conspired against single people:

> Every twenty yards or so, where a tree overhung the pavement, or at the farthest point between two street lamps, they passed a couple pressed against the wall or pushed into a gateway. Some of the couples were speaking in low voices and some were quite quiet. As she passed them Katherine would draw away from Robert, just a little and without meaning to: just a very slightly wider strip of pavement between them. He came near again, not noticing. 'They're like us,' he said. 'Nowhere to go.'

They marry eventually — secretly at first, to avoid losing their rooms and Katherine losing her job. But Robert invents a new formula for a make-up remover and the royalties allow them to rent a small house in the suburbs, complete with hired furniture, wireless, and vacuum cleaner. Of course, being out in the suburbs has its disadvantages, so soon they buy a car on installment as well.

And if you know 20th century history, you know what comes next:

> In the last week of September the bank rate rose to six per cent; the Stock Exchange closed for two days; England went off the gold standard. On the first of October Robert lost his job.

Robert joins the army of unemployed, and one by one the appliances, then the car, and finally the house is lost and the couple find themselves trapped together in a dismal pair of rooms, with nothing to do but scour the job notices, write ever-more-desperate letters of application, and grow more frustrated with each other. Katherine takes a job at a sad girl's school run out of a Bayswater house and allows her contempt for Robert's failures to show more openly. Each day he brushes off his one last threadbare suit and heads into the city with a few pence in his pocket; each day he comes home defeated.

> He knew he had to get a job, because of Kath. Kath couldn't go on, he couldn't go on letting Kath. He plodded along with his eyes on the windows, hair-cut and small tailors, Apprentice wanted, Smart Lad to learn. He knew there was a job somewhere, and he had to find it. He turned a corner and came face to face across the street with a slab of house-high hoardings, Bovo for Bonny Bairns, and a grinning crane-top in a gap between roofs. He knew suddenly with certainty that he would never get a job. He stopped short

and read it over, Bovo for Bonny Bairns. It meant nothing to him and the crane meant nothing, and it meant nothing that a dingy house or two had been pulled down and hoardings were up house-high along the site. But when he had first seen the five-foot blue letters on the red ground, and the slanting crane-head and a yard or so of tiles on the next roof, he had known he would never get a job.

It takes sixteen months for Robert to find a job, by which point he hovers just short of suicide. Trevelyan's depiction of the grim ordeal of unemployment rivals anything in the first half of Orwell's *The Road to Wigan Pier*. And Trevelyan shares Orwell's cynical assessment of capitalism's effects on the individual. 'They might always have been like that, he a coward and she not really caring about anything, but they hadn't known it,' Robert thinks. 'That was what the machine had done to them, shown them one another. Each had seen the other as something the machine didn't want.'

The source of Trevelyan's rather odd title reveals much about her perspective on the situation of her two individuals in the larger context of their world:

> Thus, whereas in China there was an adult working male population of, say, 100 millions, in the United States there was added to the 25 million working males something *like two thousand million man power* [emphasis added] in machinery. And the result is that whereas in China consumers out-number producers by 4 to 1, in the United States producers outnumber consumers by 20 to 1.

This comes from an article by Ian D. Colvin in an encyclopedic work titled *Universal History of the World* published in

1927. Colvin's 'Social Survey of the World To-Day' carries the ominous subtitle, 'Lines of Weakness revealed in Western Civilization by the Shock of War and the Reactions of Democracy to Responsibility.'

Colvin's essay is, tellingly, the last in this eight-volume, 5,000-page survey of world history. It betrays the influence of Oswald Spengler, whose *Decline of the West* was then at the height of its popularity. Yet Colvin was also familiar with Marx and the view that much of what was wrong in the world stemmed from the conflict between labour and capital. His chief concern for the future of mankind, though, was in the anonymizing effect of systems of mass production. When their fortunes take a turn again for the better, Katherine grows harder and colder (her hair in 'tight, metallic waves'), like a well-tempered piece of machinery. Robert, on the other hand, edges closer and closer to insanity:

> When he thinks about it, he can see the rims of his glasses, he tries to push the glasses further on so that he can't see the rims; he finds he can always see them; now he has once seen them he can't stop seeing them: he is conscious of seeing everything through the small round portholes of his glasses, as if he were seeing it through the end of a tunnel; he can always see the frame edging the picture. It gets on his nerves, always seeing the rims: he blinks, and the blink becomes a habit; he frowns, and stretches his brown and frowns, trying to drag the frame further on.

Robert's disillusionment illustrates Colvin's caution about the spiritual emptiness underlying the myth of technological progress:

While the work of industrial civilization, in the form of mass production, goes on under tremendous external pressure, it is losing inner vitality and significance for the human individual, and becoming more and more of a burden to be endured for the sake of the money wages which compensate for it. And since no exact method of compensation can ever be found for work in which the worker takes no interest, it is probable that the restlessness of those who have to do it will continually increase.

Trevelyan's discontent with the status quo is even more apparent in her most experimental novel, *Theme with Variations* (1937). 'Samuel Smith was the best part of thirty before anyone told him he was a wage-slave,' the book opens. Trevelyan's theme is entrapment and its effects on a personality. Her variations are three individuals — a working man, a wife and an ambitious young woman — each trapped in their own cage. The bars may be economic circumstances, class prejudices, social mores, fear, or just bad luck, but they rule out any possibility of escape and freedom as effectively as those made of steel. The saddest of Trevelyan's three trapped specimens is Evie Robinson, a bright girl held back by her family's mutual enabling society. Evie's younger sister, Maisie, suffers from some unnamed disability — something physical but also mental — that draws in all the family's energies. Her mother and father look to Evie to take over the burden of caring for Maisie, but Evie has the spunk to plan her escape. And she does, at least at first, training as a secretary, reaching the head of her class, gaining a spot in a local business, cramming for the civil service exam. 'I've got to get out. I've got to do *something*', she thinks as she contemplates taking a post in a government office. But the power of her family's dependency overwhelms her. 'Dear Sirs, I am sorry that owing to family reasons I am not able to take up any appointment', she writes tearfully at her father's insistence, all the while wondering, 'Oh lord, now what am I going to do?'

Trevelyan's last novel, *Trance by Appointment* (1939), continues her study of the exploitation of individuals with a simple but exotic story. Jean, the middle daughter of a working-class London family, is a psychic. As she grows, her family comes to recognize this talent and introduce her to Madame Eva, who runs a fortune-telling business from a basement flat in Bayswater. There, Jean meets and soon marries an astrologer who sees the commercial possibilities of a 'trance by appointment' business.

From this point forward the story will be familiar to anyone who has read Tolstoy's *Kholstomer*, usually translated as 'Strider: The Story of a Horse': a vital resource used up in a relentless quest for profit, then tossed aside in contempt. Lacking the will to resist, Jean is ground down from an innocent girl with a magical gift into a money-making machine whose sole purpose is to churn through her daily allotment of clients. Despite Trevelyan's novel choice of protagonist, a few reviewers recognized her success in immersing the reader in the world as experienced by Jean, who is simultaneously capable of psychic insight and utterly bewildered by much of what goes on around her. 'Once again Miss Trevelyan gives us an insight into human minds that is quite uncanny, and her Jean, though such an unusual character, is completely convincing,' wrote Leonora Eyles in the *Times Literary Supplement*.

Trevelyan might have continued to write ground-breaking fiction and become recognized as one of the leading novelists of her generation. Unfortunately, on the night of 8

October 1940, a German bomb struck 107 Lansdowne Road and Trevelyan's room of her own was destroyed. Though rescued from its ruins, she had been severely injured and died a few months later on 24 February 1941 while being cared for at her parents' home in Bath. Her death certificate identified her as 'Spinster — An Authoress'.

For the next seventy-some years, Trevelyan disappeared from English literary history. From the world-wide fame of her Newdigate Prize and the steady critical acclaim of her novels, she was quickly and ruthlessly transformed into a non-entity. Her name appears in no survey of the literature of the 1930s, in no study of the 20th Century English novel, in no memoir or biography of her contemporaries.

I first came across Gertrude Trevelyan almost 80 years after her death. A brief description ('a spinster tries to raise an ape as a human') led me to locate a used copy of *Appius and Virginia*, which I then wrote about on my Neglected Books website. The power of Trevelyan's writing and the near-complete absence of any mention of her work in any sources I could locate online or off led me to hunt down copies of her other novels and write about them over the course of the next year. In several cases, there were no used copies to be found for any price and I had to resort to reading them at the British Library, one of a handful of libraries worldwide where Trevelyan's books can be found.

A chance conversation I had with the publisher Scott Pack in early 2020 led to his decision to reissue *Appius and Virginia* under the Abandoned Bookshop imprint. The book's publication attracted significant attention, most notably an article in *The Guardian* that took a quote from Pack for its headline: 'If she was a bloke, she'd still be in print.' And now, as part of the Recovered Books series, Boiler House Press is publishing

Two Thousand Million Man-Power and plans to follow with the best of Trevelyan's remaining novels. With any luck, these reissues will encourage more readers and researchers to discover Trevelyan's work and begin to bring her place in literary history from the shadows in which it has been hidden for decades. In her novels, Trevelyan consistently portrayed metamorphosis as a matter of degradation and destruction. Her reputation need not suffer the same fate.

Two Thousand Million Man-Power
By Gertrude Eileen Trevelyan

First published in this edition by Boiler House Press, 2022
Part of UEA Publishing Project
Two Thousand Million Man-Power copyright ©
Gertrude Eileen Trevelyan, 1937
Introduction copyright © Rachel Hore, 2022
Afterword copyright © Brad Bigelow, 2022

Proofreading by Lindsay Hause

Photography of Gertrude Trevelyan by license from the
National Portrait Gallery
Cover photograph (Flight demonstrations at the Hendon
Air Show, June 29, 1935) by permission of Austrian Archives/
Brandstaetter Images/picturedesk.com

The right of Gertrude Eileen Trevelyan to be identified as the
Author of this work has been asserted by her in accordance
with the Copyright, Design & Patents Act, 1988.

Cover Design and Typesetting by Louise Aspinall
Typeset in Arnhem Pro
Printed by Tallinn Book Printers
Distributed by Ingram Publisher Services UK

ISBN: 978-1-913861-85-8